HER BIKER DRAGON

THE COMPLETE COLLECTION

AJ TIPTON

Illustrated by
ZAMAJK

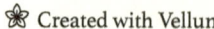 Created with Vellum

HER VALIANT DRAGON

Dylan Masters took another swig of beer and slammed the mug down on the bar top's stained surface. He wasn't a large man, just well built, with Asiatic features and long dreadlocks, but there was enough force behind his blow to chip the mug's edge.

"The Dragon High Counsel denied my plea. By the time I got home, my wife was dead." Dylan tilted the mug back to capture the last inch of beer, now slightly warm and watery with backwash. He coughed and slid the mug across the counter for a refill.

He wasn't sure how the AUDREY'S bartender, Lola, had gotten him to talk about what happened to his late wife three years ago. He hated to talk about it. His inner dragon was curled in a tight ball under his skin, quiet and still like it had been for the past few years since that horrible night. Dylan remembered walking into the house after flying the week-long journey home in dragon form, practicing how to tell her about the Counsel's rejection, when he realized the house was too still, too quiet to be inhabited. He tore through each room calling out her name. He found her in his favorite chair, wearing his sweatshirt and curled up with a book. She had been dead for days.

"Would you have gone against the Counsel's decree and given her your scales to cure her?" Lola asked, refilling his beer and sliding it back to him. The bartender was beautiful in a way that was alarming rather than alluring. Her mass of small braids stood out from her head like a sea of swaying snakes moving in different directions around her face. Her purple eyes had an ageless wisdom Dylan was only used to seeing in the most ancient of dragon clan leaders. The wicked curve of her smile matched the red rose tattoo curling across her chest and down into her ample décolletage. Dylan couldn't shake the feeling she already knew everything he was about to say.

"Of course I would have saved her. She was the love of my life. The doctors told us she still had months. If I knew just how little time we actually had, I would've--" His voice broke, thinking back to those dark days. Knowing what he knew now, he wouldn't have bothered to beg the Dragon High Counsel for permission; he would have shed a few scales, ground them into a powder, and fed them to her. It was a carefully guarded secret among dragon shifters--Dylan couldn't fathom how Lola knew--but dragon scales, ground to a powder called Puff, could cure humans of most illnesses. Back then, Dylan had still believed in the clan rules that forbade giving Puff to humans. He believed in the system. He'd thought the Counsel would protect and care for him and his family because that was what they were supposed to do. Now he knew the truth.

A scuffling sound came from behind him, and Dylan's body was turning to address the threat before his brain caught up. A fireball was halfway up his already-shifted throat, ready to be unleashed in a furious blaze that would probably raze the bar to the ground.

A pixie stared at him with enormous blue eyes, flowers growing from her head, and bright green vines curling in her blond hair. Her dress was overlapping pink and blue petals and her dainty mouth had dropped open in warning, a swarm of bees waiting right in front of her mouth to retaliate if he attacked.

Dylan held up his hands and deliberately sat back in his seat, shifting his face back to human, feeling foolish.

"Sorry about that," he said to the pixie. "It's been a rough few years."

The pixie made a little chirping sound, ordered her

drink, and went back to her table. Dylan's eyes widened as he looked at the pixie's companions: a tiger shifter in a leather bodysuit, a ten-foot tall troll with so many warts his green skin was barely visible, and a red-haired witch juggling balls of ice and fire, giggling when she dropped them to the scorched floor. A couple of vampires nursed blood cocktails in the corner, and two leprechauns made out enthusiastically, stumbling and giggling as they made their way to a door labeled "Back Room".

"Is this, um, normal around here?" Dylan asked, tying back his long dreadlocks.

"This is AUDREY'S, sweetie," Lola smiled, showing a few too many teeth. "We don't do normal."

Dylan sipped his beer, thinking. The last few years had felt like an unending series of dive bars and unanswered questions. After his wife's death, he'd spent the first year mourning and trying to carry on despite the enormous hole in his life where she used to be. He'd sold their house, quit his job as an investigator, told the clan leaders exactly where they could shove it, bought a motorcycle, and hit the road. It was in the middle of the second year after her death that he started to hear the rumors. The stories were almost too good to be true, but the possibility the Iron Claws might be real kept him moving, hunting for the elusive outlaw motorcycle club. Looking around at AUDREY'S, Dylan figured this bar seemed like exactly the kind of place where he might get some answers.

"Maybe you can help me," he said, trying to keep his face a mask of nonchalance. "I heard a rumor about a biker club, the Iron Claws. Apparently they're a group of outcast dragons who distribute Puff."

"That sounds admirable of them," Lola said, her hair

waving around her head in extra agitation like a cat's thrashing tail.

"I've been searching for them for the last couple of years, but I've always been a step behind. They keep moving so fast after each distribution that by the time I find where they've been, they've already gone."

"What are you going to do if you find them?" Lola said, her voice disinterested as she mixed something bright green and glowing for the troll.

Dylan's dragon rolled and stretched inside him, roused by the rare feeling of hope beginning to stir in Dylan's chest. Could they really be close? Lola obviously knew about them. The careful way she stood, the way she avoided his eyes for the first time since he walked in the door...she knew something. And if his deductions were correct, she was deciding if she could trust him with this information.

Dylan could understand her hesitation. The High Counsel would love to find the elusive motorcycle club and shut them down. He'd seen signs of the Counsel's goons in a few towns he'd been in, heard rumors of violence in bars that sounded like the kind of awful the goons got up to when they stretched the Counsel's leash. But he needed to find the Iron Claws.

Lola caught his eye, waiting for his answer.

"If I find them, I'll join them," he said. For the first time, he wondered if they'd have him. He had many skills to offer as a fighter and investigator, but would his past blind obedience to clan tradition make them not trust him?

Lola grinned. "Well, sugar, in that case, you might want to check out the flea market tomorrow at the Winter Wondernasium. Ask for the *special brownies*. They pack a little extra kick."

DYLAN SPOTTED the dragon shifters nearly immediately. Being a private investigator for so many years, Dylan had been trained to notice the little details others would have missed. To the casual observer--or the dozens of humans wandering around checking out the flea market--the baked goods table set up between a flower booth and a homemade soap and lotion stand looked completely innocuous.

A large black man in a leather jacket was handing a box of pre-sliced brownies to a middle-aged woman shopping with her son. Similar transactions were happening all around the flea market. What others wouldn't think to notice, however, was the relaxed sigh as the woman took the box, like a weight was being lifted off her shoulders, or the way the son's eyes flicked around them like he was checking out who was paying attention to their purchase.

Others wouldn't notice the way the enormous man at the booth stood, awesome power in every muscle bulging under his leather jacket, but with a relaxed stance like he was trying to mute his presence rather than play it up for attention.

With Dylan's heightened dragon senses, he could smell motor oil on the man's patched clothes and dark skin, the smell so strong it almost overpowered the subtle scent of dragon underneath. From the size of him, this man would be a monstrous dragon shifter, possibly an alpha, power and confidence clear in every gesture. But the gentle way he talked with the woman and her son hinted at a very different personality than Dylan was used to seeing among the very competitive, dominant dragon alphas.

The second dragon shifter manning the tent confused Dylan at first. He had assumed the second seller was a woman from the knock-out curves barely perceptible under the leather jacket. After a second look, Dylan deduced from both the way the man stood and the inexplicable energy coming off of him that he was distinctly male. He had heard one of the Iron Claws was transgender. The man--Dylan was fairly certain the trans member of the Iron Claws identified as male--had olive dark skin, a pointed chin, and the delicate features Dylan associated with the Middle Eastern dragon clans. He was paying closer attention to their surroundings than his enormous leader, his eyes scanning the crowds. Dylan turned away and pretended to check out a rack of vintage postcards as the second man's eyes swept over him.

Dylan bit down on the inside of his cheek to keep his excitement from showing on his face. He'd found them! After seeking the Iron Claws for so long, he could barely contain his joy. He picked out a few other members of the club wandering around the crowded flea market. They'd found different ways to try and mask their dragon smells, either under colognes or motor grease like their leader, but the way they moved marked them as part of the same group. Each had at least one other member of the club in their peripheral vision at all times and, no matter where they moved around the market, they never seemed to totally turn their backs toward the others.

Dylan felt a hunger he'd forgotten about after so many years without a clan. Dragons weren't meant to be alone. They were clan creatures. He didn't know very much about the club except that the Iron Claws were made up of dragon shifters who had left or been exiled from their family clans. While dragon clans tended to be monochromatic--from the same geographical and family lines--this group was pleasantly more diverse, with outcasts originating from all over the globe. And yet the misfit castaways of this secret club were more in sync than any clan Dylan had seen, moving with coordination and following unspoken commands like a single unit. It was a closeness Dylan hadn't known in too many years.

How do I approach these guys? Dylan ran through a series of scenarios in his head, finally deciding to be direct. He made it halfway across the aisle, close enough to catch the scent of the crushed dragon scale drug, Puff, in the brownies when a hand thumped across his chest.

"Hi pal," said a voice to Dylan's right. "What's a dragon shifter like you doing in a place like this?" Dylan followed the hand's owner to a wiry man with dark, rough features, stylized wavy hair, and guitar calluses on his fingertips. Tattoos covered the tops of his hands and disappeared under his leather jacket, with hints of larger designs peeking out from the top of his shirt and winding up his neck. Behind him stood two other dragon shifters: a woman in a tight tank top that read, "Faster Than a Speeding Ticket" and showed off her impressive biceps, and a smaller Asian boy who looked to be either in his late teens or early twenties. The woman looked ready to bash Dylan's head in if threatened, while the boy was shaking in his metal-studded boots, despite attempts to keep a tough expression on his face.

"Yeah, what are you doing here, mister?" the kid said, obviously trying too hard. The dragon with the musician hands let out an annoyed sigh, but didn't waver in his hard look at Dylan. The woman just smiled.

"My name's Dylan Masters. I'm clanless. I've been looking for you for the last two years."

"And why is that?" the kid asked. "You looking for some trouble?" He flexed his muscles and pounded a fist against his other palm. Dylan was pretty sure he'd seen tough guys in movies do that, but he'd never seen it in real life. The kid was adorable.

The large shifter at the brownie booth hadn't moved, but Dylan could see he had the big man's attention. Dylan was tempted to muscle his way past the welcome committee and talk to the leader directly, but it was probably best not to make enemies this early. From the way she stood, Dylan also wasn't positive he'd be able to get past the woman blocking his way.

"I'm not looking for any trouble. I'm looking to help. I have a rough history with the Counsel for wanting to give Puff to humans who need it," Dylan said. "I heard rumors about you all and what you've been doing. I wanted to see if you could use another pair of eyes and fists."

"And what do you think we're doing?" the woman said, speaking for the first time. Her voice had a musical lilt to it, a hint of slight accent Dylan couldn't quite place. The beauty of her voice gave her face a softness that wasn't in her stance or posture. He still didn't want to mess with her.

"I think you're slipping Puff into the *special brownies* over there to help sick people get better."

"We don't slip things!" the kid blurted out, immediately reddening when he realized what he admitted.

"Ned, go help Alec at the booth before you hurt something," the woman said, sighing slightly. Ned slumped his shoulders and plodded over to join his club members.

"He's young," Dylan commented.

"He's old enough to know better," the woman said. "I'm Emma."

The musician covered in tattoos stepped forward, holding out his palm for Dylan to shake. "I'm Caesar. Our leader over there is Big Joe, and our tech guy next to him is

Alec." Caesar nodded back at the booth. "Ned wasn't wrong; we don't slip anything to anybody. Our customers get to us through referrals and they know what they're asking for."

Dylan's voice came out as skeptical as he felt. "They know they're eating powdered dragon scales?"

Caesar laughed. "Hell no, we're not that stupid. They think they're taking an experimental drug that doesn't have FDA approval yet. We sell it cheap, and they can't argue with the results."

"That's--" Dylan started to say, then stopped when he saw purposeful movement out of the corner of his eye. The smell of dragon shifters came from a new direction. Strange men with suspicious bulges like hidden weapons. Conspicuous touches to the ear like checking on hidden earpieces. "The Red Guard--Counsel goons. They're here."

"What? Where?" Caesar and Emma were already moving back towards the booth. Big Joe, Alec, and Ned pulled out a small metal vat from under the table and started to dump the Puff-laced brownies into it. Dylan turned away from the harsh smell of chemicals.

Smart, he thought. If they destroyed the evidence, the goons wouldn't have anything to take back to their bosses as proof. Puff wasn't difficult to make. The hardest part of replacing that stash would be mixing up the brownies.

The five Counsel goons dropped their attempt at subtlety and started to move in. The flea market crowd must have picked up on the fact that something was going down because they started to hurry away, clearing the space in front of the bakery booth.

Dylan hoped they wouldn't have to shift to dragon form--casualties were almost inevitable when dragon flame was involved--but if they did, he took comfort that most humans wouldn't see their true forms. Only a few humans had the enlightened sight to actually see the supernatural creatures they lived alongside every day, but even humans without the sight could sense the danger brewing in the market and ran.

Daggers popped out of the goons' sleeves as they advanced, long wicked blades that shined a little too brightly in the light and--if Dylan wasn't imagining it-- *hummed* slightly with an ominous buzz.

"That can't be good," Dylan muttered.

"Friend, you better get out of here if you don't want to be caught up in this," Big Joe said, his deep voice resonant and commanding. Dylan wasn't short, but his head still barely went past Big Joe's shoulder. Dylan smelled brimstone and saw Big Joe's neck transform into dragon form, lengthening slightly and covering with hard, green scales. It was an impressive level of control. With his neck and, presumably, inner chest transformed, Big Joe would be able to control his fire bursts.

"I'm not going anywhere," Dylan said.

Big Joe nodded. "If we all survive this, we'll talk." Behind him, Dylan saw Emma and Alec step forward as the second line of defense around the booth.

"Yes, sir," Dylan said.

There wasn't time to say more. The goons descended on them all at once, slashing with their blades at Dylan, Big Joe, Alec, and Emma, trying to get around them to attack Caesar and Ned as they quickly finished up destroying the brownies.

Three of the goons came at Dylan at once, one of their punches catching him in the shoulder as Dylan dodged another blow meant for his face. He lashed out, knocking down one of them with a single blow to the face while the others launched themselves at him with renewed fury.

Dylan lost himself in the fury of the fight: punches,

kicks, and the swish of air as a knife slashed so close to his face he could feel the breeze. One knife caught him in the side, but he shrugged it off, adrenaline keeping him on his feet.

He could hear screaming from the assembled humans, the sounds of crashes and breaking pottery from the direction of the flower booth, and a sharp cry that wrenched his gut, but he didn't have the time to look to see who had cried out. The last goon still standing was larger than the rest. He had two blades in his hands and the steady expression of a trained killer.

Dylan balanced on the balls of his feet, his eyes on the man's chest, waiting for the tell-tale movement of his opponent's muscles that would signal the blades' next movements. The wound on Dylan's side was taking longer to heal than he anticipated, slowing him down by crucial seconds. The man hedged left, but Dylan was waiting for the trick and dodged under the swing of the right blade, rolling under the arm of his assailant. He could feel his wound tearing further as he rolled, but he ignored the pain. Dylan lashed out with a flying back kick that sent the goon sprawling and one of the knives tumbling from his hand. Dylan grabbed it as the goon flipped up to his feet. Dylan blocked a knife slash aimed for his throat and struck back.

"Dylan! Down!"

Dylan didn't hesitate to obey Big Joe's command. He dropped to the ground, his arms protectively above his head as a roar of flame blazed above him, hitting the goon with full force. The goon was a dragon shifter, so fire wasn't going to hurt him, but his clothes instantly caught fire, engulfing the man in flames. It was enough of a distraction for Alec to rush in and take him down with a spinning kick to the head. Dylan looked over to see Big Joe shifting back into a fully human form, his neck and chest transforming back into skin.

Dylan got to his feet, looking around at the fight's aftermath. His wound still hurt with a fury that threatened to keep him crouched on the ground, but all he needed was time for that to heal. He stumbled to his feet, holding the wound closed with one hand and waiting for his dragon healing to kick in.

The flower booth had tipped over, spilling plants and broken pots. An unconscious goon lay with his face deep in a purple thistle plant that looked distinctly uncomfortable. The soap stand looked relatively undamaged, although it appeared that someone--Dylan guessed Ned--had been using the products as projectiles since colorful soaps littered the ground for twenty feet in all directions. His eye kept moving until it stopped at the tiny broken body lying next to the bakery table.

Ned.

Caesar and Emma were bent over him, talking to keep the kid conscious and wrapping up bleeding wounds on his arms and side.

Dylan rushed over, not sure how he could contribute. "I don't know much about field medicine," he said. The kid looked really roughed up. "He's a shifter. Why isn't he healing faster?"

"Bastards used hex blades," Caesar cursed.

Hex blades? Dylan's hand clutched the wound on his side. It wasn't healing as fast as it should. Was the knife that sliced him cursed?

"I should have stayed in the hotel business," Ned moaned softly. Big Joe put a hand on the kid's shoulder and squeezed.

"You were real brave, kid. You did just fine. Now we'll just have to get you patched up," he said. Big Joe turned to Alec. "Call Marie. Have her meet us at the clubhouse as soon as she can."

"Already called her," Emma said. "She's on her way."

Big Joe nodded and turned to Dylan. "You did good back there. We might have use for you after all. As long as you're down with being hunted by our former leaders just because we want to help people."

"I think I can get behind that," Dylan smiled.

"Grab your bike and follow us. We need to get this one to Marie."

"Who's Marie?" Dylan asked.

Big Joe exchanged a glance with Emma. "You'll see. I think you'll like her."

MARIE LOOKED down at the puddles of blood leading to the clubhouse door and sighed. *What have these boys gotten into this time?* She gripped the handle of her medical bag and walked faster towards the clubhouse. The building did not impress in the harsh light of day--the clubhouse looked like a dive bar had a baby with a barn--and the exterior was crisscrossed in burn marks splattered with blood, puke, and the other disgusting fluids one would expect outside a biker bar. The place hardly met the sanitary requirements she preferred when stitching up injuries, but the Iron Claws always avoided the hospital if they thought they could get away with it.

"Doc!" Big Joe's voice echoed across the empty bar as Marie crossed the threshold. "Over here!"

Of course it's Ned. Marie resisted the urge to coo and fuss over the smaller man. Big Joe and Emma had laid Ned on one of the pool tables near the bar. He bled from several deep cuts along his body, and he moaned and squirmed, spreading blood around the table's fuzzy green surface. *Poor little guy.*

Marie went to work straightaway, cutting off what remained of Ned's clothing and then sterilizing and stitching his wounds, one by one. *Looks like another hex blade attack.* She sighed. It seemed like there were more and more of the damned things in circulation every day.

Alec, Big Joe, and Emma hovered around her as she worked, the low-hanging fluorescent light sputtering above Marie as she stitched up Ned. She didn't mind; she was used to stitching up these guys in less-than-ideal situations. A pool table was far better than the time she had to patch Emma up in the middle of the desert with sand blowing into everything.

"I dunno, Doc. He doesn't look so good." Big Joe blocked the light as he moved over her shoulder.

"We should probably put him down," Emma joked, pushing Big Joe out of the way so Marie could see. "They *do* say it's just like going to sleep."

"Nah, he's scrappy. He'll probably outlive us all." A blood-splattered Asian man with long dreadlocks she didn't recognize strode towards them, grinning broadly. She had no idea what he was doing there or how he had gotten involved with the fight, but she hoped the Claws would keep him around for a long while. He was *gorgeous.* The way his eyes seemed to take in all of her, from her rounded curves to the stains on her hospital scrubs to her slightly-smeared eye makeup. She wanted to slide up and down his body.

Ned let out a quick yelp of pain.

Marie could feel her face burn red as she realized she had been tugging on the last stitch while staring at the newcomer. *Holy shit.* She'd never thought lust-at-first-sight could be so powerful. He was leaning slightly like his side pained him, but most of the blood on him didn't appear to be his. Even covered in blood and possibly injured, the way he held himself exuded confidence, his sly smile made her melt, and the muscles revealed through the rips and tears in his clothes hinted at a near-perfect male form.

"Doc, this is Dylan Masters. Dylan, this is the Doc. Watch out, she likes to stitch her initials in us sometimes." Alec laughed.

"It's Marie, actually." She smiled, pulling off a latex glove to shake Dylan's hand. She felt a tiny zing as their skin touched. "And I only do that when Alec pisses me off." His hand was huge compared to hers, and she could feel rough calluses lining his palm. *Hard worker. Good to know.*

She tried to keep her facial expression neutral as images of how he got those calluses raced through her mind: Dylan as a cowboy, riding horses shirtless while roping cattle; Dylan as a farmer, working the land, coaxing life out of the dirt, sweating underneath the hot prairie sun; Dylan as a fireman, his shirt burned to tatters, rescuing a kitten from a towering inferno.

"Doc? He's probably going to need that hand back," Emma stage-whispered with a knowing grin.

"What? Oh, right." Marie released him from her grip, the feeling of coming back to reality like a quick slap across the face.

"I wasn't complaining." Dylan walked away towards the bar, his gaze strangely hungry as he looked at her. She felt warm all over, but she pulled on a new glove and turned her attention back to Ned.

"So what exactly happened out there?" Marie raised a

suspicious eyebrow at Big Joe as she cleaned up the bits of suture and gauze from the pool table.

"Oh, you know Ned." Big Joe leaned against a column.

"He's such a klutz." Emma took a sip from a steaming cup of coffee.

"Huge klutz." Big Joe grinned. "He tripped and fell."

"Wow." Marie snapped off her gloves, tossing them into a nearby trash can. "That *sure* is unlucky. What are the odds of Ned here slicing himself over and over, almost like a knife fight?"

"Pretty slim odds," Emma cut in. "We should make him buy a lotto ticket today."

Marie cleared her throat and waited, wearing her best displeased principal face. The room fell still.

"It was my fault." Dylan broke the silence. "Some huge goons from the Counsel were lurking around and..."

"We responded appropriately." Emma flexed, grinning. "Those dickbags were packing hex blades though." She helped Ned up off the pool table. "Takes all the fun out of it."

"Although it does give us this quality time together." Marie pulled out a shiny green apple-flavored lollipop and handed it to Ned. He promptly stuck it in his mouth. "You're gonna be just fine, kiddo." She gathered up the bits of gauze and tape leftover from her work and turned to Alec. "Actually, we have some business."

Business, as Marie always called it, was the part of her job she loved the most. As a registered nurse, she spent her days using the latest technology and FDA-approved drugs available to heal people, but sometimes it wasn't enough.

"Even with the disruption today, we were able to get Puff out to fifty patients," Alec said, opening up his laptop.

Marie shrugged. "It's a start." Marie remembered five

years ago when her own cancer had spread faster and further than the doctors could cut out. She could barely move, was unable to eat, and spent her days staring at the ceiling of her hospital room, wracked with pain, wondering when death would come.

"Fifty people?" Dylan said, moving to look over Alec's shoulder. "How have you managed to stay under the radar for so long?" Marie wasn't sure if it was the lighting, but Dylan looked paler than when he'd first walked in the door.

"Very carefully," Alec said, his delicate lips curling in a smile.

Back when she met the Iron Claws, the club hadn't been so careful. With no one on the inside passing them referrals, Big Joe had to skulk around the oncology ward looking for people who would benefit from Puff. One morning he snuck into her room, all muscles and sass, and convinced her to try a new treatment, a 'special' new medication, as he called it. With nothing to lose, Marie agreed, drinking down the Puff-filled glass of water he handed her. If he'd told her at the time she was consuming powdered dragon scales, she liked to think she would have thrown it at the wall, but she would have swallowed eye of newt if someone claimed it would decrease the pain.

"It's worth it. Think of all the people who could benefit from Puff. The Counsel won't help humans because they're afraid of our kind being hunted down if the humans were ever to find out. They're not helping people, letting innocent people die, because of *fear*. We have to be better than that." Big Joe turned to Alec. "If the goons hadn't come by, how many more people were on the list who didn't have the chance to collect?"

Alec just shrugged, big bound breasts pushing at the front of his jacket.

Marie looked at the somber faces around her. Even Emma, who rarely showed any emotion except anger, looked sad.

"We'll get more at the next distribution, right?" Ned asked, his voice sounding especially young and innocent.

Big Joe laughed, a booming guffaw, and ruffled Ned's hair. "Yes, kid. We will. We can't be afraid to help them all." Marie glanced over at Dylan and then looked away at the expression of awe on his face. She'd been with the Iron Claws so long now sometimes she took for granted how unusual they were.

"Ned, go do inventory," Alec said. Marie was about to protest, but Ned smiled broadly at being trusted with a task and bounced away, only wincing slightly as his stitches pulled. *This is what I love about these people: their boundless optimism*, Marie smiled.

Their optimism had saved her. Everyone on the hospital staff had assumed Marie was done for. They had shifted attention and resources to other patients and left Marie to die, making her "as comfortable as possible". Week after week, Big Joe had shown up, patiently waiting for Marie to finish each drop of her new "medicine." Everyone had given up on her, except Big Joe and his family of outcast dragon shifters.

After the first week, Marie's appetite returned and she tore through the hospital's sub-par menu with gusto. After the second week, her doctors were agape at how swiftly she was recovering, and scrambled over each other like school-children to claim credit. She looked around at the Iron Claws' renewed smiles. She would never be able to repay her debt to them. As soon as she could hold herself upright, she followed Big Joe back from the hospital and discovered his club, all tattoos and scars. Marie immediately pledged her loyalty. She could still remember their dumbfounded faces, each insisting in their own way that she should go off and live the life she was so nearly denied. It was Emma who saw what Marie could be for the club: a medical resource for identifying patients, an inlet of legitimacy in a tight-knit industry, and an on-demand medic for a group that regularly got into scrapes.

"You sure he's going to be okay, Marie?" Caesar asked, looking at Ned's retreating back. Marie smiled. Emma and Big Joe might joke about Ned's injuries, but Caesar had always been the sensitive one of the club. He was also the only one who occasionally lapsed into using her real name rather than the honorific "Doc" the rest called her.

"Looks like our Little Ned is going to be dancing at the concert on Saturday after all," Emma said, elbowing Big Joe in the side.

"Yeah, with all his left feet," Big Joe said, finishing her thought with a shared smile that the group all ignored.

Marie chuckled, resisting the temptation to jab at Big Joe and Emma for being adorable. "You guys make sure he shifts to dragon form for a few hours tonight. That should speed up the healing," she said. "And cut down on those knife fights; they're bad for your health."

She pointed at each face in turn, wagging her index finger at them. Big Joe and Emma looked slightly annoyed, while Alec just looked amused and Caesar grinned unabashedly. She looked around for Dylan and felt a near-palpable panic course through her when she saw him. Dylan had fallen to the dirty cement floor behind the group, his face ashen, his hands covered in blood, his shirt soaked through with crimson. Marie's heart hammered in her chest as she ran to his side.

D<small>YLAN BLINKED</small> awake to the sound of a steady beeping, a sharp pain in his arm, and the harsh smell of disinfectant and latex. He reached over to try and ease the pain in his arm, but a small hand stopped him.

"Wait, Dylan. You need that."

His eyes finally focused on the most beautiful face he had ever seen. Marie. She was standing over him, backlit by the florescent lights so it looked like her face was surrounded by a halo of light. His inner dragon squirmed and thrashed, truly awake and aware for the first time in what felt like forever. His dragon focused in on Marie, the stunning Latina nurse he'd met at the clubhouse. Since they met, he never wanted to look away, his beast quivering with the need to touch her.

Dylan looked around. He was strapped into a hospital bed, an IV stuck in his arm and a machine beeping with the pace of his heart.

"What happened?" he said, his throat feeling rough and dry.

"You were seriously bleeding and decided to keep it to yourself. That wasn't very clever," she said, moving around the room to check his chart and click a few buttons on the heart monitor.

"How long have I been here?"

"You were unconscious for the last few hours as I stitched you up. You're going to be fine, but you'll need to rest a bit longer and keep that IV in your arm." She adjusted the nearly-empty saline bag on its perch. "Why didn't you tell anyone you were wounded? If I had gotten to this sooner, you would be in much better shape."

He shrugged, then winced as the movement pulled at

his stitches. "I didn't want to make a big deal about it. I'm a shifter. I should be healing faster than this."

She chuckled. "Not make a big deal? You were cut with a hex blade. You *know* that a hex blade injures you the same way a normal knife would hurt a human."

Dylan almost smiled in relief. *Oh, a hex blade! I'm not a total wimp.* "What the hell were these guys doing with hex blades?"

"Emma told me they're all registered and tightly regulated, but it seems like the Counsel has no problem handing them out to their goons when we're the target. You should know better than to try and keep that kind of injury secret, even a big strong guy like you." Her hand wandered along his arm in a way that didn't seem entirely professional. Dylan was thrilled.

"What about you, Marie?" Her name felt good on his lips. It was beautiful. Ever since he first set eyes on her at the clubhouse, he'd been drawn to her. The way she'd taken care of Ned showed gentleness, competence, and a kindness he was unused to seeing in his years on the road. She had a goodness that shone out of her eyes and hid in the corners of her smile that made him want to be near her. It didn't hurt that she was beautiful: brown eyes that glittered like gems, luscious black hair he wanted to weave his fingers through, and a rounded figure of ample curves he wanted to feel under his hands. His dragon wanted her, badly. He hadn't felt this kind of intense warmth for a woman since his wife died, and the depth of his attraction surprised him.

"What about what?" she said. Her voice was a little breathless as she looked down at him. He noticed her hands lingered on his shoulders, her touch scorching him through the thin hospital gown.

"Shouldn't a woman as skilled and beautiful as you be

staying away from criminals? And shifter criminals at that? Why are you helping me?"

She bit down on the side of her mouth, and he had to will himself not to become instantly hard.

"I met up with the Claws after they used Puff to cure me. But I was already on the run. And *that's* a long story, and not one I should talk about here," she said, her eyes glancing at the window to his hospital room.

"Then maybe we should go someplace where you can tell me about it?" he said, reaching out with his non-IV laden hand to touch her hand. She blushed and smiled, the expression so sexy he lost the battle to keep his attraction from showing. The hospital gown did nothing to hide it, tenting up around his erection.

"Oh!" she sighed. For a second, it looked like she was going to reach forward to rub his shaft, and his whole dick twitched with the intense need to have her skin against his. He imagined tearing off the gown, ripping off her scrubs, and pulling her down to straddle him. He could visualize all too well the blush on her cheeks as she rode him, her abundant breasts bouncing against her chest until he caught one of the globes in his teeth. She would bite her lip as he thrust up into her. Then he'd bend her over the side of the bed and fuck her until she screamed his name.

"Dylan?" Her voice, so filled with concern, broke his reverie. "Are you okay? Are you in pain?"

His inner dragon roared with hunger. He wanted her. He wanted her in his bed, for her smile and her kindness to warm his days. His entire body burned for her.

"I'm fine." He had to be fine. He had to convince her he could make her happy, show her how he could make her body sing.

She looked at him, biting her lip again in a way that

made him think of those lips all over his body. "If you feel well enough, we should get you to the roof where you can shift. Your IV is done and," she glanced at the heart monitor, "you've stabilized now. Even with a hexed wound, you'll heal faster if you can shift to dragon form."

Dylan couldn't argue with that. Just thinking about shifting made him feel better. She helped him to the roof, checking to make the sure the coast was clear of other nurses and orderlies before half-carrying him up a back stairwell to the roof. Dylan felt slightly weak, but he enjoyed putting an extra stumble in his step, making Marie rush forward to allow him to lean heavily against her.

"Thanks for helping me," Dylan said, leaning down to whisper in her ear, letting his breath stir the fine hairs on the back of her neck. Her skin pebbled into goose bumps and she smiled.

"It's no problem. I'm *so sorry* you're having such trouble walking. Are you sure you feel strong enough to shift?" From the look on her face, she knew perfectly well that he was fully capable of getting up the stairs if he wanted to. Dylan felt himself returning her smile, feeling a lightness in his chest he hadn't felt in a long time. Was this what *fun* felt like?

Her hands roamed his side as she supported him, while his hands wandered across her shoulders and then down her back. Only a mockingly stern look from her kept his hands from skimming all the way down to her ass. Her ass in her light blue hospital scrubs was definitely a sight to behold, but he kept his hands off. Delaying satisfaction would make finally getting his hands on her curves all the more exhilarating.

The wind blew in whistling gusts across the roof. Marie went out first to check the coast was clear; the last thing they needed was a nurse sneaking up to the roof to have a cigarette and catching Marie as she smuggled out a patient in a hospital gown who then transformed into a dragon.

As soon as she confirmed they were alone, Dylan looked inward at his inner dragon, allowing the beast's essence to fill him, pushing out from his human shell and expanding outward. He felt his muscles lengthen and shift, bones breaking and expanding into new shapes. The change had been uncomfortable when he was young, but now it was so much a part of him. His body surging out of his skin felt like a blessed relief, making the enormity of his insides finally match his outsides.

In less than a minute the transformation was complete, and most of the roof was taken up by Dylan in his dragon form: not as large as the dragons in the Counsel or a true alpha dragon, but still huge. He was covered in gold and dark blue scales and stood larger than a bus with a fifty-foot wingspan.

"What do you think?" Dylan asked, his voice in dragon form gruff and deep.

"It's, um... different," Marie said.

Dylan huffed, and a tiny tendril of smoke puffed out of his mouth. "That's it? I'm a majestic, terrifying beast and all I get is 'different'?"

Marie burst out laughing, holding her sides. It was an amazing sound, and Dylan was determined to make her laugh as often as possible going forward.

"Truly, I didn't mean to question your dragonhood," she giggled. "I've seen all the club members in dragon form. You beasts are all very impressive."

"Then what's with the 'different'?" he said.

"Would it make you feel better if I like you more as a man than a giant lizard?" she said, blushing slightly.

"Oh? You like me, do you?" he said, a smile feeling unfamiliar on his draconian face.

"Please stop making that face. I can tell you're smiling, but it really looks like you're about to eat me."

Just the last few moments in dragon form made his wound feel better. The pain had ebbed, and he could feel muscles and skin knitting together as his dragon form's increased healing powers attacked the hexed wound.

"Maybe I do want to eat you," he said, feeling his body shift back into his human form. His hospital gown had shredded to pieces as he transformed into his dragon form, so now he felt the breeze all over. Marie's eyes looked south, her face reddened, and she looked hurriedly back up again, her eyes fastened on his face. He walked forward to cup her face in his hands.

"Maybe I want to eat you all up," he whispered, leaning down close to smell the aroused musk coming off of her in waves. She smelled exquisite, and he wanted to bury his face between her legs and lick her senseless.

"Eat--" she started to say, then stopped. "We barely know each other," she said.

"Then come have drinks with me. Get to know me."

"I don't know," she said. "If you're going to be part of the club, I probably shouldn't. I work with them. I practically live with them. If this becomes a thing and then it doesn't work out, it could be--"

He stopped her by leaning down and kissing her soundly on the mouth. She hesitated for a second, and then her arms went up around his neck, pulling him close. Her scent surrounded and filled him, making him feel stronger and more content than he'd been in years. His hands massaged the back of her head and she leaned in closer to him, her hands surprising him as they came down to squeeze his ass. Hard.

"Marie," he said, pulling back just far enough to rest his cheek against the side of her face. "I would love to take you on the top of this roof, but you mentioned getting to know each other better. We should probably do that."

"Spoilsport," Marie breathed under her breath, but not too softly for supernatural hearing to catch it. And, from her smirk, she knew it too.

This woman is awesome.

"So tomorrow... drinks and dinner and getting to know each other?" he said quickly, before he could change his mind and tear off her clothes right there and then.

She squeezed his ass so hard he jumped.

"Absolutely."

If I don't get out of here, I'm going to take her on this roof.

"Until tomorrow, then," Dylan said, making a running leap for the side of the building. He transformed as he fell, his dragon form overwhelming his weak human form and soaring above the clouds. The sights and smells of the town below came alive in his dragon form, but the only sound he cared about was back on the roof: Marie's tiny frustrated sigh as she said his name.

MARIE STIFLED a snort as the bubbles from her cocktail tickled her nose. She had been to AUDREY'S many times, but had never felt so comfortable or at home as right now. It must be the company.

Dylan cleaned up very nicely, looking handsome yet casual in his tight jeans, close-fitting t-shirt and leather jacket. He was behaving like a perfect gentleman, giving her plenty of physical space and striking up substantive conversation, but the look in his eyes made it clear he wanted her.

Marie wasn't sure how much more gentleman-ing she could take. She bit back a sigh as she remembered Dylan's gown tenting at the hospital, her mere presence causing such a rise in him. Her pulse quickened and she slid her small, tan hand across the scarred wooden table, sliding it into Dylan's palm, marveling at how perfectly it fit. His fingers closed around hers almost instinctually, but he continued speaking.

"So, you travel all around the country with the Iron Claws? That's got to be a pain, always being on the move like that."

Marie took a gulp of her cocktail--something fizzy and blue that Lola had made--and forced a smile. *I hate telling this story.*

"The club has to stay on the move to be ahead of the Counsel." She tried to pull her hand away, but Dylan had it captured, almost like he was afraid she would run. "You've got eighteen stitches that prove how necessary it is to stay ahead of their Red Guard. It was perfect for me though because I was already..." she paused, searching for the right euphemism, "nomadic."

"Can't be pinned down, eh?" Dylan's eyes were lit with mischief, no doubt picturing the carefree life of a roamer, all impermanence and free love.

"Something like that." It was nothing like that. She had a life, she had a *home,* and then everything was torn away.

"I was a nurse at this huge hospital back home." She remembered how excited she had been to get the job she had spent years working towards. She had a ton of friends, she went to karaoke nights, she was *normal.* On the start of a night shift she made her rounds early, checking in on patients slightly before she was meant to, just so she could watch the finale of some stupid TV show back at the nurse's station. It was the rustling of the blankets that had drawn her into the room.

"Somebody was murdered, and I saw it happen." She thought someone was tossing and turning in their sleep, her strong maternal instincts compelling her to soothe the tortured soul. Every day she thanked her lucky stars for her comfortable work shoes that made no sound as she walked, gave the assailant no hint he wasn't alone. The room was completely dark, but a car's headlights flashed through the window in a brief beam, pointing a spotlight at his scarred face. She would never forget that face. Vinny the Fist. She wouldn't know his name until later, but his face haunted her nightmares.

Dylan squeezed her hand gently, all hint of mirth gone from his face. "That must have been terrible."

Worse than that. "It wasn't that big of a deal. At hospitals people die all the time, so it wasn't exactly new." The man in the bed struggled and squirmed under Vinny's grasp. Marie dove to the ground behind a crash cart, cloaked by darkness. The crack of the man's neck snapping echoed sharply through the room, making her stomach drop. The room spun--she couldn't breathe, she wanted to pass out, to disappear, to run from this murderer and the patient she failed. But she just hid, trying not to be detected by the vicious predator only a few feet away.

"There was this whole trial, and I had to testify." She waved her hand dismissively, struggling to smile. "Something happened and they called a mistrial. I think the arresting officer goofed." The evidence of the officer's mistake didn't come to light until halfway through the trial, and Marie had already testified. She had already faced

Vinny the Fist, the muscle for a very powerful crime syndicate, the Fratellis. Marie pointed at him, identified him as the murderer, and she could see how the veins in his square neck pulsed and his fists clenched as she spoke. He could kill her without breaking a sweat, and she had just given him good reason to.

"They came after me. I didn't qualify for witness protection, so I figured it was a good idea to get out of town." The memory of that night coursed through her mind for what felt like the hundredth time. She woke up freezing, snow and cold air streaming through a window she had definitely closed before sleeping. Fear gripped her heart. Someone was inside her home. She grabbed her phone from the nightstand and ran. A hulking shadow closed on her, and she dove out the open window of her first floor apartment. She sprinted towards the bright lights of a nearby 24-hour diner, the cold air stinging her lungs, the snow biting against her bare feet. She managed to get some distance and finish dialing 9-1-1 before the Fist's bullet shredded her shoulder.

"After a few years moving around I got sick, the Big C, and then Big Joe found me. The club gave me Puff to bring me back to health, and now I use it on my patients to sort of pay it forward." She didn't have the words for what it meant when Big Joe and the rest agreed to make her part of their family. After so many years, terrified of Vinny and the Fratellis finding her, being surrounded by badass dragon shifters had turned her life from a terrifying series of narrow escapes into a glorious crusade to bring miraculous healing powders to the masses. She took a long sip from her cocktail and chuckled. "So, that's how a girl like me ended up in a place like this." She gestured at AUDREY'S eclectic clientele.

"I'm so sorry you had to go through that." The look in Dylan's eyes wasn't pity, it wasn't sympathy. It was almost *pride*. "You're an amazing person to come out the other end and still want to help others."

She could feel the blush rise in her cheeks, and she locked eyes with Dylan. A rush of anticipation coursed through her. She didn't want to think about Vinny or the Fratellis. She didn't want to think about cancer or death. She only wanted to think about the fact that a wonderful, handsome guy was looking at her like she was a goddess. Her pulse raced as she leaned towards him across the table, displaying her ample cleavage in her low-cut top for his gaze.

"Have you ever heard of AUDREY'S back room?"

DYLAN DIDN'T WAIT for her to ask a second time. He pulled her off of her stool, lifting her up as she made a happy squeal and carrying her in the direction Lola pointed. He could still smell old fear off of Marie's skin, could see the strain in the corner of her eyes from talking about a part of her life she obviously hated to relive. Even as she told her abbreviated version, he could see from the tenseness of her body it had been much worse than she described. He felt like an asshole for even asking about it, but he was glad he understood her better. It made sense now how someone as amazing as Marie could have fallen into the role of motorcycle club medic. She relied on their protection rather than the human law enforcement system that failed to keep her safe.

That was something else they had in common: the system had failed them. But she didn't seem embittered by it. She still worked as a nurse at hospitals and clinics wherever the club set up, helping people and using Puff to save those who would otherwise not be saved. Her strength and kindness floored him.

He kicked open the door of AUDREY'S back room, still holding Marie in his arms. The room was small, one wall covered in boxes while most of the room was filled by a cot barely large enough for one person. He gently lay her down on the blankets, leaning down to kiss her.

"Marie, you're never going to go through that again. I promise," Dylan said, pushing up her shirt to kiss her stomach.

She grabbed the back of his head by the hair and pulled him away from her torso so she could look into his eyes.

"Don't you dare treat me like I'm fragile," she said. "I'm a big girl and I want you hard and dirty, Dylan Masters."

Holy dragon lords.

His whole body felt heightened and arousal coursed through him. He briefly transformed a single finger into a dragon claw and slashed through her blouse, ripping it off her body. Her tan skin glowed with sweat, and her chest's aroused blush was like an arrow drawing his attention to her beautiful breasts. She was the most glorious creature he'd ever seen, all womanly curves he ached to hold onto. The strength in her eyes and the stubborn set of her chin appealed to his dragon, who roared with appreciation of a mate who could match him.

She unhooked her bra and threw it across the room, sitting up on her knees to get closer to him and undo his belt. She yanked down his jeans and his boxers so his hardness was in front of her face. She bit down on her lip and Dylan groaned, his hips unconsciously thrusting toward her mouth.

"I don't know what conclusion you've reached from my fucked up life story," she said, using his precum to lubricate his shaft, running her hand up and down his dick as her other hand cupped his balls. "But I'm a nurse and a motorcycle chick and a friend and a hundred other things before I'm a witness on the run." She took a deep breath and her breasts rose and fell.

"Do you know what else you are?" Dylan said, reaching down to grab her breasts with both hands, pinching her nipples hard between his fingers. She arched back, pushing her breasts more firmly into his hands. Her breasts were large enough their flesh overflowed his grip, and he loved it.

"What else?" Her voice was breathless now, and he could smell the musk of her arousal in the air. He hadn't thought his cock could become harder, but knowing she was aroused and wanted him drove him crazy. He needed her slick passage around his dick. Now.

"Sexy as fuck." He pulled her to her feet, pulling off her skirt and underwear and pushing her chest up against the door.

"Yes!" she cried, her hips thrusting backward toward him. He spread her legs with his hands and pushed two fingers deep into her.

"You're so wet," he said, biting her shoulder hard enough to mark her. She screamed and the scent of her arousal increased, her passage soaking his fingers. He withdrew and positioned his dick at her entrance, then thrust in hard. She felt so tight, and he moaned and grabbed her breast, pinching the nipple the way she liked it as she squirmed and bucked. Her body flexed around his cock, consuming him, helping him lose himself in the soft wetness of her. He withdrew and thrust back in slowly, stretching her and waiting for her to adjust to his girth.

"Dylan, fuck me! Harder! I need, oh God, fuck!" her words tumbled incoherently, but he couldn't deny her. Pushing her against the door, her breasts pressed against the wood. He slammed into her, roughly holding her ass, then lifting up one of her legs to get a better angle to push his dick all the way in and fuck her hard.

"Yes!"

He could feel her beginning to come, her insides clenching as her screams grew higher, and she roared. Her whole body writhed and stretched, her fists pounding against the door as he felt her pussy spasm around his shaft. He reached the hand on her breast down to flick her delicate clit, prolonging her pleasure as she surged up and down against his cock. She finally slumped, exhausted against the door, and he withdrew, still holding her naked body close to his.

"That was--"she started to say, but Dylan flipped her around so her back was pressed to the door, lifting up her legs so they wrapped around his hips.

"Did you think we were done?" he said, his voice rough. He lifted up her hips so she came down hard on his cock, buried deep as he leveraged her against the door to thrust up into her, gravity pulling her down hard on his shaft. "You have a lot higher to fly, my dragon."

Her eyes were bright and her face was still flushed from her first orgasm, but her legs' grip around his hips was steady and strong.

"I'm not a dragon. I'm a human," she said, laughing as she levered herself up to rub her breasts against his chest.

He lifted her up again, impaling her so deep with his dick she gasped and fell back against the door. He adjusted his grip along her ass until he reached the right angle, then plunged into her again.

"You're a dragon in your soul. My dragon knows when he's met his match."

Her eyes went wide, but he didn't give her a chance to respond. He leaned forward to kiss her, biting at her lip and rolling his tongue in her mouth as his thrusts picked up the pace. She moaned into his mouth, biting at his lip while her tongue explored and thrust into his mouth at the same rhythm his cock fucked her. The aroused noises she was making drove him wild as his thrusts came closer together, throwing them both against the door in furious strokes. He could feel her passage clench around him again as she came a second time. It was the extra edge he needed to come, pouring himself into her and roaring with jubilation.

He blinked back to awareness after what felt like an hour of blissful stars. Marie's face was close to his, her expression equally befuddled with post-coital calm.

"Marie--" He didn't know what he wanted to say. It was too early to use words like love, but he felt like he needed to say something to convey the rightness it felt to be here with her. "You're amazing."

"You better not continue that sentence with a but," she said, her eyes flashing in warning.

"No, you are only an 'and,' no 'buts'," he smiled. "Unless you really like butts," he said, sliding his hand around to cup her ass. She laughed.

"Butts are for another time," she said, an eyebrow raising. His cock twitched at the thought of another time. As they gathered their clothes and dressed--she had to borrow his jacket after he'd destroyed her blouse--he couldn't shake the feeling that he needed to remember every detail of this night. This was the beginning of something special. *She* was someone special. And, in his experience, the special ones didn't last long.

SETTING up the merchandise stand next to a speaker had been a huge mistake, Marie realized. The music itself wasn't a problem--the band Caesar was playing with this time was amazing--but Marie couldn't help but feel a little disappointed she wasn't able to talk with Dylan over the thumping bass. He fascinated her in every way: how he could understand the parts of her story she never spoke, how his eyes occasionally grew dark and sad when he thought nobody was looking, the way he mercilessly pounded into her, over and over...

"May I have one *special edition* CD, please?" an elderly woman in a floral dress asked Marie. The woman looked so small and weak, her blue veins showing brightly through her near-translucent skin. Marie recognized the woman from the hospital. She had four grandkids she talked about constantly. She was one of the clients Marie had hoped would make it to the first drop-off at the flea market. The converted clubhouse wasn't exactly a comfortable meeting spot for the over-seventy crowd.

"Looks like it's on sale today! Only ten bucks." Marie smiled, trying not to let pity creep into her facial expression. She remembered hating the piteous stares during her time as a witness to a grisly murder, and especially years later when she was sick.

The least I can do is give her a real smile with the drugs, Marie thought.

Marie tried to look natural, like she wasn't distributing drugs at a concert like some terrible cliché from an after-school special. Concerts drew in a younger crowd, and young people meant camera phones. *Everywhere*. Setting up the distribution spot here had been risky, but in this small town, opportunities were low on the ground. She was pretty sure nobody could so much as sneeze at the bar tonight without it ending up on YouTube.

The old woman gripped the CD jewel case in both hands, shaking and smiling, a tear streaming down her cheek. The joy in the woman's face reminded Marie of why they did this work. The "special edition CD"--code for a CD case filled with bags of Puff--came complete with instructional liner notes printed up. Big Joe had coordinated with Caesar to make Puff's dosage instructions lyrical enough to pass as actual songs to someone who didn't know his music.

"Thank you, this means so much to me." The old woman grasped Marie's hand quickly, giving a squeeze before she tottered off, the crowd of punks and thugs parting to make room for her. Marie chuckled as Big Joe lifted a skulking teenager out of her path.

He bared his teeth and let out a roar: "Make way for Nana!"

Marie turned to deposit the money into the cashbox and ran into a wall of warmth and muscles. *Shit. I need to look where I'm going.* She tilted her face upwards to see Dylan grinning broadly down at her. He wrapped an arm around her waist, pulling her close, and shouted into her ear.

The speaker boomed and hummed, drowning out his words.

Marie stood up on her tiptoes and tried to mouth "What?" to him using exaggerated movements. He responded with a vague gesture that she couldn't understand; it looked like two birds fighting or perhaps a turtle dying.

"I can't hear you!" Marie cried, pointing at her ear and trying to shout over the music. He pointed toward the center of the room and made the same gesture again. This time

Marie was almost certain he was miming someone making pizza.

Emma walked over from Marie's side of the merch table and waved her hand out to the mass of dancing concert-goers.

"GO!" Emma said, moving her mouth deliberately so they could read her lips and shooing Dylan and Marie towards the dance floor. Marie could feel her face grow hot. Dylan had been asking her to dance and she completely missed it.

I'm going to hear about this tomorrow, Marie thought, dreading the jibes she was going to receive. She looked at Dylan's face. The lines of his jaw were *perfect*. The inevitable razzing was absolutely worth it.

Marie felt Dylan's hand encompass her palm, her sexy dragon leading her away from the deafening speaker. The bar where the club lived and worked wasn't huge, but it was sufficient for Caesar's concerts. Marie worried the rickety building might shake apart from the sheer volume emanating from Alec's speaker setup, but as she and Dylan walked away from the merch & Puff table, the music stopped and then started up again, slower and sweeter. Marie tried to stifle a laugh as they moved together. Of course it was time for the power ballad.

"May I have this dance?" Dylan was all charm in his Henley shirt and ripped jeans. His voice was low, and goose bumps tingled along her skin.

Marie nodded, stepping closer into his embrace. His hands felt warm on her sides, and she ran her fingers across his shoulders before leaning in so the tops of her breasts brushed against his chest. They swayed gently, pressing into one another as the music rang out around them. Marie could feel the beat of his heart as they moved, and it skipped when she snaked her arms around his neck, gripping the long coils of hair that went down his back.

"I can't stop thinking about you." He brushed a stray eyelash off her cheek, and she felt her breath hitch. "It sounds so stupid saying it out loud, but it's true."

"Is that so?" Marie cocked an eyebrow at him, keeping her face close to his. Marie inhaled deeply, breathing in his scent. He smelled of leather, grease, and sweat--all man. Being so close made her want to taste him again, and she tingled with anticipation. The power ballad seemed to cushion and surround them, the music deep and throbbing. Dancing with Dylan felt as natural as breathing, the easy ebb and sway of their bodies like floating.

"If you can't stop thinking about me, that might be a medical issue." She winked, pulling him off the dance floor to the stairs leading to the loft apartments above the bar. "I'm a medical professional. I should probably take a look to make sure you're okay."

"Yes, nurse." Dylan crushed her against the wall of the stairwell, capturing her mouth with his own, probing intensely with his tongue while his hands roamed all over her. She met him with equal ferocity, bruising his lips with her own. This time, she was determined to be in charge.

Breathless, she broke away from him, pulling him by the arm as she nearly ran up the stairs to her apartment. Her hands shook with excitement as she fumbled with her keys, her attempts to work the lock hampered by the distraction of Dylan's mouth on the back of her neck.

They burst into her apartment, laughing and kissing. Her place was bare-bones. The club moved around so often it didn't make sense to own more than could be thrown in a car or strapped to a bike. Her sole belongings consisted of two duffel bags of clothes next to the bed.

"So, my patient, you'll need to get undressed so I can examine you." Marie pointed towards her bed, "On the examination table."

Dylan removed his shirt in one swift motion, the fabric flying over his head to reveal tight muscles. Marie resisted the urge to run her hands all over his tempting body. *Not yet.*

He slowly unbuttoned his jeans, never breaking eye contact as he moved, kicking off his shoes and dropping his pants to the ground. His erection tented his lion-print boxers, the last piece of clothing remaining, and he paused, making her wait.

She stepped forward and hooked her fingers into his boxers and dragged them to the floor, kneeling in front of him. She licked the precum off of his dick, running her fingers gently along the shaft.

"It looks like you have some localized swelling." She remembered their role play. "Lie back on the exam table so I can take a look."

Dylan did as he was told, lying on his back on the bed, breathing heavily. Marie could tell how much she was turning him on, and it sent a thrill to her core.

"Stick your tongue out and say 'ah.' " Marie kneeled next to him on the mattress. As soon as he complied she struck, covering his mouth with her own, licking and sucking on his tongue. His hands found her waist and he tried to pull her closer.

Marie pulled away. "No touching the nurse, sir." She ran her fingers along the strong contours of his jaw and down his neck, caressing his exposed skin. "Let's find out what's causing this swelling."

"Nurse, I feel tingly all over." Dylan's voice came out in a low grumble. He gripped at the blankets beneath him, his knuckles white with the struggle to keep his hands off of her. "It feels better where you touch me," he said in a play-fully hopeful tone.

Marie brought her mouth to Dylan's neck, nipping and sucking at him. She could feel his pulse racing under his skin as her hands explored his broad chest.

"Interesting." She sat up, slowly unbuttoning her shirt. "Increased skin-on-skin contact soothes the patient." She stripped as she spoke, throwing her jeans in a pile next to Dylan's. "Anything to make my patient feel better." Marie, completely bare now, pushed Dylan's hands down away from her.

She ran her hands through the deep grooves in Dylan's abs, and he let out a low moan. She leaned forward, pressing her naked flesh into his, completely on top of him now. She kissed him quickly.

"Tell me where it hurts."

Breathless, he pointed at his throbbing cock, purple and swollen with want. Marie kissed her way down his body, stopping to suck at his nipples, until she was gripping his thighs. She ran her fingers along his length, moving in to lick and suck at his balls. His hand twined through her long dark hair as she moved, his touch gentle, not guiding.

She licked him, slowly up one side, circling across the tip, and down the other, reveling in the sounds he made as she teased him.

"I think I can cure you." She briefly took him inside her mouth, releasing him with a pop. "But you'll have to trust me."

"Yes, nurse." Dylan was breathing so hard, Marie could barely hear his response as she positioned herself above him. She lowered herself down slowly, impaling herself on his cock, marveling at the expression of joy on his face. She slammed down on him, surprising herself with her rough-ness, riding him hard.

His hands gripped her waist as Dylan plunged into her, meeting her thrusts with upward bursts of his own. Still moving, he pulled her down towards him, capturing one of her nipples in his mouth. He sucked and bit at her tender flesh, growling with pleasure as he pounded into her. She was so close it was like nearing the edge of a cliff. Her breath came quick and she tightened her grip on his hard stomach, urging him to go faster and take her over.

Dylan quickly pulled her off of him and rolled, posi-tioning Marie on her back. He slid down her body, keeping one hand massaging and rolling her breast. She groaned, wanting him inside her.

"Nurse, you're all wet down here." He slid his tongue over her core in one long movement. "May I lick this up?"

"Oh, god yes." Marie squirmed under his touch, trying not to thrust against his face. She had been so close to coming when he was inside of her, and she longed for release.

Dylan kissed her folds, his tongue flicking out to devour her. His mouth latched on her clit briefly, and the feeling of him sucking at her sensitive spot made Marie's head swim. His mouth moved once more, licking every inch of her pussy in unpredictable ways, darting then slow, licking then sucking. It was driving her mad.

Her legs began to shake around him as he moved once more to her clit, flicking his tongue at it. He thrust two fingers inside of her suddenly, and it was too much. She came, screaming his name, convulsing around his fingers as the fiery ecstasy raced through her.

Dylan slid back up her body, his large hands circling her face gently as he softly kissed her. She could taste herself on him, and it made her blood rush. She was ready for more. She moaned, squirming beneath him, purposefully rubbing against his erection. His eyes glazed over with lust as her small hand encircled his shaft, positioning it at her entrance.

"Fuck me," she whispered.

Dylan's response was immediate, slamming into her fully, making her gasp. He was so huge, so thick, he hit every sensitive spot at once. His hand found her clit and rubbed it furiously as he fucked her hard, slamming the bed against the wall. The thumping of the bed synchronized with the thumping of the bass from the bar beneath them, and Marie could feel another orgasm building.

"Come for me again, baby." Dylan sat up, placing Marie's ankles over his shoulders. He pounded her even deeper in this new position. It was more than she could take. She came again, her final explosion met with Dylan's hot cum as he emptied himself into her, howling with pleasure as his thrusts slowed to a stop.

The last thing Marie remembered was being pulled close by strong arms, and a deep voice telling her something about love.

She woke with a start, the night silent except for the sound of Dylan's soft snoring and crickets outside her cracked window. Her phone glowed on the nightstand next to her, "1 New Message" displayed on the screen.

She slid away from Dylan slowly, to not wake him up, and read the message. She had to bite her hand to keep from screaming. The text message was from a blocked number. It read simply: "found you". Beneath was a screenshot of a YouTube video from last night's concert. In the picture Marie was smiling, dancing with Dylan under a sign marked "The Claw".

Vinny the Fist.

I am going to die.

DYLAN FLEXED his shoulders and forced himself not to check again to confirm his knife was still secure and ready on his belt. His back felt sore from being so tense for so long. He hadn't relaxed in the last eight hours since the creepy-ass text had come through from Marie's long-ago tormentor. After the text came through, she woke him up and he'd roused the rest of the club to high alert. A trained murderer was coming, and Dylan doubted the man would come alone.

The clubhouse was a squat two-story building in the middle of a clearing on the edge of town with enough space around to park the bikes and give clear line of sight for any attackers. But Dylan didn't trust the side streets. He would rather identify any enemies before they'd gotten the chance to come within shooting distance of the building. He'd convinced Big Joe to send club members to scout out the other radiating streets and paths leading up to the house, with no one going far enough they couldn't run back and protect The Claw if trouble came calling.

Dylan could smell Caesar on the breeze one street over, his distinctive smell of aftershave and guitar polish clear and comforting. Dylan wasn't sure about the man as a fighter, but Caesar moved quickly and with enough confidence Dylan was glad he was so close. Ned, newly healed and ready for action, was on the other street, smelling of the licorice hidden in his pockets and his coconut shampoo. Ned probably didn't realize it, but Dylan could also pick up Alec's scent tailing the youngster a few feet behind, the man identifiable by his distinct smell of solder and coffee. It had been so long since Dylan went into a fight with a pack; he had forgotten how good it felt to know there were people close by who had his back. He liked the feeling of belonging to something again.

If anything happened to Marie, Dylan wasn't sure what he would do. Just a few days with her and he felt like his entire self was transformed into something more. Falling in love with her would be easy and it was there, a tantalizing promise just around the corner. She excited and soothed him, challenged and relaxed him. She was fun, yet serious, drop dead gorgeous with her curves, yet apparently unaware of the fact.

He stalked the streets looking for signs of anyone who shouldn't be there. A grandmother out shopping with her grandson, an exhausted-looking father holding two shopping bags of diapers, a couple of tiger shifters fucking against the wall in the alley behind the convenience store, a witch lighting a clove cigarette with her finger talking to a friend about going to happy hour at AUDREY'S, and there... a man leaning against the doorframe of a hardware store.

The man looked like he was leaning, but his feet were placed with perfect balance. It was a very distinctive stance. His hands were in his pockets, the edges of his fingers wrapped around larger objects under his jacket. The man's clothes were dipped in something that smelled extra cloying, the harsh smell of cherry air freshener disguising his actual scent. A Counsel goon.

The goon was talking to another man just around the corner out of Dylan's sight. Dylan ducked behind a parked truck, grateful he was downwind and the goon hadn't gotten a whiff of him yet. He focused on the conversation happening in front of him, actively ignoring the grunting from the tiger shifters and the witches' conversation.

"--that bitch has this coming," said the man inside the building. There was something about the man's voice that was slimy and unsettling. Dylan's inner dragon roared and thrashed, wanting to be released to attack. But Dylan made himself stay still. There were more cloying smells in the building, and too many other men standing around who didn't seem to have a purpose to be there. He was outnumbered; attacking them now would be suicide.

"Just be sure all of your men have the blades we gave you," the goon said. Dylan could hear the annoyance in the goon's voice. "Don't make me regret allying with you."

"Those bastards won't see us coming," Fist grunted.

Yes we will, Dylan thought. He pulled out his phone and sent a blast text to the club.

"GOONS WITH VINNY, MOB HAS HEX BLADES," Dylan wrote. A second later, another blast text came through from Big Joe.

"EVERYONE BACK TO THE CLUB NOW."

Dylan approved. Now that they knew the extent of their enemies' weapons and resources, they would be safer on their home turf, with better access to their weapons. The mob was joining up with the Red Guard; the Iron Claws would need every advantage. The clearing around the club also gave them the space--if necessary--to shift to dragon form. Looking over at the elderly woman standing in front of the candy store window, Dylan knew having the fight right here would result in too many innocent casualties.

"I still don't see why we can't just use guns," Fist was saying. Every word the man said made Dylan want to rip him up with his claws. "I've got a sniper who could just shoot through the damn window--"

"You don't know who you're dealing with, Fist," the goon's voice was hard. "These are dragons. Your bullets would just bounce off, and they'd hear the click of your gun before your man had a chance to fire. Have your men stick close to us and we'll all get what we want: your snitch in the grave and our nuisances burned to the ground."

Dylan started to back away. He'd heard enough, and he should regroup with the rest of the Claws.

"Just so long as you can get me a few minutes with that bitch before you all burn that motherfucking place to the ground," Fist said.

Dylan froze.

"There's going to be a battle, Fist," the goon said, sounding annoyed. "Just get rid of our problem. We won't have time for--"

"I don't care about your fucking dragon politics. That bitch is going to suffer, and I'm going to make it slow."

Dylan didn't stop to think. He felt his dragon erupting out of him with the instinctual need to protect his mate. His neck elongated and his jaws emerged while flames ripped from his chest and spurted into the house filled with Fist and the Counsel goons.

The goon in front of the door shifted his arm to a giant fireproof wing at the last possible second, blocking Dylan's flame from striking the men. Dylan roared with frustration, dodging the goon's responding ball of flame. The goon's fire rolled over the truck Dylan had been hiding behind, exploding it in a ball of metal and gasoline. Screaming filled the streets as bystanders ran for cover.

Behind him, Dylan heard another explosion coming from The Claw and the sound of metal against metal. The clubhouse was under attack. His blood went cold, and he completed the transition to his full dragon shape, flying back toward the clubhouse.

I must get back to Marie.

He sent one baleful glare back toward the house where Fist was still hiding behind the goon's wing. It was so tempting to burn the whole building from here and screw the consequences to the surrounding buildings. But Fist would come to him soon enough. Right now, Dylan needed to get back and protect the club.

He just hoped he wasn't already too late.

IT WAS all going so wrong.

Ever since she received the text from Vinny the Fist, everything flew into chaos.

The Claw's main area was designed as a bar and sometimes music venue, not for defense. It was open with a raised stage at one end, the only protected area behind the bar. A few pool tables clustered near one wall, along with a few smaller high tables. Large windows took up most of the walls. They'd built an escape hatch through the floor behind the bar for emergencies, but Marie hoped they wouldn't have to use it.

Ned, Caesar, and Alec had gone with Dylan to scout out any Fratellis coming their way, leaving her alone in the house with only Big Joe and Emma. Of course those two couldn't be in a room alone without sniping at each other, and as Marie got her medical supplies in order, she contemplated throwing water at them. *Seriously, guys? You're going to hone that sexual tension now?*

Marie wasn't too worried. After all, she had befriended

the biggest, baddest kids on the playground. Her enemies had bullets and knives? Well, she had talons and fire.

Her phone buzzed with a text from Dylan. *The mob has hex blades.* Marie's hands shook as she read his warning. The goons were coming for her and her dragons, and they could do real damage.

Emma cried out a warning and Marie dropped to the ground behind the bar as a burst of flame erupted through the window. Emma bellowed a warrior cry and ran out the door, shifting as soon as she crossed the threshold, her grey scales winking in the sun. Big Joe shot off a quick text to the group ordering everyone home before he sprinted after Emma.

Three men burst through the door wearing Fratelli colors, and Marie ducked behind the bar as the clashing of swords and flames turned the world into madness. Hollers alerted her the rest of the club had returned from their scouting, but she couldn't hear Dylan's voice. Marie gripped her med kit, huddled behind the bar, listening to the sounds of screams and breaking glass shattering on the floor.

"Get the fuck out of here!" Caesar roared as he dove over the hardwood bar top, barely dodging a hex blade aimed at his throat. He huddled down amongst the liquor bottles, quickly thrusting a fist upward into the chin of the closest attacker. Caesar's pursuer fell still, and Caesar pulled his limp body down next to him on the floor. Marie rushed forward to confirm the goon still had a pulse, sighing with relief the limp goon wasn't dead.

Caesar gently pushed her aside, grabbing blades and guns off the man's body. He used the gun to blindly shoot over the edge of the bar. Bullets wouldn't hurt any of the dragon club members, but it would keep the Fratelli goons at bay for a few seconds. Caesar tore off his shirt, revealing the complex pattern of tattoos covering his chest, and shifting his head and neck partially to dragon form. His neck glowed orange as the fire grew inside of him.

"Marie, you have to get the fuck out of here. Use the back door. Run for the woods," Caesar yelled before letting out a blast of flame.

Marie clenched her teeth. She wasn't going anywhere. She clasped her med kit tightly to her chest. *I'm club medic. I'm not leaving my friends to die.* The battle raged all around her: Caesar fighting next to her, Ned and Alec inside the concert space in human form, flanked by the Red Guard and mob hitters, their fighting restricted to knives, guns, and swords by the smallness of the room. Through a shattered window Marie could see the rest of the club as fully-shifted dragons battling mid-air, latching on to Counsel goons with razor-sharp talons and dripping fangs.

Marie heard someone inside give out a howl--it sounded like Alec--and she sprinted towards the pool tables where the sound originated. A rush of adrenaline surged through her as the wall next to her head splintered and exploded outwards, probably from a stray bullet or a thrown dagger; she didn't stop to see what.

Ducking around the debris, Marie saw Alec holding an onyx-colored sword in his left hand, bellowing as he lopped off the head of the Red Guard about to stab him with a hex blade. The disembodied head bounced to the ground with a sickening sound as Alec slid to the floor, gripping a wound on his right shoulder. He tried to rip off the bottom of his shirt to staunch the wound, but Marie grabbed his hand.

"Hey, leave this to the professionals," Marie said as she ducked down under the pool table, gently moving Alec's bloody hand from his wound. She moved quickly, whipping items out of her med kit with practiced expertise as she tended to the gaping hole in Alec's shoulder.

"Thanks, Doc." Alec had gone pale and twitched painfully at her touch. "How we lookin' out there?"

"Caesar's almost done--" A loud bang shook the bar, and the sound of newly-formed flames filled the room. "Caesar *is* done handling the guy that was after him." She breathed a sigh of relief as she heard the sounds of a fire extinguisher being deployed. "Counting Headless over here, we've got one more of their guys on the inside. Emma, Big Joe, and Dylan are outside, shifted and giving them hell. "

"Do you have eyes on the last guy standing in here?" Alec was shaking now, and losing a lot of blood. Marie scanned the room for him as she grabbed a suture kit from her bag.

A loud, surprisingly high-pitched scream rang out, and Ned suddenly appeared, slamming into the wall beside them and pulling the table down on its side for better cover.

"Shit, Alec, you okay?" he said.

"I'll be fine if you handle the last fucker!" Alec's eyes flashed furiously as he threw Ned the onyx blade.

Ned gripped the blade's hilt with both hands, lifting the sword over his head. He bellowed at the top of his lungs, leaping over the pool table and sprinting across the room towards his opponent. The man had been leaning over one of the other fallen goons and was so surprised at tiny Ned's sudden ferocity he didn't have time to stop the blade from running straight through his torso.

Ned immediately vomited. Marie felt tempted to do the same.

"Ned! Come over here and keep an eye on Alec!" Marie finished the last suture and ran back to the bar. She hurried back from the fridge with a bag of blood labeled "Alec" and hooked it up to a vein in Alec's arm. Alec winced as Marie inserted the needle, and Marie bit back her angry, "Told you!" Alec had been one of the club members who called her paranoid for insisting they stock their blood for emergencies.

"Alec, keep an eye on Ned," Marie whispered. "Caesar! You okay?"

"I'll be better once I kick some Counsel goon ass!" Caesar grinned as he emerged from behind the bar, a small trickle of blood winding its way down his forehead.

Marie and Caesar ran outside where the beat of dragons' wings was blowing around anything not nailed down. Caesar shifted immediately, leaving Marie alone to watch the behemoths battle against the bright blue sky.

She gasped, her chest tight with wonder and fear. The sky seemed to be filled with dragons of every color, blasting flame, swiping razor-sharp claws, and whipping pointed tails at their opponents' unprotected bellies and faces.

Marie had heard about all the politics and bullshit that came with being a shifter. She never really wanted to be part of that world, never felt jealous about not being able to change her physical appearance so drastically. Until today. She would have given anything to be able to transform and join her Iron Claws family in the air, fighting to protect their group as much as for herself.

All the club members were faced off against the Red Guard. Emma was up against two--one dark green and the other mustard-colored. The green dragon was bleeding heavily from the neck and thrashed as Emma tore at its throat, peeling away protective layers of scales as she clawed and gnawed through its flesh. The green dragon stilled, staring with blank, unseeing eyes. It fell from the sky with a loud thump that shook the ground. A second thump from the other side of the house made Marie jump. Another goon down, killed by one of the club members.

Tears welled up in Marie's eyes. Killing went against everything she believed in. Even if the Red Guard and the Fratellis were murderers, she hated their deaths. She hated that, because of her, Ned had to kill someone back in the bar, and that this all happened because the Iron Claws had taken her in.

Marie counted. She recognized Dylan, Big Joe, Emma, and Caesar, leaving two Counsel dragons left she didn't know. With the two goons down, the battle was quickly becoming one-sided, with the enemy dragons struggling to escape the beating they were taking from the Iron Claws. One of the purple-colored goons had a long tear in his wing, while the other black dragon had a massive wound on its stomach. Marie felt tears running freely down her face as she watched the majestic creatures destroying their own kind.

She must have made a sound because Dylan turned to look at her across the distance, and she locked eyes with him.

"Stop this," she mouthed to him.

Dylan spun and beat his wings so the air pushed the goons away from the throng, then turned to block his fellow Iron Claws from pursuing them. The other Iron Claw dragons seemed to understand what he was doing: letting the others escape back to their masters, ending the fight.

"Marie! You're going to want to take a look at this!" Alec's voice yelled from the other side of the clubhouse.

Marie ran toward his voice, trying to figure out who could possibly be injured. As she rounded the bend, she heard the sound of dragons landing around her: Emma, Big Joe, and Dylan coming close to protect her if necessary.

Vinny the Fist lay bleeding on the ground, a deep wound from a talon straight through his gut. He was feet away from the back entrance to the clubhouse. Someone must have spotted him trying to get in the back way through the barroom floor and stopped him before he reached it. He was still breathing, but only just.

"Call 911!" Marie yelled at Ned. "We need an ambulance." She tried to move to Vinny's side, but Big Joe stepped in front of her.

"What are you doing? This man brought the goons down on us!"

"He's hurt," Marie said. "Get out of my fucking way and let me do my job."

Big Joe nodded and stepped out of the way. Marie started to wipe down the area around the wound with antiseptic and gave him a sedative to numb the pain, keeping constant pressure on the bleeding wound. Vinny the Fist was still conscious and looking at her like she was insane.

"I was going to kill you," he muttered, his voice slurred.

"Yes, and now I'm trying to save your life," she said as she brought out a fresh suture kit and began to close up his wound.

Big Joe ordered the rest of the Iron Claws back into the clubhouse to start getting packed up to leave before the goons came back, leaving Dylan and Emma on guard in case Vinny tried anything.

Vinny was quiet for so long Marie thought he'd fallen unconscious. She could hear the ambulance coming closer and she let out a deep breath. If he'd lasted this long, there was a good chance he'd make it.

"I owe you now, woman," Vinny finally said. "I'll call off the hit."

Emma stepped forward to kneel next to his face. "Yeah,

because next time I'm going to slash off your head, not your gullet," she said. Marie shivered. Her friends were a little scary sometimes, but she was grateful they were on her side.

As the ambulance pulled up, Marie heard the roar of motorcycle engines coming to life on the other side of the building.

Time to go.

DYLAN FELT a warm contentment fill his chest. Another town, another distribution point. This time, they were selling Puff out of an auto repair shop run by a pair of friendly werewolves--supporters of the Iron Claws' work. Local humans heard about the "experimental treatment" from Marie at the local clinic, and word spread fast. They approached cautiously, shyly coming forward with hope on their faces. This time the Claws were selling "double premium-grade oil": oil cans filled with packets of Puff, labeled with instructions for proper use.

The whole club was there. Big Joe and Emma bickered away (even as they finished each other's sentences) while they put together packets and instruction manuals in the back room. Caesar lounged against a wall with his guitar, jotting down new lyrics as he strummed a few chords. Alec worked the register and took careful notes on his tablet of the recipients and their dosages. Ned stood at the distribution table looking uncomfortable, his expression far away.

"We need to find Ned a girl," Marie said, coming up to stand beside Dylan. He figured she deserved a break from greeting her patients as they came by and reminding them the proper code word to get the miraculous "experimental treatment."

"He's been acting strangely for the last week. It's possible he already has a girl," Dylan said.

Dylan was just happy they hadn't seen any sign of the Counsel or the Red Guard in months, and he'd gotten word through the grapevine the Fratellis had officially stopped their hunt for Marie. Vinny the Fist had lived and kept his word, it seemed. The day the club found out, Dylan and Marie had made love for three hours against every surface of his bedroom, rejoicing in their new sense of freedom. Marie was safe, at least until the Counsel caught up with them again.

Dylan wrapped his arms around Marie and breathed in her scent, letting it calm and settle him. He loved knowing she was close and safe. It was only a matter of time, of course, before the goons came back, more prepared this time for the Iron Claws' defenses. In the meantime, Dylan was happy to enjoy being surrounded by his new friends and family.

"Marie?"

"Hmm?" she said, snuggling close to his side. Her eyes followed a small family, a mother and father pushing a pale child in a stroller in front of them. They took the canister of Puff from Ned, paid Alec, and left, their footsteps lighter than when they walked in.

"You know I love you, right?" he said.

"Well, you haven't told me in the last three days, but I'm glad to see it's still valid," she said, reaching up to kiss the tip of his nose playfully. "I still love you too, in case you were wondering."

He responded by grabbing the back of her head and swallowing her mouth in a passionate kiss. The werewolf owners of the auto repair shop made comical gagging sounds. Dylan ignored them.

"And how would you feel about spending the rest of your life mated to me?" he said, looking deep into her eyes. He couldn't think of a better place to ask her than surrounded by the club's work helping and healing people. This was the part of being an Iron Claw that mattered, not fighting and killing to protect themselves, but this: using what they had to make the world better.

Marie looked up at him, her eyes filling with tears. For a second, Dylan felt panic--*I made her cry!*--until he realized she was laughing.

"Of course, my sexy dragon. I thought you'd never ask."

Dylan picked her up in the middle of the repair shop, lifting her legs to wrap around his waist, and kissing her deeply, thrusting his tongue into her mouth. He distantly heard a scuffling noise and then Big Joe's voice from close by.

"Back room is clear, you two. Get in there before you scare the children."

Dylan didn't stop kissing Marie as he carried her to the back room and kicked the door closed behind them. From the other side of the wall, he could hear the whole club cheering.

His last conscious thought as he dissolved into passion was,

I'm home.

HER DELICIOUS DRAGON

Don't *fuck this up.* Ned fumbled with two plastic containers of cream puffs, each the size of a microwave, as he waited outside the intimidating mansion. He almost dropped the precious cargo twice on his way up the tiger shifters' long driveway lined with stone statues of naked couples and threesomes mid-thrust. Tigers had a reputation for extreme sexual appetites and—if the decor of their alpha's mansion was any indication—they earned it.

Ned gulped, staring up at the mansion's large wooden doors, each taller than two Neds standing atop one another. He floundered with the boxes for a second before success-fully striking the doorbell with his elbow. *Nailed it.* He smiled.

Ned waited for someone to answer, tapping his foot impatiently. He told himself there were worse things than being the Iron Claws' errand boy, always being sent out for jobs that didn't require physical strength, technical skills, or pure cunning. Each member of the motorcycle club was a clanless dragon shifter, but they all brought really useful, unique skills to the table.

All but me.

"Yes?" A suspicious voice made him focus on the job at hand.

Ned looked up into the most gorgeous brown eyes he'd ever seen. The woman glared at him expectantly, dressed simply in a tight black tank top and jeans with a taser on her hip. She was breathtaking. Her stunning amber-colored skin, fierce eyes, and the shining red bindi between her eyebrows almost made Ned forget why he was there. The woman tossed her long hair, twisted into a complicated braid, over her shoulder and Ned realized she was awaiting his response.

"Hi, I'm Ned." He fumbled to try and shake her hand while still holding the large parcels of desserts. He finally gave up after the cream puffs slid in the box at extreme angles and settled for what he hoped looked like a cool nod. "From the Iron Claws? They sent me to drop these off for Gita?" A droplet of sweat worked its way down the side of Ned's face. "Am I at the right place?"

"*You're* with the Iron Claws?" The woman smiled, stepping close to Ned. "I thought you would be..."

"Bigger?" Ned guessed. He heard it all the time. He wasn't exactly short—Ned stood just shy of six feet tall—but his fellow Claws dwarfed him in comparison.

"I was going to say *dirtier*. For a motorcycle guy, you clean up nice." The woman took the containers from Ned's hands and set them down. "Now spread 'em."

"What?"

"I'm Maya Bethi, head of security for Alpha Raj. I need to check you for weapons and the like."

"S-sure, I guess?" Ned willed his body not to react as Maya's hands slid down his outstretched arms, over his shoulders, and all along the muscles of his chest. He tried to think of anything other than how wonderful her touch felt as she knelt to the ground before him, sliding her hands from his ankles up to his calves, his thighs, his...

"Okay you're good." She smiled, now eyeing the desserts she had set aside. "So what's with the pastries?"

"The box with the sticker is for Gita. We heard your alpha's favorite..." Ned felt his face turn hot as he blushed furiously "...consort was sick, so I baked some of our Puff into these chocolate ganache cream puffs so she can get better."

"I heard you crazy kids were distributing Puff to humans." Maya smiled approvingly. "Bold."

She thinks I'm tough! "It's a dangerous job. The High Dragon Council strictly forbids it, so we're in constant danger, getting into fights and shootouts. We don't really care about the Council and their hitmen and their rules," Ned bragged. Puff, a powder of ground-up dragon scales, had miraculous healing effects on humans. Just a few doses could heal or even bring a human back from the brink of death. The High Council forbade distribution of Puff, paranoid that humans would return to hunting dragons for their scales like they had centuries before.

"Okay, killer," Maya said dryly. "Gita's room is up the stairs to the left." She stopped Ned before he crossed the threshold. "You mentioned Gita's medicine is in one of the boxes. What's in the other?"

Ned shuffled the boxes so the unlabeled one was on top. He popped open the lid and grinned widely. "These are chocolate ganache cream puffs with no Puff in them. I thought some of your clan might like them."

Maya delicately dipped her hand into the box, removing a wax paper-wrapped pastry while bearing an unreadable expression on her face. "Thanks. Now get in there." She nodded her head towards the main stairwell leading from the foyer.

Ned walked up the stairs, careful not to jostle the cream puffs as he moved. The stairs wound gently to the second floor and Ned paused at the bend to see if Maya would take a bite. She slowly unwrapped the dessert.

Is she a squinter? He loved trying to guess how people would react to his food. Some gave little gasps, others just crinkled their eyes and sighed. Maya popped the cream puff into her mouth and Ned held his breath. A small moan escaped Mona's lips and she closed her eyes, chewing slowly and deliberately.

This is why I cook. Ned smiled.

Ned hurried on before Maya caught him staring. His feet sank deeply into the plush carpeting as he moved down the hall. *Did she say left or right?* He looked around for some hint of where Gita's room was.

As he wound through the long hallways, Ned handed out the non-Puff laced pastries to the tiger shifters bustling about their business. He noted their reactions with glee, his feet feeling lighter as he walked. Gasper, squinter, gobbler. No other moaners, but one was enough for one day. Even the more subtle reactions made Ned happy.

The corridors all blended together after a while. The only difference in the hallways was the artwork dotting the walls, all depicting their subjects in various states of love-making. Ned stopped to stare at one particularly striking photo of a woman in the throes of joy being serviced by two men and another woman.

"You! Are you the Claws' boy?" a smoky voice asked. "I'm Gita's healer."

Ned tried to stifle his embarrassment as he turned to the woman. "Boy" was a relative term. He wanted to declare he wasn't a kid. He was twenty-five and a half, damn it. The woman wore a blue scrap of fabric around her waist and a smile. Ned tried to actively ignore the woman's nudity as she walked towards him, her bare breasts swaying gently with the movement of her body.

"I'm Ned." He handed her the labeled container. "This has Gita's medicine. There are instructions attached on the top, and this should stay refrigerated..."

The woman pressed a finger to his lips. "Don't move." She disappeared into a room on the other side of the hall with the Puff-laced desserts balanced on one of her sashaying hips.

Ned shifted his weight as he waited, trying to not stare at the painting of a couple contorted into an angle that should be impossible. The healer stepped out of the room after a few moments.

"Gita is grateful for your club's assistance." Her hands began to roam Ned's body and she moved closer. "I am *also* grateful."

The strange woman's body was so close Ned could feel the heat coming off of her skin. She leaned forward, the hard points of her nipples poking into Ned's chest, and took his earlobe between her teeth, nipping gently. Her hands slid down Ned's body slowly, teasing him with a light touch before she reached his belt.

"Let me show you how grateful we are." She tilted her head slightly, her lips upturned in a catlike smile.

Ned could feel his heart pounding in his chest as his body reacted to the stranger's touch. It would be so easy to listen to his urges, to allow this woman to undress him right there in the hallway. He'd never had sex with a tiger shifter before, and if the stories were to be believed...

"No." Ned backed away. "I mean, thank you for the kind and generous offer, but I don't do that." He stammered. "I mean I do *that*, the sex and all." He ran his fingers through his hair, gripping at the ends as he tried to get the words out. "I don't do the anonymous sex...thing."

The woman nodded and gave him a quick peck on the cheek. "My name's Crystal. Perhaps I'll see you another time now that I'm not"—she turned back to Gita's room, then winked over her shoulder—"Anonymous."

Ned jogged down the hallway away from her until he found the main stairwell leading to the foyer. At the bottom of the curved staircase stood Maya, looking radiant despite the chocolate smeared around her mouth. Ned wanted to walk over and wipe the chocolate off just for the excuse to feel her lips. Or perhaps, even better, he could kiss the chocolate off, tasting the flavor of his cooking and her mouth all at once.

"So you're all set?" Maya asked.

"Absolutely. Crystal gave the cream puffs to Gita. She should be well soon." Ned hefted one now-empty plastic container under his arm.

"I see they cleaned you out of the non-medicinal ones?"

Ned almost heard a hint of regret in Maya's voice. He grinned, pulling a lone cream puff wrapped in wax paper out of his jacket pocket.

"Almost. I saved this one for you."

Maya's face lit up as she grabbed the cream puff from Ned's hand. She took a giant bite of cream puff.

"Hey, what are you up to tonight?" she said.

MAYA WATCHED Ned gaze around the celebration with a slight smile. He looked so amazed, it was a little sweet. Everything about him was sweet; it made the tiger inside her want to lick every inch of him and see if he tasted as delicious as his cooking.

But she wasn't going to.

The party was supposed to be for Gita. Gita wasn't even better yet, but the possibility she *might* become well was reason enough for Raj to throw a party. When Gita was further recovered, there would be another party and when she was *almost* well there would be yet another party. And then when she was *actually* well, there would be...again and again until the clan came up with a new excuse to party.

Maya stifled a bored sigh. All of these gatherings were

the same. The sounds of the orgy in the back room were beginning to grow in pitch, although they wouldn't be deafening for another forty-five minutes or so. The tigers who hadn't made it back to the orgy yet were quickly finding partners, grabbing quick kisses in romantically-lit corners and rubbing themselves against soon-to-be lovers.

The other tigers and their consorts knew well enough not to proposition Maya anymore, but she could feel a few pairs of eyes following her. The more competitive shifters always watched her closely to see if tonight would be the night Maya decided to fall into line with her people's expectations and give up her deviant, prudish ways. They couldn't understand why she took sex so *personally*, avoiding it when it was with someone who saw her body as a toy or a trophy.

"Um, Maya?" Ned asked, looking at her face. He was tall enough to look her straight in the eye, which she appreciated. After so many dates who liked to bend down to make her feel small, it was nice to talk to a man she wasn't craning her neck to see. "Are you okay? You look upset."

Observant as well as cute, Maya thought, forcing a smile onto her face. She leaned against the wall, crossing her arms. Without thinking about it, she'd chosen the wall with the best visibility of all corners of the room. Once security, always security.

"How are you enjoying your first tiger party?" she said, ignoring his question. "You ready to go yank one out in the bathroom yet?" She smiled.

"Is it that obvious?" Ned said, blushing and smiling back.

He's a blusher. Adorable. Maya chuckled, but her eyes moved beyond him to watch a tiger alpha from another clan sniffing at one of Maya's off-duty security men. She waited until her employee grabbed the strange alpha's balls and massaged them tenderly—*good, consent*—before her eyes moved onto another possible threat. Raj had given her strict instructions to turn off her professional vigilance for a night and get laid, but she couldn't stop herself from scanning the room for any signs of trouble.

"Ned, you've been gripping your belt tight enough to turn your knuckles white ever since you walked in here," Maya replied.

"I've just never seen quite this much, you know, out in the open—" His voice trailed off as he watched three women kissing each other on the sofa, one naked redhead in the middle with a blonde kissing her neck while a brunette licked her way down the redhead's stomach. The redhead in the middle was groaning, both her hands up the blonde's and brunette's mini-skirts, her fingers working their pussies with enthusiasm. The two women moaned.

"It's our way," Maya said, wincing at the sharpness of her voice. Unattached sex might be the tiger shifter way, but it wasn't *her* way. "But that's not why I invited you here tonight."

"Oh?" Ned said, sounding distracted.

He turned away from the three women to look at Maya, but his face flushed even deeper. Maya looked behind her to see what had inspired his new blush: two couples were talking to each other with drinks in their hands. It could have been a scene from any non-tiger party, except two of the politely-chatting shifters were grinding on each other hard, one man's leather pants flush with a woman's wide ass as she thrust back into him. Neither spilled a drop of their drinks, and they maintained an animated conversation with the couple across from them. None of the four batted an eye as the man from the opposite couple reached across to pull down the woman's pants and rub her clit.

"This is what you guys do all the time?" Ned asked, his voice adorably high.

"Only when there's nothing good on TV." Maya tried to keep her tone light. She knew she might be happier if she could let go and join in the fun with the rest of the clan, but something stopped her every time.

A chorus of groans sang out from the back room and Ned and Maya both looked at the entrance in time to see a woman wearing a red bikini top and nothing else fall out of the door and then run back in, a look of determination and hunger on her face.

"I need to look into that," Maya said. "I'm sorry, but all this only works if everybody plays nice." Maya gave Ned one last look of apology and then hurried over to the orgy room. The woman in the bikini top was trying to find a way back into the melee, but all of the men and women on this side of the action were too distracted to notice her attempts. Red Bikini grabbed a nearby ass, but the man—his lips deeply buried in another woman's pussy—only lifted his head enough to growl angrily at the interruption.

"But I want it!" Red Bikini whined, grabbing his ass harder and grinding herself against his backside. His head whipped up and around, his growl now escalated to a roar at the intruder, showing sharp teeth. Red Bikini shifted her mouth to its tiger state, showing fangs and snarling back.

That's quite enough of that, Maya thought, looking around for her on-duty security. Nelson was working the party tonight and was already on his way over, but Maya was closer and waved him away. She transformed just the tips of her fingers to claws and advanced on Red Bikini, moving stealthily towards her target. Maya hooked her claws under the surprised woman's neck, making eye contact with the male to signal him to back off. He bowed his head in submission, diving back into the pussy awaiting him.

"For failure to obtain consent, you are banished from the next three parties," Maya growled in the woman's ear, her claws tightening just enough to form little pin-prick cuts along the woman's collarbone. The cuts would heal in moments, but the pain was sharp enough to shock the woman away from whatever was driving her.

"But I was just—" the woman whimpered.

Maya tightened her claws deeper, pulling the woman to the door. "Consent, kitten. Go to your room and think about it until the message gets through to your upstairs brain. If this kind of disgrace *ever* happens again, you'll be exiled from the clan." Maya nodded to Nelson to escort the woman to her room, and then stuck around long enough for him to confirm it was done and watch him return to his post.

"I'll make sure it doesn't happen again, sir," Nelson murmured.

"See that it doesn't," Maya said.

"Weren't you supposed to get laid tonight? Alpha's orders," Nelson said as Maya turned to return to the front room. Nelson was one of her recruits, working up the ranks over the last five years to become one of her most trusted guards. He was built like a nacho chip, broad shoulders with a narrow waist, but he was smarter than his looks implied. Folks tended to underestimate him, which made him a very valuable asset.

Maya frowned at him. "Raj is my Alpha and I'll protect him with my life. But some orders are outside of his authority to give." She turned on her heel and left the orgy room just as the sounds began to escalate in a chorus of orgasms.

The coolness of the front room felt welcome in comparison. She looked around for Ned and her steps slowed when she saw him: eyes shut, fists clenched, sitting on a window seat with a naked woman licking down his neck, while another was on her knees, slowly caressing her way up his inner thigh. Maya pushed down her flash of disappointment.

The woman on her knees said something Maya couldn't hear over the growing din, but whatever it was made Ned's eyes fly open and his hands make fast gestures for the women to move away. Maya felt her feet speed up to enforce his lack of consent, but the tigers were already leaving, kissing each other in consolation.

"Enjoying the party?" Maya said once she got close.

"Maya! I didn't see you there!" Ned cried. "I'm so sorry. I wasn't doing anything, just sitting here, and they just came up and started, you know, um, and when they asked me up to their room, I said no and..."

"Ned, it's okay. Tiger shifters aren't monogamous. In fact, it's frowned upon," Maya said, feeling a blush in her cheeks. "Just because I invited you to the party doesn't mean I was making any sort of claim..." Her voice trailed away.

Isn't that exactly what I was doing when I invited him? she thought. His pastries were the best thing she'd tasted in her life. She still had the wrapper in her pocket to sniff at and remember the taste luxuriating on her tongue.

"Oh." He said again. "I guess I had hoped..." She could see the unhappiness in his drooping shoulders and it made her chest ache. Had he wanted her to make a claim? What did that even look like? Tigers didn't claim people. They may or may not consent to someone in the moment and whether they consented to the same person later was based on whim, not obligation or duty or emotional attachments. She'd always hated it, but no lover she'd ever taken among the tigers had ever understood her expectation for them to actually *care*.

"So, tell me about you?" Maya tried. That's what non-tigers did, right? They talked about themselves, got to know each other as people? That's what they did in movies at any rate. "What do you do with the Iron Claws?"

"Nothing really, I guess." He said, looking down. "I mean, I'm the cook. I bake all of our Puff-laced brownies and desserts, and I make all the dinners for the club based on what we can afford at the time." He shrugged. "I like feeding people. And during fights I help out, of course. A few months ago this human mob came after our healer, Marie, along with a whole mess of Council goons, and I went into battle with everyone else. I even killed a guy with a sword." He tried to say the last like a boast, but it came out like a half gurgle of guilt. He didn't like killing people. She felt her respect for him ratchet up a notch. Too many of the warriors she knew saw other people's death as trophies. Ned regretted the death of an enemy, and that made him special.

"Sounds like you actually do a lot," Maya said. The sounds from the back room were getting so loud now she was having a hard time hearing Ned. The smell of sex was stronger than before, a pungent scent of oil, sweat, and heated bodies. The orgy was beginning to spill out into the front room as couples who had been seducing each other during the first half of the evening began to consummate their meetings all over the room.

"There's a lot they won't let me do," Ned said. The three women on the couch were now enthusiastically fucking in a daisy chain and Ned stared for a long second before closing his eyes. "The Claws still treat me a like a kid." He said. "They keep saying I'm not ready for full clan responsibilities. I'm only at this party because they wanted me to be their errand boy and drop off Gita's medicine while they were out defying the Council distributing Puff."

"And that's why the Claws came to town? For Puff distribution?" Maya didn't know a lot about the work the Iron Claws did, but knowing they were illegally distributing drugs—even drugs that helped people—in her city worried her. Illegal activities tended to draw trouble, no matter how well-intentioned.

"It's mostly Raj's doing we're here at all. In our last town, the Council's Red Guard goons were coming after us hard; we barely made it out alive. We were figuring out where to go when we heard Gita was sick. It seemed a good enough reason to come here. Raj is a friend of Emma's from long back." From the expression on Ned's face, he hadn't really thought until this moment about what kind of "friend" Raj might have been to his fellow Claw member in the past. "Anyway, we hadn't been around this area in a while and it was an opportunity to help Gita." He smiled at her and Maya felt a little happy feeling in her stomach. "I'm very glad we came."

"Oh gods! I'm going to cum!" One of the women on the couch—it might have been the redhead—screamed loud enough to rattle the windows. Ned blushed to the roots of his hair and continued to concentrate on the wallpaper. He probably hadn't realized yet the wallpaper pattern was suggestively intertwined bananas and orchids.

Ned sported such an enormous erection in his pants Maya was impressed he could form coherent sentences. His fellow clan members clearly didn't recognize Ned's self-control if they were still treating him like a kid. From the width of his shoulders and the strength she could see in his hands from all that cooking and baking, he was most certainly *not* a kid.

"I'm glad you came, too," Maya said, stepping closer to him and nearly running into a large, sweaty back.

Two men were making out wildly with one another while a woman on her knees between them scrambled to keep giving one a blow job while also jerking off the other. Maya sidestepped around them, but the threesome's balancing act collapsed and the trio fell directly between where Maya and Ned were standing.

Ned looked like he was torn between asking them if they needed any help and trying to flee to safety.

"How about we go talk someplace else where we're not surrounded by an orgy?" Maya said.

Ned nodded, a wide smile growing across his face. "I have my bike parked outside. How about we leave right now?"

Even though the trio had fallen on the ground, they barely stopped for breath before changing positions, with one man firmly fucking the other man in the ass, who in turn speared the woman bent over on all fours. The woman thrust back so hard her naked breasts jutted against Maya's shin.

"Yes, right now sounds great," Maya said.

NED FELT the familiar buzz of his motorcycle working beneath him as he rode around to the front of the mansion to pick up Maya. He always felt more confident when he was on his bike; it was the one place he was always in control, never clumsy or faltering like everywhere else in his life.

"Hey, mister, give a girl a ride?" Maya was breathtaking in a long tangerine dress with a slit all the way up to the thigh and strappy silver sandals. She slid the spare helmet he handed her over her head, adjusting her long hair so it hung free down her back.

Her touch felt electric as she placed one hand on Ned's shoulder, supporting herself as she swung a leg over the humming machine. Her hands snaked around Ned's body, gripping his abs as she scooted close to him, pressing herself against his back.

Be cool, Ned willed himself as he drove them to the restaurant. The night air felt cool as it whipped around him, a sharp contrast to Maya's warmth against his body. *You're a badass motorcycle guy. You can do this.*

They roared up to the art deco awning of Chez Fenêtre, a five-star restaurant that had a year-long waiting list for reservations. It was a good thing Big Joe was on a first name basis with the chef—a bear shifter's mate—and made a call on Ned's behalf.

Ned tossed his keys at a confused-looking valet and helped Maya off the bike. Her hand felt so small and soft in his that he didn't want to let go.

"This place is…" Maya's voice trailed off as she walked into Chez Fenêtre. The restaurant was absolutely magical. The lighting was low and romantic, the tables far enough apart to provide an intimate dining experience, and a piano player was playing La Vie en Rose softly on a raised stage in the middle of the room. The maître d' greeted them at the door by name and swept them to their table, helping Maya into her chair.

Ned tried to smile and look casual, as if dining at the finest restaurant in town was an everyday experience. He stared down at his place setting. Six different forks and seven different spoons stared up at him accusingly. *I'm way out of my league.*

Ned tried a couple bland conversational gambits about

the weather and the lack of traffic on the ride over before asking what he really wanted to know.

"So...are all tiger shifters so"—Ned fumbled for the correct word—"amorous?"

Maya unfolded her crisp napkin from its origami swan shape and laid it delicately across her lap.

"Most of us are. It's just the way things are done." She fiddled with the pages of the intimidatingly-large wine menu. "Not me, though. I'm a little..."

"Different?" Ned offered, immediately regretting chiming in. *Don't call your date weird. What's wrong with you?*

Maya smiled warmly, gently placing her hand in Ned's. "Exactly."

"Sir. Mademoiselle." An uncomfortably-thin man in an overly-starched uniform stood alongside their table. "I am Anton. It will be my great pleasure to ensure you have everything you need this evening." His attempt at a gracious smile was stopped by his immobile cheeks and cold eyes.

Ned could feel pricks of sweat forming on his palms and quickly moved his hand away from Maya's, dragging the tablecloth with him. His tug sent their water glasses flying and he felt the cold splash strike him in the face a second before the melodic crash reached his ears. Ice water spilled across the table, drenching Ned and the waiter.

Anton was not amused.

Apologizing profusely, Ned managed to place their order for wine and appetizers to a red-faced Anton, who was barely feigning calm. Anton's lip twitched and flinched every time Ned mentioned a specific wine or food, his disapproval at their choices painfully apparent.

"Sorry about that," Ned muttered, but Maya wasn't looking at him or the water dripping down his shirt. Her eyes were scanning the room, dancing to the wine opener in

Anton's apron before flicking to the exits, the kitchen, the restrooms.

"You take this security stuff seriously, huh? You're acting like you're still on the clock."

"Excuse me?" Maya set her wine glass down purposefully, giving Ned her full attention.

Her expression was so terrifying that Ned's blood ran cold. *Shit.* "I didn't mean that in a *bad* way..."

"I am responsible for the safety...the *lives* of everyone in my clan. Yes, I take that seriously. If I goof off, if I turn off, my people are vulnerable." Her hand shook as she brought the wine glass up to her lips. She closed her eyes for a moment, breathing deeply. "Besides the wine openers with knives all the wait staff is carrying, I count two tasers, three daggers, and one loaded gun in this room *right now*."

Ned whipped his head around, trying to spot the armed diners in the room. Everyone was dressed to the nines, innocently sipping their drinks or delicately eating their meals. Nobody showed any signs of packing heat. *Damn, she is good.*

Anton dropped off their appetizers: sautéed duck foie gras with toast points, baked brie in puff pastry, and chèvre truffles.

The waiter sneered as he turned to leave, muttering something that sounded like, "Enjoy your selections from the *children's* menu."

Maya shot up from her chair, knocking their table over and grabbing the arm of the man at a neighboring table in an especially posh tuxedo. The shocked man was rotund and pasty, his lips stained red from his wine. He struggled against Maya's grip, a wrinkled, veiny hand grasping a long dagger.

"Put. That." Maya twisted the man's wrist, eliciting a high-pitched shriek, "Down."

The dagger dropped to the floor, pinging as it bounced against the restaurant's marble floor.

"Unhand me!" The man shook, making his jowls sway slightly above his bobbing chins. "This is unacceptable!"

Maya released the man, picking up the discarded blade with her cloth napkin, wrapping it delicately.

"You have the audacity to pull a weapon and then call *me* unacceptable?" she hissed.

Anton's feet slipped a bit as his dress shoes struggled to gain purchase on food-covered marble.

"This is Mr. Fry, a longtime customer and entrepreneur." A vein in Anton's neck throbbed. "He is a procurer of rare objects and was here to conduct a *sale*."

Maya's face turned pale "So this was just a—"

"Business transaction!" Mr. Fry's mouth sprayed spit as he snatched the dagger back from Maya's outstretched hand.

Ned wiped the foie gras from his hair, letting out a long breath as he desperately tried to figure out how to possibly save the evening.

"Bah!" Maya's laughter echoed through the restaurant, startling a few diners and almost making a waitress balancing a tray with five drinks lose her grip. Maya blushed bright red.

She's adorable. Ned grinned. "I don't think this place is really..."

"Us?" Maya offered.

Anton looked like he heartily agreed, but was smart enough not to say anything while Maya was still so close to the ornate knife.

"If you're still up for dessert," Ned said, "I have a few options at my place." He tried to keep his facial expression neutral as he realized what he'd just asked. *Oh shit, it sounds like I'm trying to get her into bed!*

"Well..."

"I mean, not like that!" Ned's flailing hands nearly smacked a busboy. "Not that I don't want to..."

Maya raised an eyebrow.

"I mean, you're very..." Ned slumped back into the soft cushion of his chair. "Sometimes I like to cook, and there are some desserts I think you might like. But those desserts just *happen* to be at my apartment, and..."

Maya pressed her finger to Ned's lips, cutting off his rambling. "That sounds like a lovely idea, Ned."

Anton already had their coats in his hands, waiting for them.

The ride home was even more charged than the one to the restaurant. Ned wove through back streets on his motorcycle with Maya wrapped around him, taking the long route home just to have a few extra minutes with her. Being close to her felt so right.

"Nice place." Maya gave him a wry smile.

She was right to mock him. The apartment was small and sparse; the Iron Claws moved around the country so often it was unreasonable to have more than a few bags' worth of possessions. Usually the whole club would rent a place large enough to stay together, but this time they hadn't been able to find a clubhouse on short notice and had separated into smaller apartments in the same neighborhood. Ned knew his place was tiny, but he hadn't minded until he realized how dismal it was compared to where Maya worked.

The entrance led directly into the kitchen, which transitioned into a bedroom after a few feet, with a bathroom off to the side. Ned had one bag of clothes and one bag of kitchenware to his name. The clothes were—Ned noted with a relieved sigh—almost all crammed out of sight into his large duffel, but his cooking implements were *everywhere.*

The kitchen looked like a flour bomb had gone off. The sink was stacked with dirty dishes and the table in the center of the room was covered in racks of bourbon pecan pie, four different kinds of cakes, and peach tarts.

"You were not kidding when you said you like to cook." Maya took a quick swipe at the Boston cream cake sitting on the table, slipping her finger into her mouth to suck off the chocolate frosting. She made a little groaning sound as she tasted it, which charged Ned's skin from head to toe.

"You haven't even seen the best part." Ned grinned, opening the fridge. It was stacked with pumpkin cheese-cake, chocolate éclairs, and ramekins of crème brulee. He produced a small cooking torch from a nearby drawer. "Have you ever set your dessert on fire?"

"Ooo, gimme!" Maya's bright smile lit up the dingy apartment.

Ned showed her how much sugar to sprinkle over the crème brulee surface and how to work the torch. The fire was meant to be administered in small circles over the dessert, caramelizing the sugar, but Maya's technique was too blunt and she kept burning it.

"Actually, it's more like this." Ned stood behind Maya, not too close, but close enough to feel the warmth radiating off her body. He slid his hands down her arms, resting them over her hands.

Ned could feel his pulse race as he pressed the small 'on' button, igniting the torch. He guided Maya and together they moved in precise circles, controlling the fire with their combined touch.

Maya turned off the small kitchen torch and turned her head, her mouth so close to his they were practically kissing.

"I did it!"

Ned pulled strands of Maya's long hair away from her neck, his fingers dancing along her skin longer than they needed to. He could feel her blood race under his fingertips where he touched her. Her skin was so soft and warm; she smelled like honey and raspberries.

Ned spun Maya around. Her mouth opened in a surprised "o" and he captured her lips with hungry urgency. He tried to convey everything he believed about her in one kiss, pouring out his admiration and longing. *She's incredible and has no idea.*

Maya moaned into Ned's mouth, her tongue darting in to dance with his own. She slid her hands up his chest, locking behind his neck as she pulled him close. The long, drugging kiss made Ned want more and it took all of his willpower to break away. He took a step back as he ran his fingers through his hair. "We should probably—"

"Stop. You're right." Maya smiled a little sadly and stepped away.

She snatched a few desserts off the table and took a big bite from one of the peach tarts she was holding. Her eyes rolled back in her head and she moaned.

"I love that sound."

She took another bite and made an exaggerated moaning sound. "What? *That* sound?"

Ned laughed. "Yes, that's the one."

Maya smiled, then looked down at the dessert and back at him.

"Ned, I can see how your whole face lights up when you feed people. Why aren't you a chef somewhere? Why ride with the Claws?"

"That's a long story." He moved so the table was between them. He hated thinking about his life before he joined the Claws.

"You don't have to talk about it if you don't want to."

"No, it's okay." Ned gulped. "I was kicked out of my clan." Speaking the words out loud rekindled a dull ache in his chest. "My clan was my family, but they wanted me to use my position at a shifter hotel to spy on other supernaturals." Ned couldn't look at her, just traced patterns in the spilled flour on the table. "But I wasn't any good. A busboy doesn't really have access to a ton of secrets and I just couldn't betray my boss by snooping around. And I was a coward. Whenever one of the guests lost their tempers and shot poisonous gas or made vines grow out of the floor, I just got security to handle it. I was a dragon who didn't want to fight. I wasn't a valuable resource for the clan, and—without any living relatives—there wasn't anyone to take my side, so...the clan kicked me out."

"Ned, I'm so sorry—" Maya reached out to touch him. "I know what it feels like to not fit in with your people."

"I didn't just not fit in, I was *useless*. You have skills. You're the head of security. After my clan kicked me out, I wasn't *anything*. I just flew around, occasionally shifting to human form to find food. A pack of werewolves found me, tried to challenge me to a fight, but I didn't want to engage. The Iron Claws happened to be close by, stepped in, and let me tag along with them ever since."

"You do more than tag along," Maya started to say, but Ned waved her words away.

"I'm just a baker." Ned forced a smile. "And you haven't even tried my cheesecake yet." He moved around the fridge to pull out a box.

Maya smiled at him, but the smile was sad. "I have to get

going. I have an early shift in the morning. But I want you to know"—she walked forward to place a hand on the side of his face—"I will be back for that cheesecake."

Ned was still smiling as he fell asleep that night.

MAYA STOPPED herself from looking at the clock for the fifth time that morning. Ned was supposed to arrive sometime before noon to bring a new selection of Puff-laced desserts for Gita.

"Your *boyfriend* hasn't arrived yet?" Nelson said the word like it was a sickness. He held up his hands before Maya had a chance to snap at him. "I didn't mean anything by it. Everyone saw you leaving with the guy last night. We're just happy you finally got laid. It's been a really long time."

"You're on duty." Maya said. "Shouldn't you be patrolling?"

"Lunch break." Nelson waved the paper coffee cup he was holding at Maya. "Fadi's doing my walkthrough until I get back."

"Oh." Maya waited a full minute before adding. "And it hasn't been *that* long."

Nelson smiled. "We got a pool going for how long you can go without getting some. It's just not natural. We're tigers. We have sex at least two or three times a *day*. And you've gone without since—"

"Say it and I'm putting you on orgy room cleanup duty for a week," she said, not quite able to keep the smile off her face. Just thinking about Ned made her mouth inch upwards into a smile.

"Fine. Your boyfriend is coming up the drive now."

Nelson pointed out a nearby window. "Maybe he'll put you in a better mood."

What? Maya forced herself not to fix her hair. Nelson would tell the rest of the guards and she'd never live it down.

Maya watched Ned's motorcycle roar up the street, his plastic containers of desserts strapped to the back. A familiar black car followed him until Ned turned up the mansion's driveway, at which point it slowed and turned to continue down the side street.

The hairs on the back of Maya's neck prickled. She recognized that car. It had been behind them as they rode to the restaurant, and then on the way to Ned's, parked across the street from his apartment. Now the creeper was here and Maya didn't like it one bit.

She opened the door for Ned before he had a chance to knock, hustling him inside the door and closing it quickly.

"How long has that black car been following you?" she said.

"And hello to you too, Maya." Ned said, holding out a dessert container wrapped in a red bow. "I made you a chocolate chip cookie dough cheesecake." Maya felt her unease sharpen. Ned was simply too adorable.

Nelson behind her made a loud coughing sound. "Guess you haven't gotten laid yet." He coughed again.

"Keep watch and mark every time that black car comes back. And I want you to get me that license plate number," Maya snapped. Nelson sobered up immediately and started scrolling through security camera feeds at the front desk, telling the security detail through his earpiece to keep an eye on the side streets.

At least he can take security seriously, Maya thought.

"What's going on?" Ned said.

"A too-familiar black sedan. I think you have a tail."

"What would anyone want with me?" Ned asked, his voice steady.

Maya was impressed—he didn't sound scared or worried. Ned looked ready to do what needed to be done. He was a lot braver than the Iron Claws gave him credit for.

"It's possible your club's enemies think the cook is an easy target. If someone knows the Iron Claws are here, then they might go after you to hurt the whole group."

"That's ridiculous." Ned said. "No one knows me. I'm the small one, the insignificant—"

"You said you killed one of their goons in battle." She said, cutting Ned off before he had the chance to start listing how little his fellows thought of him. "Enemies pay attention to who's responsible for a body count." Ned looked so upset at the mention of the man he killed, Maya wanted to smooth away the stress lines away from his forehead. One of these days she was going to give his club members a piece of her mind for making Ned think he was worthless. "Go. Bring your desserts to Gita. I'm sure it's fine. I might be overreacting."

Ned nodded, looking uncertain as he went up the stairs toward Gita's room.

"You almost never overreact," Nelson said from the desk. "Even if you're wrong about the car in this case, I'm sure there really was a black car last night."

"I know that and you know that." Maya said. "But Ned doesn't need to know that. He's not a violent guy; he's a baker. I don't want him nervous about this. I want him to keep being him: happy and funny and adorable."

"Wow, you really like this guy." Nelson sounded impressed and a little confused.

"He's not like anyone I've ever met," Maya said, so low

only enhanced shifter ears could hear it.

"Then why haven't you banged his brains out yet?" Nelson said, sounding genuinely interested. "And I think I see the car." He looked out the window.

Maya shifted her eyes for long-distance detail vision and shook her head. "That's a different model. And my love life is none of your business."

"Oh *come on*, kissing and telling is what we *do* around here." Nelson smiled.

"Not me."

"Then how about just kissing him? It might help you unwind a little."

"I'm on duty."

"Then go keep a lookout from the second floor. It has a better view of the road and you can give us a longer head start if you see the car again. I'll man the door and bring Sahab off the north woods side to help cover here."

Ned was on the second floor. Maya felt a small flash of pride. Nelson had been awful at strategy before she started to train him as part of her security team.

"Fine, but not Sahab. He knows the woods better than anyone else. Call up one of the off-duty guards. They'll have rested eyes."

Maya walked upstairs fast enough she could pretend not to hear Nelson's grumbling about how annoyed the off-duty guards were going to be.

The twisting hallways on the second story were built to facilitate romantic interludes on corner couches, not efficiency or security. The blonde and the brunette from the sofa last night were making out with desperate passion a couple of hallways down and Maya wondered if the redhead from the middle of their sandwich had found a new playmate.

But they weren't her problem. A black car was following Ned and that couldn't mean anything good. The front northwest bedroom had the best view of the two main streets that crossed the mansion's drive. She raised her binoculars and counted cars, listening to updates on the headset.

"Well, aren't you sweet looking?" a sultry voice said from the hallway behind her. Maya shook her head, focusing on the road. A perfume Maya recognized as belonging to the redhead from the couch wafted into the room and Maya stilled.

"Hi, I think you were at that party last night, right?"

Ned.

Ned was flirting with the redhead in the hallway. Maya's fingers shifted to claws before her brain caught up and she let them dig into her palms. She wouldn't be jealous.

Not jealous.

They had agreed to nothing, spoken no words of commitment or affection or love. They had a nice night. That was all. He owed her nothing.

"Yes, I remember you from last night, too," the redhead's voice purred. Maya could picture what the redhead was doing right now all too vividly. "You liked watching me," the voice continued. The redhead would be doing what all tiger shifter women did: seducing the living hell out of him. "I liked you watching me." And Ned would be a tumbled mess on the floor, sated and jaded like all the rest. "It made me wet to think of you watching me. Your eyes on me, watching me cum—I liked it." The redhead's voice became muffled for a second, like her mouth was full of something else, and Maya thought she might cry. "I want to feel like that again." The same muffled sound, then Ned's voice making a strangled cry, part moan and part startled yelp. "I can feel you; I can feel how much you want me."

Maya couldn't see the road anymore through the tears swimming in front of her eyes. On the other side of the door, less than ten feet away, Ned was proving he was just like everyone else. Maya wiped her eyes away and concentrated on the street. Red car. Yellow car. Grey car. Another grey car. Minivan. She counted them.

Maya's mother hadn't been a tiger; she was a human. She'd fallen in love with a tiger, loving everything about his strong body and the way he made her body sing. She thought that the beauty of their lovemaking meant their love was equally strong. She thought great sex meant he was committed to her and to her future. When she became pregnant, he told her that lactation wasn't his kink and introduced her to his best friend who loved to fuck pregnant women.

"Ummm, what big muscles you have. You shouldn't hide those big hands of yours." The woman's voice carried far too well.

Some kinds of pain passed down through generations.

"That's very nice of you to say," Ned replied, his tone a little strangled.

Maya pressed the binoculars hard to her face, focusing on the bruising feeling of the hard metal against her face. A childhood of hearing about the heartlessness and fickleness of tigers hadn't helped her learn how to trust easily. It made a career in security and looking out for trouble come naturally, and she was good at her job.

Mom was right. She used to say all men—no matter what animal supposedly lived under their skin—are actually pigs deep down.

"This shirt would look so much better if you unbuttoned it a little. You look so hot."

Maya had lived with the tiger shifters since she was

eleven and her mother found a new husband: a werewolf who didn't want a cat in his house. From a distance of years —and several decades living with the tigers—Maya understood her tiger father hadn't meant to be cruel. In his way, he had cared for her mother and only wanted to make her feel good. He thought he was giving her what she needed: sex. He simply never understood that some humans wanted something different, *more*, and longer lasting than a couple of naked days or weeks. And although her tiger kin tried to impress on Maya she should simply accept that sex was the end-all, be-all of earthly pleasures, Maya was still her mother's daughter.

She wanted love. She wanted someone to want her for who she was, not for her convenient holes.

"Sorry, but I really can't do that," Ned said, his tone firm.

What? Maya put down the binoculars.

"You're very pretty," he said. "You're gorgeous actually, don't get me wrong. I mean, yeah, you're beautiful."

"Then what's the problem?" The redhead's voice was quickly shifting from sultry to pouting.

"There's someone else."

"Then bring them along!" The redhead said, the confidence in her voice returning so fast Maya thought there might be something wrong with the woman. "I always like a third. Or a fourth. More hands are always, hmmm, handy."

"Please don't!" Ned cried.

Maya sprinted across the room, poised to strike. Maya opened the door enough to see Ned push the redhead away from him. The redhead—dressed in a long, purple dress so sheer it left nothing to the imagination—hesitated, keeping a few feet between her and Ned. Maya paused, waiting to see how things played out, but ready to jump in and enforce consent if it was necessary.

"I know it's not how you all do things, but there's someone I care about," Ned said, his hands fisted in a defensive stance like he was ready to actually *fight* the redhead off. "And she's smart and kind and badass and beautiful and the most amazing person I've ever met."

The redhead smiled, but it wasn't a nice smile. "If your object of affection is a tiger, sugar, trust me, she's probably off in the west wing screwing three guys out of every entrance. She would be the first one to tell you to go with this." She stepped forward again and Ned stepped back, keeping the distance.

Ned sighed, not relaxing his fists. "You may be right. I don't know her life. But I know me. And I know how I feel about her. And I can't be with you when all I can think about is being with her."

Maya felt like someone had ignited a kitchen torch inside her chest.

He really does care.

The redhead tossed her hair and muttered something about his loss and walked away, her hips' sway so extreme Maya hoped the woman would fall over. Maya opened the door wider, ready to run into Ned's arms.

"Maya," Nelson's voice came crackling through her headset and Maya bit back a curse at the interruption. "We have eyes on the car."

"Model?" she said, running back to the window and adjusting her eyesight so she wouldn't need the binoculars.

"Early 2000s Lincoln Towncar. It's been circling; this is the third time. We got our hands on last night's security footage from Chez Fenêtre to confirm, but this is the one."

"Copy that," she said into the headset. "Get everyone off their asses. We're going to need all hands on deck tonight to protect the house. And Nelson?"

"Yeah?" his voice said over the line, his worry clear even in one syllable.

"You're in charge tonight. There's someplace I have to be."

THE SAFE HOUSE wasn't pretty, but the property was in Maya's mother's name and was totally unknown to the shifters, tiger and dragon alike. The furniture smelled musty under the dust cloths and several generations of spiders were massacring mosquitoes in the corner of the bathroom.

"It's, um, cozy," Ned said, looking around the dust-covered kitchen.

"It's temporary," Maya said.

Ned had been a surprisingly good sport about agreeing to go with her to the safe house, smuggled in the backseat of her car so the tailing sedan wouldn't see Ned leave the mansion. Maya had been amused when the redhead—whose name was apparently Charlotte—volunteered to disguise herself in Ned's helmet and jacket and roar away on his motorcycle to draw the goons away. Considering the look on Nelson's face when he helped Charlotte into her Ned costume, Charlotte would achieve her goal for the afternoon. Maya found she no longer cared if Charlotte got laid, so long as it wasn't with Ned.

"What are the odds I'm going to find eggs and flour?" Ned said, rummaging through cupboards with an increasingly frustrated expression.

"Sorry, I haven't been here in a few years. We're going to be lucky to find canned soup."

Ned winced. "Canned soup." He shook his head, cringing at the offending provisions. "You sure whatever the goons have planned for me is really *that* bad? Because I'm pretty sure torture on the rack might be better than canned soup." He opened the freezer and pulled out a frozen pizza, examining the box. "A week from the expiration date! We're saved!"

"Did you mean what you said to Charlotte?" Maya blurted, then wanted to clasp her hand over her mouth to take back the words.

"What are you talking about?" Ned asked. He stopped unwrapping the pizza and looked at Maya with an adorable grin that made her want to step into his arms and never let him go.

"I heard you, back at the house. You turned Charlotte down because you said you wanted to be with me," Maya said.

"Yes." He said, running his hand through his hair so it looked even messier than before. "I hope I'm not moving too fast. I mean, I realize we've only had one real date. But I like you. I really like you. And some day, I'd like to—"

Maya rushed forward and pressed her lips to his. He tasted just as sweet as she remembered. She devoured his mouth, her tongue teasing his lips as his hands wrapped around her back, pulling her closer.

"You'd like to what?" She breathed into his neck as she nibbled on his ear, her hands roaming down his back and toward his ass.

"This." He moaned. "But not only this. I want to know you, everything about you. I want to know what your favorite foods are in the morning and late at night. I'm going to cook them for you and—"

"Ned, shut up," Maya said, kissing him again. "I want to know you, too. And I promise I don't want to be with anyone else."

She felt herself dissolve in his arms, fitting perfectly

against his body. She gasped as he shifted his fingers to dragon claws and shredded her tank top to ribbons.

Two can play that game. Maya shifted her fingers to tiger claws and tore off his shirt and the side of his pants, revealing the flame-print boxers underneath.

A pile of torn fabric grew at their feet as they stripped each other down until finally flame-patterned boxers twisted alongside a heap of shredded lace panties.

She shifted her fingers back, unable to get enough of the feeling of his skin under her hands.

"We'll get to know each other better," Maya said, her voice low as she pushed him back towards the couch. "Tomorrow. Right now, I need you."

Ned gave a wicked smile and pulled her in for a long, drugging kiss. Maya's head swam and her blood rushed through her body with excitement. She gave a surprised squeal as Ned lifted her in the air, gently depositing her on her back on the couch.

He grabbed her hands and rested them on the sofa arm above her head. "Don't move." He breathed. "Keep holding on." She nodded, feeling her eyes go wide.

True to character, Ned started slow, gently massaging Maya's calves and peppering them with featherlight kisses. Maya squirmed beneath him, trying to make contact with his bare skin without moving her hands. Not touching him was torture.

Ned licked a line up Maya's leg, taking a moment to tickle the sensitive flesh behind her knee with his tongue.

Maya let out a whimper, gripping the sofa arm so hard she felt the seams burst.

Ned kissed up Maya's thighs, harder now, nibbling and sucking as he worked toward her core.

Maya wanted to scream with relief when his mouth

found her soaking pussy. Ned slowly licked her folds, brushing gently against her clit as he made pass after pass.

"Ned...please." Maya was panting now. She couldn't stand it and let go one hand to roll and tease an erect nipple with her fingertips.

Ned thrust two fingers into her suddenly and Maya's head fell back to the couch's scratchy surface. He latched onto her clit with his mouth, sucking and flicking his tongue at the delicate bundle of nerves.

"That feels so fucking good," Maya shrieked, unable to hold back. She grabbed onto the couch beneath her, trying to hold onto something as Ned fucked her with his fingers. He began to rub her clit hard with the other hand and she came apart around him, screaming and moaning as she crashed over the edge.

Ned stood, smiling proudly. His erection was large enough to make any tiger proud and seeing his want made Maya's inner tiger come alive once more.

Maya stood on shaky legs, pushing Ned onto his back on the couch. She positioned herself above his cock and leaned towards Ned.

She whispered, "Fuck me."

Ned didn't say a word, just pulled her hips down onto his cock and thrust deep into her. The sway of their bodies moved perfectly in sync, his thrusts in perfect counterpoint to the sharp bucks of her body. Each powerful thrust rubbed her clit against him and she could feel her climax growing once more.

"I'm so close." She screamed, riding him harder, pressing his torso deeper into the couch as he pushed his cock deeper into her.

Without warning, Ned grabbed Maya and flipped her so she was on her back, her legs wrapped around him as he pounded into her from a new angle, pulling her legs up so he could push deeper.

"That's it, take it, take all of it," Ned groaned. "Moan for me, Maya. Moan like I like it."

She could barely hear him, her senses so overwhelmed by the pulsing orgasm building in her core that her awareness seemed to spread throughout her body in delicious waves. As the shocking rush of the orgasm hit her, she moaned deep in her throat, closing her eyes and arching her back in ecstasy.

His fingers reached between their bodies to rub her sensitive nub, prolonging her orgasm until the exhilaration rolled like thunder all the way down to her curling toes.

Just when she thought her body couldn't take any more pleasure, Maya felt the warmth of his seed pour into her and his deep groan as his entire body tensed on top of hers. The last words she heard as she collapsed into sleep were, "Maya, I'm yours."

NED WASN'T sure how long he'd been awake. Hell, he wasn't even sure if he *was* awake. The past few days had been like some sort of beautiful dream that he never wanted to leave.

"Mmm...good morning," Maya muttered as she rolled over, the sheets sliding down to expose her bare breasts. She grabbed a pack of gum from his pants pocket on the floor, popping it in her mouth as she passed Ned a small rectangle of his own.

Ned chewed the gum with a grin, enjoying the minty taste as he took in the radiant sight before him. The sun streamed in through a break in the curtains and struck Maya with an angelic glow. The sheets were still twisted from the second round of last night's exertions and barely covered Maya's naked body, her soft skin rippling with hard-earned muscle. He leaned over and gave her a long kiss, loving how the taste of the mint on her tongue tickled his nose.

"Good morning. How are you this fine day?" He kissed her shoulder as he pulled her body close to his own. He could feel how his blood rushed just from being close to her.

"Let's just say I'm happy the Claws sent you to deliver Gita's medicine." Maya kissed Ned on the chin, squirming so the pointed tips of her nipples rubbed against Ned's bare chest. She kissed along his jawline up to his ear, licking and nibbling at his lobe.

"Me too." Ned moved his hands along Maya's side, caressing her soft skin. "If you met any of the big, tough members of the club, you wouldn't have looked twice at me." He dipped his head and took one of Maya's nipples in his mouth, sucking at the sensitive flesh.

Maya pulled away. "Is that what you think? You're less than the other Iron Claws?" She looked horrified.

Crap. "No, sorry, forget I said anything." He pulled her close, hands pressed against her lower back as he peppered her neck with kisses.

She pushed him away. "Ned. I am not spending time with you because you were the first guy I saw. How can you believe that?" Her face looked appalled and Ned reached out for her again.

"No, that's not what I was saying. I just—"

"You think I'd have fallen in bed with whoever showed up that day." Maya's eyes flashed, her forehead furrowed in furious wrinkles.

"I just thought someone like you deserved someone..." Ned's voice came out almost as a whisper. "...better."

"You think you're not a big, strong guy?" Maya gripped Ned's bicep. "Look at you! You're certainly strong..." Her hand slid down Ned's side, cupping his length. She began to stroke him as his manhood engorged at her attention. "And as for big, you've certainly got that covered."

She rolled on top of him, kissing him fiercely. "I want *you*, Ned." She slid down his body, rubbing herself against him as she kissed his nipples and his abs. "Nobody but you." She licked up the side of his throbbing erection, stopping to kiss the tip. She parted her lips, flicking her tongue along his length as she took him in her mouth. Maya moaned and looked up at Ned, moving slowly at first, and picking up speed.

Ned let out a groan and wound his fingers through Maya's hair, loving the sight of her giving him pleasure. He guided her as she moved, slowing her down when he got too close to the edge, and pushing himself deeper and deeper. Her hands caressed his balls and he nearly came right then. Ned pulled her off of him, panting.

"I need you *now*."

Maya positioned herself over Ned, leaning backwards and supporting herself by gripping his thighs. She took Ned's hard cock in her hand and slowly lowered herself, gasping as he stretched her.

She's breathtaking. Ned gazed up at Maya, impaled on his dick, mouth slightly open in a silent moan.

Her skin was flawless, her body sculpted from years of security work, and her perfect breasts heaved slightly with the pace of her excited breathing. She deserved so much better than him, but he couldn't give her up. Then, she began to move on him and all thought fled his mind.

He thrust upward to meet her movements, pushing himself deeper and deeper into her velvety passage. She cried out and leaned forward onto him, her hands gripping his sides as she approached the edge. Ned pulled one of her nipples to his mouth, bit gently, and felt her fall apart, screaming his name as she came, pulsing around his dick.

She fell forward, panting, into Ned's arms.

"You want more?" Ned asked, gently lifting her so he could look into her eyes.

"Show me what you got." She winked and he felt seven feet tall.

Ned flipped her over, positioning Maya on all fours and began to tease her soaked passage with his penis. He buried himself to the hilt in one swift thrust.

"Yes!" Maya threw her head back as she screamed.

Ned gripped Maya's thighs as he moved in her, plunging relentlessly into her. She met him thrust for thrust, teasing her own breasts with one hand while supporting herself with the other.

Ned could feel himself getting close and snaked a hand around her hip, capturing her clit between two fingers as he rolled it roughly, pounding into her tight cavern over and over. He let out a roar as he came, bucking as he exploded into her. She followed him over the edge, her body milking every last drop from him.

They fell, laughing, into a sweaty heap amidst the twisted sheets. "I could sleep for a week," Maya whispered, curling into a tight ball.

Ned pulled her close, the soft skin of Maya's back against his hard chest. He could feel the tension that usually coursed through her body lessen, her shoulders relaxing and her breathing steady in his arms.

Maya snored gently and Ned suppressed a chuckle, carefully untangling himself from her. She slept on as he slid off the bed and padded over to the kitchen, excited to make her a first-class breakfast.

The culinary options really were dismal; Ned's options were instant coffee, ramen, or a dented can of pork and beans. *This is unacceptable.* Maya deserved something special. He scrawled out a quick note on a scrap of paper, "Buying real food. Back soon. Ned."

He remembered passing a grocery store on the way in, only a few blocks away from the safe house. He'd be able to walk there and back in less than an hour. She'd never even know he was gone. Ned whistled happily as he locked the safe house door behind him, feeling a little goofy. *Who cares? I'm in love!*

The red-hot shock of pain coursed from the top of his head, radiating throughout his body. His vision blurred as darkness closed in around him and he faintly heard the man holding a bloody tire iron behind him say, "We got him."

Maya stretched, her arm reaching out toward where Ned had been lying when she fell asleep. The sheets were cold and her eyes focused on the scrap of paper on the bedside.

Shit, shit, shit. He went outside.

She looked at the clock. 11:06 Am. She never slept this late. He could have been gone for hours.

Pulling on her clothes, she rushed to the security room and scrolled through the footage from the security cameras stationed around all the corners of the safe house. Maya couldn't stop her small cry when she finally found Ned's smiling face as he exited the apartment, timestamped from two hours ago. The bewildered expression on his face as he crumpled to the ground broke her heart.

Whoever took Ned must have noticed the security cameras and managed to keep his face frustratingly out of view. From the way the man moved, Maya had him pegged as a shifter, but that was really all she had to go on. *I'm going to need some help.*

Fifteen minutes was all she needed to activate her team, find the location of the Iron Claw's main base in town, get permission from Raj to use clan resources to save Ned once they had confirmation he was alive, and fill her car with enough weapons to level a city block.

"Tigers aren't usually about mates," Raj said after giving his blessing to do whatever she had to do to get Ned back. "But it looks like you found yours."

"Thanks, boss," she said, hanging up the phone and putting the car into drive.

Maya concentrated on the road in front of her, trying not to think about what could have happened to Ned in the hours she was sleeping. *Sleeping! How could I have been so careless?*

She beat the steering wheel with her fist. Convincing Raj to help her get Ned back was easy. Raj wanted her to be happy, and Ned supplying the Puff to save Gita's life put the tigers in debt to the Iron Claws. If Ned was in danger because he helped Gita—however indirectly—then Raj was happy to rally his people to defend him.

Convincing the Iron Claws they needed to risk everything to save Ned was going to be another story.

Thinking about Ned's face whenever he talked about how little he was worth to the Claws made her want to rip open their dragon hides and tear out their hearts. Ned was loyal, kind, extremely skilled—she felt her face heating when she remembered just how skilled he was in certain areas—and was a better man than the lot of them *combined*.

If those goddamn dragons don't mount up to save Ned, I will rip off their wings with my bare hands.

Maya pulled up to the apartment the Iron Claws were using as their home base in town. It didn't look like much, but it was still a step up from the safe house. She caught the eye of an enormous Asian man with dreadlocks cascading down his back. He leaned against the front step talking with a wirier guy with tattoos running up his arms and neck. Both moved too smoothly to be human.

She'd pulled up the clan's files on the Iron Claws before coming here. The guy with the dreads was Dylan Masters, the head of Iron Claws' security and their newest member. Tattoos was Caesar de la Vega, soldier and musician.

Dylan approached her, his gaze wary as his eyes swept her, taking in all of the details.

"What does the head of Raj's security want with us?" Dylan's voice was deep, cautious. Maya didn't need to ask how he knew who she was. Their files didn't have a lot on Dylan, but he stood like he had a long background in security. If he didn't know the faces of the local clan leaders and their security, he'd be shit at his job.

"You have a problem. I need to talk to Big Joe. Now."

Caesar stepped forward. "Sorry, but we need to know if you're a threat to our leader, lady." He stretched out his arm like he was going to block her way.

"She's not a threat," Dylan said, stepping aside.

Maya bristled. "You aren't worried I could be dangerous?"

Dylan smiled and Caesar relaxed slightly, the smile some kind of signal Caesar was waiting for. Dylan turned to Maya. "You didn't finish braiding your hair, you still have pillow indentations on the side of your face, and your shirt is on inside out. You came running here within an hour of waking up. If you'd been planning to attack us, you wouldn't have done it so spur-of-the-moment."

"She could just have done all those things to put you off the scent," Caesar said, his tone light.

"Perhaps, but I smell Ned and his favorite chewing gum on her skin and I don't think she faked that," Dylan said, walking toward the door and gesturing for Maya to go in front of him.

The inside of the headquarters was almost bare, reminding her of Ned's apartment. A pile of travel bags lay in a pile in the corner with the names of the clan members written on the side, ready for each of them to grab if they had to leave in a hurry. The names felt familiar from Ned's stories: Big Joe (their leader), Alec (the trans tech wiz who covered their tracks), Emma (their most badass warrior who never talked about her past), Caesar and Dylan she had met out front. And Ned. Her heart constricted just thinking of Ned. *He's going to be fine*, Maya told herself.

A Latina woman wearing hospital scrubs with a large medical kit over one shoulder rounded the corner: Marie, the human medic who married Dylan last year.

"What were you saying about Ned?" Marie said. She walked over to stand next to Dylan, her arm going around his waist in an automatic gesture of intimacy that made Maya stare for a second. In a tiger clan, her hand would have gone directly down his pants, but here Marie seemed content to just rest it lightly on Dylan's side. Easy contact, not sex. "Is Ned okay?" Marie asked.

"I need to talk to Big Joe," Maya said, proud her voice sounded so steady.

"Big Joe is out stretching his wings." It took Maya a

second to recognize Alec from his photo. He had the body of a gorgeous woman, all curves and enormous breasts only partially disguised by the baggy jacket he wore to cover them. He held up a small device and pressed a code into it. "I sent out a high-frequency pulse. He and Emma will be back in a second."

"I'm here," a deep voice boomed, as two figures entered from the back door. Big Joe was enormous, easily the largest man Maya had ever seen. He had to duck to fit through the doorway, and his dark skin seemed to glisten in the fluorescent light overhead. An intense, tall woman walked at his side, bulging muscles showing through her tank top and knives strapped to each hip. This had to be Emma, his second-in-command.

"Ned hasn't checked in this morning," Emma said.

"The last we heard, he was with you," Big Joe said. "What happened?"

"Ned's in trouble. You have to help him. He has far more value than you realize, he is—"

"We know exactly how valuable Ned is," Big Joe said, stopping her. Maya figured he was about to give her a list of reasons why they couldn't risk themselves for a lowly errand boy and the thought filled her with rage. She ran forward, grabbing Big Joe by the front of his shirt. She knew she risked angering him—her head didn't even reach his shoulders—but the idea the Iron Claws might not help was driving her crazy.

"Ned isn't disposable! He's one of your men and he's in trouble. If you won't step up to protect one of your own, even if you think he's some kind of weak link, then—"

"Whoa! Nobody's saying that," Big Joe said, at the same moment Emma stepped forward and pried Maya's hands off Big Joe's shirt.

"Ned isn't weak!" Emma said, pushing Maya back. "And if you're about to come in here and say crap like that, then you're itching for a fight."

Caesar, Alec, and Dylan quickly surrounded Maya, boxing her in. Scales were beginning to appear on their necks, a first sign they were shifting to partial dragon form to breathe fire.

"I'm not saying Ned is inferior! I'm saying he's amazing," Maya said.

"We know that," Alec said.

"Yes, we all know that. Ned is one of the most valued members of our club," Dylan said.

"We love him. He's our family," Marie said.

Maya looked around at their faces. Their expressions weren't filled with pity or disgust. They just looked scared for Ned, and ready to rip off Maya's head if she said another bad word about him.

"Then why does Ned think you all look down on him?" Maya said carefully, shifting out of her defensive stance and taking her hand off her taser.

"That's all Ned," Emma said, speaking softly.

"He thinks because he doesn't like violence that we'll abandon him the same way his clan did," Alec said.

"Which is bullshit," Caesar added.

"But why isn't he with you? Where is he?" Dylan said.

Big Joe's phone rang at that second, a trill of a Taylor Swift song that made Emma smile. He clicked the phone on, but didn't say a word, just listened for a long second before turning the phone off. The whole room waited in silence.

"The Red Guards—the High Council's goons—they have Ned." He paused.

"What do they want?" Emma asked.

"They want me. They want me to turn myself over for

Ned," Big Joe said.

"This smells like a trap," Emma said.

"Yeah, they just want us all in one place so they can spring whatever they've been planning on us," Caesar said.

"Did they give proof of life?" Maya asked, fighting to decelerate the too-fast beating of her heart. "None of this even matters if they've killed Ned."

"I could hear Ned in the background, and he sounded fine. It almost sounded like he was cooking." He looked at Dylan. "We're going to need all of our firepower."

"And you're going to need me," Maya said, stepping forward.

Big Joe looked her up and down, then glanced at Emma, who nodded.

"Right, gear up. We're going to save Ned or die trying."

"THIS LITTLE GUY CAN COOK!" somebody blurted, their voice muffled like their mouth was full of food.

Ned blinked awake to a world of pain. He didn't know where he was, but it smelled awful.

"You're disgusting!" a gravelly voice responded from close by. He looked around and saw two strange men lounging on crappy motel chairs next to the window. They were eating a box of desserts he'd made for the Iron Claws' Puff distribution tomorrow.

"What? It's good! It just has a little Puff in it," the first voice said.

"Puff? What?" Ned moaned. He tried to focus as the world dipped and swayed before his blurry eyes. *Yep, that's a concussion*, he thought dismally. The room looked like a cheap extended stay motel room: the stained carpet, laughably generic art on the walls, and ancient kitchen appliances were all dead giveaways. He tried to move, to stand, to flee, but a painful tugging at his wrists and ankles stopped him.

Ned looked down, the pain in his head throbbing out in a syncopated cha-cha. Thick chains confined him to the chair on which he sat.

"Puff's just powered dragon scales! It's practically skin cells. Trust me, buddy, everything you've ever eaten had skin cells in it." The stranger eating Ned's brownies was tall and well-muscled with dark hair. He made loud, chomping sounds as he guzzled the chocolate, flecks of the dessert flying from his mouth in large spitballs as he spoke.

"You're still disgusting, Scott," the other man, a wiry blond, said as he ran his fingers through his greasy, thinning hair.

"Oh *I'm* the gross one, Carl? Well *you*--," The dark haired man yelled.

"Shut up. The kid's awake."

Ned concentrated, waiting to feel the telltale movement of his bones. These idiots had chained him up? *I am an effing dragon!*

Nothing happened. He looked at the chains again. Elaborate markings etched each link and Ned felt a shiver of fear race down his spine.

Ned coughed, "So, what's going on here?"

The blond—Carl, apparently—spoke. "These chains have been hexed. You can't shift while they're touching you. Just sit tight and be a good little bait for your friends."

Ned wriggled in the chains, testing them for weakness. They were definitely hexed; they sat heavy and burned where they made contact with his exposed skin. He glanced over at the box of brownies sitting on the mucus-colored Formica countertop. It had the Iron Claws' seal on it; these goons had finally managed to get their hands on some product. *They must have a few humans in their pocket.* The Claws would never sell to shifters, especially stupid dicks like these guys.

"Hey, fellas, don't you think these chains are a bit much?" Ned slouched, trying to look smaller and weaker as he spoke. "I'm just the cook."

"Sure, and without those chains you're going to just sit there calmly waiting for a rescue instead of shifting and flying away," the greasy blond said. "Because you're an honest guy like that." His voice dripped with sarcasm.

"Your friend there is almost at the bottom of that box of brownies. He strikes me as the type to get a bit..." Ned paused. "...grumpy when his blood sugar drops."

"I could eat." Scott belched, scraping at the bottom of the now-empty box of brownies.

"You're an idiot," Carl sneered.

"What's this guy gonna do, whisk us to death?" Scott scratched at his stomach thoughtfully. "We'll take enough chains off so he can cook, but leave enough on so he can't shift. It's not like there's anything else to do until this thing gets started."

"Fine. But if this shit goes sideways, I'm selling you out to the High Council so fast it'll make your head spin."

Ned sighed in relief as the goons—if they were name-checking the High Council, they had to be Red Guard—unwound the heavy chains from his arms and legs. The pain immediately abated and Ned took a deep breath to steady himself. They secured a single loop of chain around his left arm, tethering him to an exposed support beam.

Ned opened the fridge and rummaged through the pantry. The place was pretty well-stocked.

"So...cupcakes?" Ned turned to his captors with a smile

that he hoped looked convincing.

"What did you call us?" Scott's face turned bright red and his substantial midsection jiggled as he dove across the room. He captured Ned's throat in his hands, the hairs on his knuckles tickling Ned's earlobes uncomfortably.

"I meant..." It was getting harder to breathe, let alone speak. "Do you want...cupcakes?"

Ned gasped gratefully as the large man released him. Each breath was a joy. *I love air.*

"Shit, yeah, let's have some cupcakes." Scott guffawed.

Ned was still hunched on the ground panting, but managed to lift his hand to give a weak thumbs up.

"Get moving. We're heading out in about an hour. The other guys are almost done setting up." Carl lit a cigarette and leaned back into his puce-colored chair. "Make with the eats, Betty Crocker."

Ned mixed up the cupcakes from scratch, chocolate Guinness cake with Bailey's frosting. He was cooking under duress, but he had *standards*, dammit. These bastards were going to stuff themselves silly with his delicious desserts. Ned tried to keep his face passive as he poured his batter, being sure to run it through the hexed chain so all of the mixture got a nice, prolonged exposure to the chain's magic.

By the time they're done eating, he thought with a smile, *being ugly and stupid will be the least of their worries.*

THERE WAS STILL another hour before the bullshit prisoner handoff and Maya made her way stealthily around the perimeter of the quarry, avoiding both the dragons and their human guards. The more she saw, the more the battleground impressed her.

The quarry itself was an oval that ran deep into the ground, with high cliffs on every side too steep for a human to climb. It was surrounded by a desolate landscape, so flat and empty, there was nowhere to hide and any approach would be spotted from far off. On top of all that, the quarry grew narrower as it went down, a layout that would encumber the Iron Claws' wings' movement once they got to the ground but would hinder any High Council's goons on the ground as well.

Maya shook her head. The Red Guard sure knew how to set up a kill zone.

Big Joe, Emma, and Dylan--the main strategists of the club—went over every detail they could find about the trap set for them but still didn't hesitate, saying the risk was worth it for Ned.

They really do love him. Maya smiled.

Maya concentrated on staying low and quiet, hidden to the men patrolling the top of the quarry.

"Did you try the kid's cupcakes?" one of the guards standing next to a large rock said to what appeared to be the open air.

Is he talking to me? She paled.

"Yeah, that chocolate stuff on the inside is incredible. I had three." The voice seemed to come from inside the rock itself. Maya moved quickly over to the men, staying low so they wouldn't spot her as easily.

The rock wasn't really a rock; it was a hollow case painted to look like a rock. Inside, Maya could barely make out the form of a man with what looked like a cannon pointed at the air above the quarry. Maya snuck around the faux-rock and located the ammunition set up to auto-load once the cannon fired its dangerous cargo: weighted ropes to drag the Iron Claws from the sky. It would be too easy for any of the Red Guard goons waiting on the ground to attack the trapped Iron Claws with hex blades and take them to the High Council.

These guys don't mess around.

Maya moved with practiced silence along the top of the quarry, now with a better idea of what to look for. The entire rim was booby trapped with fake rocks hiding net-throwing cannons. At least ten of them, almost perfectly blended into the landscape and equally spaced along the ledge.

And it wasn't just cannons. The lip of the quarry was rigged with four large-scale explosives camouflaged on the cardinal points. *You clever bastards.* They weren't going to be taking *anybody* in to the Council. Once they had the Iron Claws netted at the bottom of the quarry, all the goons had to do was blow up the walls and let the rock avalanche take care of the rest.

They couldn't have set all this up in the few days since the Iron Claws came to town. The High Council had known the club was coming.

Maya ran back to the road and dialed Big Joe.

"We have a problem," she said.

"I really hate it when people say that. Is anyone else kidnapped?" he said.

"Not that I know of, but this whole place is a death trap. They must have been putting it together for weeks at least. Who knew you were coming here?"

"No one. We didn't tell anyone." Maya heard Big Joe pull the phone away from his face and say something muffled to someone else in the room. A second later, he returned to the phone. "Emma says we didn't even know we were coming here until a few days ago when we heard Gita was ill. We got on bikes less than twenty-four hours later."

So the High Council knew the Iron Claws would be drawn to

this particular quarry before the club even knew they would be in town.

"How did you all even know that Gita was ill in the first place?" Maya said.

"Let me ask Emma," Big Joe said.

Maya could hear the muted voices on the other end and shifted her weight, looking down into the quarry. Ned was out there somewhere, either at the bottom of that quarry or being held gods-only-knew where waiting to be used as bait. She couldn't stand that he was alone. Maya tried to ease her mind by reminding herself the goons had no need to torture him; he was just a bargaining chip.

Please underestimate him. The second they realized Ned wasn't as powerless as he looked, they'd kill him.

She wanted to shift to tiger, tear down to the bottom of the quarry, and kill them all before they even had a chance to scream. But even she had her limits. She was outgunned, outmanned, and out-planned—she *had* to wait for backup.

"You still there?" Big Joe's voice said on the other side of the phone.

"Ned isn't getting saved any faster out here," Maya said.

"Caesar says we heard about Gita at one of his gigs. Some random fan mentioned he'd heard that Raj's favorite human was sick and needed Puff." Maya could hear in his voice he'd come to the same conclusion she had: the High Council sent a spy to lead them into the trap. She would have to investigate later if they were also the cause of Gita's illness, but since Gita was getting better, the priority right now was saving Ned.

"They've been preparing this for a long time, you're going to have to be careful," Maya said.

"No shit." Big Joe sighed. "Maya, just how committed are you to getting Ned back?"

"Completely."

"Then here's what you have to do."

Night had descended on the quarry, the full moon giving the white limestone an eerie glow. Maya crouched in her tiger shape at the top of the quarry, hidden inside one of the camouflaged cannon huts. The hut's previous occupant lay bloody but breathing nearby, restrained with an impressive series of zip ties.

Alec, wearing only a robe to facilitate a quick shift once the fight got started, knelt next to her, typing fast onto a small laptop in his lap.

"Do you think this is going to work?" Alec whispered.

"It has to," Maya whispered back.

A spotlight switched on suddenly, illuminating a large group of dragons flying toward the quarry. Alec quietly pointed out the Iron Claw members to Maya, unfamiliar with their shifted forms: Big Joe, Emma, Caesar, and Dylan along with seven other High Council dragons surrounding them. Another spotlight switched on, pointing directly down and showing the quarry's depths in bright detail.

Maya couldn't help her small gasp. Ned was in chains, thick manacles around both his wrists and his ankles, chained so tightly he bent half over in his chair. He was alone. She expected he would be surrounded by guards, but then she remembered the explosives. The High Council wouldn't want their own people down there when they set off the rock slide.

She focused her sight and could see the tiny details of his chest rising and falling as he breathed, his fingernails caked in something brown. *Mud? Chocolate?* Of course. Only

Ned would be in a hostage situation with his fingers covered in frosting.

The dragons landed on top of the quarry, the Iron Claws forming a circle where they could watch each other's backs.

"I demand you bring Ned here," Big Joe roared, a spurt of flame issuing from his mouth.

The largest of the High Council dragons hovered above the quarry, his enormous wings shining black in the spotlight's glare.

"Shift to your human form, come down into the quarry alone, and we will bring you your messenger boy." The dragon's voice had a nasty nasal tone that set Maya's fur on end. "We'll even allow your people to escort you as you hand yourself over."

Yeah, so they'll all get hit by net cannons and then get caught in an avalanche, Maya thought.

"Can I trigger it now?" Alex whispered.

"Not yet," Maya whispered. "Wait for my signal."

"I am here to surrender myself in exchange for a member of my crew," Big Joe bellowed. Maya bit her lip, wanting all of this initial dance to be over. The Iron Claws knew the prisoner turnover was a trap. The High Council knew the prisoner turnover was a trap. *Just spring it so we can go get Ned!* "I demand you bring my man here. Only then will I surrender."

Big Joe launched himself into the air until he was flying directly above the quarry, right in the middle of all of the net-hurling cannons.

"That's the signal. Keep them busy up here until I can get to all the explosives."

"Copy that," Alec said as his fingers flew across the keyboard. He tapped the headset attached to his ear. "Alright, everybody, it's show time."

Emma, Dylan, and Caesar all lifted off at once, flying above the quarry to join Big Joe just as Maya started sprinting along the side of the quarry edge, running as fast as she could for the first set of explosives.

The High Council dragons launched themselves into the air at once, but hesitated to engage with the Iron Claws above the quarry. Maya smiled, but didn't stop running. *They're waiting for the cannons to go off and finish off the Iron Claws for them.*

She heard the High Council dragons' cries along the quarry's edge, shouting at each other.

"Where are the cannons? Steve, you asshat, get the cannons working!"

Maya felt a smile pull widely at the sides of her face. The key discovery of the afternoon's reconnaissance mission had been the Red Guard had more cannons than men to manually control them. They had rigged the cannons with remote triggers. It would have been a good move on their part: fewer of their men at risk. But their plan fell apart as soon as Maya snuck Alec into an unoccupied cannon hut a few hours before and let the tech wiz take over the remote cannons' control protocols.

One of the High Council dragons cut away from their main group, swooping down low to one of the camouflaged cannon huts and shifting to human form. Steve the Asshat, Maya assumed. *He's Alec's problem now*. She didn't like it, but she had to trust the hacker would be able to keep the Red Guard's tech guy from regaining control of the net-throwing cannons before she disabled all of the explosives.

Emma roared a challenge and a green High Council dragon answered her with a war cry. Maya watched out of the corner of her eye as the sleek beast flew through the air to attack Emma, followed a second later by the other six remaining High Council goons. It was hard to see details in the spotlights' glare, but the goons' shadows rocketed through the air toward the Iron Claws like monstrous demons from horror stories.

A swooshing noise and the cannons started to fire their nets at the High Council, but they evaded Alec's shots and the nets fell harmlessly down into the dark quarry bowl.

"We'll keep them busy," Caesar said over the headset, his voice gruff in dragon form.

"You better," Maya said as the second round of cannon blasts went off. This time, one hit a High Council goon from mid-air and pulled him down to the ground. The dragon's crash echoed through the quarry and Maya dared a look down.

Ned was trying to scramble out of the way of the flailing goon, hobbling on his manacled feet to get as far away as possible. *Good, he's okay.*

Maya didn't have time to worry about Ned. She had to disable the four explosive caches before the Red Guard decided to cut their losses, blow up the quarry, and take down as many Iron Claws as they could. The first explosives cache was assembled in an old fashioned design that she hadn't seen in years, but she shifted her paws to hands and got to work disarming the bomb.

She could hear the sounds of battle screeching and clawing above her as the Iron Claws clashed with the goons. She could barely see them out of the corner of her eye, but the Red Guard seemed strangely sluggish as they tried to herd the Iron Claws down into the quarry.

Bursts of flame lit up the sky as each side tried to flambé the other, but Maya could see it was in no way an even fight: the Iron Claws were outnumbered three to two.

Just keep them busy, Maya prayed. As soon as the Iron

Claws dipped below the edge of the quarry, the High Council would blow the entire place to bits.

One bomb down.

Maya shifted back to full tiger form and ran with all her might around the edge to the next explosive. She took a long look at it and cursed. This was a completely different detonator. They must have had more than one person putting these together.

"I'm going to need a couple of minutes," she shouted into her headset.

Alec's voice sounded worried in her ear. "The goon's hacker is good. He's going to take back the cannons *soon*!" he said.

"Then stop him!" Big Joe cried from above as he roared a massive blast of flame at a purple High Council dragon.

Another crash and boom and Maya dared a glance down at a second netted dragon trying to scream and claw its way out of the ropes holding it to the quarry floor. It wasn't an Iron Claw. *Thank the gods.*

Second bomb down.

A scream of pain rang out over the quarry and Maya glanced up as she ran for the third explosive. Caesar was bleeding heavily, a massive wound to his belly drawing two of the goons to circle him like sharks closing in for the kill. But they didn't attack; they bobbed and weaved, hiccuping bursts of sickly green fire. The goons' wing beats were uneven and slow like they were drunk or sick.

The cupcakes. Maya remembered the chocolate on Ned's fingers and the men mentioning Ned had made them all cupcakes. Ned poisoned the goons before any of the Claws even showed up.

I knew he was a keeper.

The third explosive cache was the same as the first and

she pulled it apart quickly, concentrating on the dangerous substances in her hand and not allowing herself to pay attention to the screaming in the sky.

Third bomb down.

"Guys! They aren't trying to get control of the cannons anymore!" Alec's voice sounded panicked through the headset. "Go get Ned now! They're going to blow the last explosive!"

Maya looked up. The High Council goons—including the hacker—were flying away as quickly as possible. The Iron Claws descended in one unified swoop into the quarry as Maya ran in the opposite direction. She wouldn't be able to get down to Ned faster than dragons' wings and she was already calculating the blast radius of the last explosive compared to where she was standing.

This is going to be close.

The explosion rocked the ground beneath her feet, the shock wave shoving her roughly onward as the sound deafened her and blew out her headset. She didn't stop running until she got to the road and shifted to human form.

Four large shapes swooped down from the sky, the Iron Claw dragons landing with varying degrees of grace before shifting to human form. Maya sprinted forward as Big Joe's claws opened to reveal a dusty, beautiful Ned. Safe and sound.

"Never! Never do that to me again!" Maya cried as she pulled the manacles off of him.

"Don't worry." Ned smiled, his released hands immediately cupping Maya's face. "The only person I'm ever allowing to chain me up is you."

The Iron Claws, all in human form, gathered around them.

"We're so glad you're okay!" Caesar said.

"Yeah, man, you had us really worried," Alec said.

"Sorry to make everyone so upset," Ned said, his expression one that Maya hadn't seen before. "You all put your lives on the line for me."

"There's nothing to feel sorry about, you didn't do anything wrong," Big Joe said, walking forward to put a hand on Ned's shoulder.

"Of course we would risk everything for you, you're our family," Emma said.

Ned smiled. "You all are my family too and you always will be, but I've been doing some thinking..."

Maya held her breath. The other Claws just looked confused.

"I don't want to be an Iron Claw anymore," Ned said.

All of the others started talking at once, saying that he was being ridiculous and they needed him, but Big Joe remained silent until he coughed and all their eyes turned to him.

"You will always be an Iron Claw," Big Joe said. "But there is no rule that all Iron Claws must ride with us all the time. I know that being constantly on the road and fighting goons isn't for you, Ned. But you are our brother and always will be."

"And you can ship us boxes of your brownies every couple of weeks when we're running low," Emma added.

Caesar and Dylan looked like they still wanted to argue, but when Ned got to his feet and put his arms around Maya, their expressions cleared.

"I want to be with you," Ned said. "Let's live here. You'll keep the tigers safe and I'll open a bakery or something. What do you think?"

Maya grinned and pulled him close. "Sounds delicious."

HER ROCK STAR DRAGON

The roar of the crowd still rang in Caesar's ears as he tried to relax backstage. The bar out front was packed to the rafters, and fans were still singing along to his songs now being played out of the bar speakers.

Caesar perched on the edge of his seat, post-concert adrenaline still surging through him. He strummed a chord on his guitar and winced. The melody was pretty solid, a catchy tune about life on the road, but the bridge just wasn't working. He hummed a couple of bars and tried a different chord. The tune shifted to something sadder, almost mournful. Caesar grimaced and strummed out the "Low Rider" base line to clear his head. He paced around the room.

"Don't suppose you have any advice?" Caesar said to his club brother, Alec, who was lounging on the ratty couch across from him. The rest of the Iron Claws motorcycle club had already left, but Alec had decided to stay backstage with Caesar.

"About doing a cover of "Low Rider"?" Alec said as he read a tech magazine while simultaneously playing a civilization-building game on his tablet. "It'll be a crowd pleaser, but don't you have more of a punk rock sound?" He grinned and turned the page of his magazine with one hand while the other prepared his digital village for a nuclear launch.

Caesar smiled. He had stopped being surprised by Alec's feats of multitasking long ago, but it never stopped being impressive.

"No, I mean advice about this." Caesar dropped back into his chair and played the new bridge again. It sounded even sadder this time.

Alec paused his game, frowning a little. "It sounds really lonely. Was that what you're going for?" He tapped his game and a digital mushroom cloud appeared on screen. "I thought you were trying to be more upbeat since that music blog called your latest album 'emo.'"

Caesar tried ending the phrase on a high note. The result sounded more upbeat, but didn't feel as *true* as the earlier chord sequence. He got up and started to pace again, walking the five feet of the small green room back and forth like a six-foot metronome.

"Fuck emo," Caesar said. "This song is supposed to be about how life on the road isn't lonely when you've got somebody you love with you." He hummed the new sequence again. Definitely too cheerful. *Maybe a lonely bridge with an upbeat chorus would be better?*

Alec rose an eyebrow at him. "That's sweet. Something you want to tell me?" For a second, Alec looked anxious. Alec was transgender; had a female body, but was a man through and through. The Claws didn't care—Alec was Alec —but Caesar knew his brother worried sometimes if his fellow male Claws paid too much attention to his female shell.

"Dude, chill," Caesar said. "It's just easier to write a song about a single romantic interest, but it's about all of us." He started pacing again, his guitar still in his hands. "I mean, the Iron Claws, we're like a family—not related, obviously— but we're still a family of a sort. I mean, we all left our clans for different reasons, but we ride together and live together and—"

Alec laughed. "I'm just giving you shit. Of course we're family. Even Ned, although he doesn't ride with us anymore." He raised a fist to his heart quickly, then returned to playing his game. "Once an Iron Claw, always an Iron Claw."

"Poor Ned, stuck in the suburbs." Caesar strummed out a few bars of "House of the Rising Sun". "I'd go insane."

"Insane would be just fine if I was also super rich and married to a sexy tiger shifter," Alec said.

Caesar chuckled and shifted the tune to "If I Were a Rich Man" in mid-refrain. "Genius bastard, figuring out how to use magic in his gluten-free desserts so that they actually taste good. Did you hear his bakery brings in six figures a quarter? Makes me almost wish I could cook."

"Rich and famous could still be in the cards for you, though. But don't sweat it. If you leave us some day and become a big, fancy rock star someplace, you'll still be an Iron Claw too." Alec smirked as he tapped out a complex sequence on his tablet that diverted an incoming comet from his village smashing into another player's village instead. "You can't get rid of us that easily."

"Hmm," Caesar said, trying out the new bridge again. He could picture it too easily: an agent appearing at one of his gigs, signing him with a major label. It was a familiar fantasy. There would be fancy recording studios and air-conditioned tour buses; adoring fans who wrote fan fiction about his love life, and buffets overflowing with gourmet food in his spotless dressing room backstage. He'd ride his bike only on nice days when he wanted some air, rather than through rain and storms to get to the next town. He'd have to hide he was a dragon shifter from humans, obviously, but there were plenty of successful shifters who were able to keep their identities secret without too much hassle.

He started to play "Homeward Bound" without really thinking about it. If he became really successful, he could call into the weekly video-chats with Ned and the rest of the team. Maybe by then more members of the club would have split away to do their own thing. Dylan, the club's second in command, and Marie, the club's medic, were married and still riding with the club, but they might want to start a family some time. And if Big Joe and Emma finally got their heads out of their asses enough to admit how much they loved each other, then they might split off too. It was hard to imagine Alec not riding with the Claws, but if he found somebody who could look past Alec's female body to see the true man under his skin—and who was smart enough to keep up with him when he started talking tech—Alec might stop his wandering ways as well.

Picturing the members of the Iron Claws scattered across the country, Caesar played the mournful bridge again. A couple of tweaks, and it might be perfect.

"What do you think you'd do if you didn't ride with the Claws anymore?" Caesar asked Alec.

"I don't know." Alec rearranged the magazine in his lap so it was tilted up with the cover facing Caesar and partially hiding Alec's face. "My job's mobile. I figure I'll keep riding, distributing Puff to the folks that need it, and keep the Iron Claws alive after you jerks all go settle down. Somebody's got to keep going; it might as well be me."

"Don't worry, I don't think I'm going to be whisked away anytime soon." Caesar's eye caught on the cover of Alec's magazine.

It can't be, Caesar thought. He stared at the face smiling at him from the glossy surface.

"Hey, mind if I take a look at that?" He pointed at the magazine.

Alec gave him a questioning look as he handed it over. "What is it? You look like you've seen the Ghost of Christmas Future, all robed and creepy."

"More like the Ghost of Christmas Past." Caesar tapped the magazine's cover. "I think I know her."

Alec nodded. "Of course you know her. That's Nina Alvarez. She's one of the most successful people in tech. You should have heard her TED talk. She's a genius." He winced. "I had tickets to see her at a conference once, but that was around the time Ned got kidnapped so I missed it. Little dude totally owes me."

"No, I mean, like, I *know* her." Caesar held the cover up to the light to see more of the details. Her hair was different, more carefully styled than he remembered, and the photographer hadn't quite captured the fire in her eyes, but it was definitely Nina. "She came to a concert a few years ago. She was a big fan and we, um, hung out after the show."

"Is that what the kids are calling it these days?" Alec rose an eyebrow. "Hanging out?"

"It wasn't like that," Caesar said, handing the magazine back to Alec. He didn't want to think about the slight pang in his chest as Alec opened the pages on his lap and Caesar couldn't see Nina's face anymore. "I mean, it *was* like that, she was a groupie and we had a good time, but that's not why I remember her. She's the one who taught me how to knit."

"Holy crap, Knitting Girl was Nina Alvarez?" Alec laughed. "Damn, the world is small."

Caesar winced. "It wasn't that big a deal." Of course, it had felt like a big deal at the time, but that was years ago. He wasn't that guy anymore who fell in love with every girl he talked to for more than twenty minutes.

"She was a big enough deal for you to write a song about her." Alec pointed at him, grinning widely.

"I write a lot of songs about a lot of people." Caesar tapped the song notes next to him on the chair. "Seriously, I barely even remember her." A lie, but Alec's knowing grin was annoying.

"Oh-ho, now the story changes. So, which is it? Do you know her, or not?" Alec was almost bouncing with glee. "You have that whole verse about her being the girl who got away. How did that go? *If I ever find the girl who knits/I'm never calling it quits/Because I have to admit/She's the girl with the wits/To keep me—*" he sang in a warbling off-rhythm imitation of the original song.

Caesar put his hands over his ears, trying to drown Alec's voice out. "Quit it!"

Alec laughed so hard he nearly fell off the couch. "You still like her!" He made kissy noises at Caesar. "Never thought I'd see the day. Is she coming to the show tonight? Did you invite her?"

"Of course not," Caesar said, picking up his guitar and gathering up the scraps of paper with his lyrics scribbled on them. "It's been years, and it was just a one-night stand. I doubt she even remembers me. She never came to another concert. And I still need to practice for tomorrow's show."

"Uh huh," Alec said. He put down the magazine to type on his tablet. "Just you wait. I bet she hasn't forgotten you either. She'll be there."

For a second, Caesar remembered Nina's smile, the gentle touch of her hands as she put the smooth needles into his hands, molding his fingers around each stitch. He'd knitted hundreds of different projects over the last few years and given them all away, but he'd held onto his first misshapen piece of rag she'd helped him make. He used to imagine it still smelled like her skin, but there was no way after so many years that was still true.

The longing to see her again--to see if she was really as spectacular as he remembered--ran through him like a jolt.

He shook his head. "No, it probably didn't mean a thing to her. She won't be there."

HE'S BACK. Nina stared in disbelief at the concert poster. Today had been another nice, normal Tuesday of coffee, clients, and coding when that single sheet of paper stopped Nina dead in her tracks. That old feeling of trepidation, adoration, and lust welled in her stomach as she looked at Caesar's picture.

"Neema, you look like you see ghost," Rada said. The older woman had mispronounced Nina's name the first time Nina came to the coffee shop, and Nina hadn't had the heart to correct her since.

"It's nothing," Nina said, although her eyes were drawn back to the poster like a magnet.

Caesar de la Vega looked magnificent. If anything, he'd gotten hotter in the last five years. The poster featured a shot of Caesar in the center, shirtless, screaming into a mic. The neon highlights of the poster drew focus to the pattern of intricate tattoos that ran all along his strong chest. The designs went all the way down his arms, ending in the compass tattoo on his right hand which he'd made the logo for his band. He'd cut his hair since she saw him last, but his same intense *presence* still jumped off the page.

"Your face says more than nothing." Rada pressed a warm cup of coffee into Nina's hand.

"Today might be a chocolate croissant day as well, Rada," Nina said. Rada smiled and bustled away.

Nina's favorite coffee shop, The Grind, had been her haven since she first came to town. Rada, The Grind's Eastern European owner, had made Nina feel at home in a way her bare, subleased apartment couldn't. The small cafe only had a few scattered tables and chairs; the perfect place to get a relatively-cheap cup of joe without the pretension. Rada also didn't mind if Nina sat there for hours working on her projects, knitting scarves for family and friends, sorting through receipts, or going through her mail.

Nina shifted the stack of papers and mail under her arm to take the croissant from Rada. Nina knew her curves didn't need another pastry, but one look at Caesar's poster was enough to declare today a comfort food day. She took a long sip of her coffee and resisted the urge to moan as the hot liquid slid down her throat.

"Mm, your coffee is perfect as always, Rada."

"I know this," Rada said, her expression skeptical. "My coffee always the same. Why ghost look?"

Nina bit her lip. "It's truly nothing, Rada." She tried to look casual as she nodded at the wall. "It's just, um, who brought in that poster?"

"Tall man. Very polite." The words tumbled out musically in Rada's thick accent. "He got big, black coffee—no sugar." Rada lowered her voice conspiratorially. "Never trust man who likes things too sweet."

"Was it the man on the poster?" Nina could feel her heart hammering in her chest. *Was he standing here? Right here?*

Rada squinted and leaned towards the poster, staring hard for a moment. "Yes. Only he didn't look so..." Her hands wobbled back and forth as she tried to find the word.

"Shirtless?" Nina offered.

"Yes. Unfortunate." Rada buzzed around the near-empty cafe, wiping down tables and chairs as she moved. "You know this man?"

Nina tried to hold back the blush overwhelming her

face. Even if five years had passed since she met Caesar, she still remembered every detail.

"A little," Nina said.

Even before she met him, Nina had loved Caesar's music. The honesty of his lyrics, the passionate heat in the driving beat; she'd listened to his album so many times her roommate had insisted she switch to headphones. She'd gone to his concert ready to enjoy the music, but been utterly blown away by him on stage. Everything about Caesar was magnificent. There was something about the way he moved on stage, like a wild beast was trying to stretch itself free under his skin, that aroused her beyond what she imagined possible.

She still couldn't believe that she managed to sneak backstage with a few lies and some strategically-visible cleavage. It was the sort of thing she'd never considered doing before, but she was willing to risk it for Caesar.

When she finally found him, she'd been tongue-tied. Everything about him radiated restless energy, from his constantly tapping fingers to the way he sat barely restrained on the edge of the faded dressing room couch. The muscles on his arms strained against his tight shirt, his hands so large they looked about to snap the guitar cradled in his arms. The chiseled lines of his jaw made her want to run her tongue along its edges, and the waves of hair falling over his face looked silky and soft. Caesar's face immediately lit up when he saw her. The sight had made her feel like she could fly.

"Neema? You okay?" Rada touched her shoulder and Nina was jerked back to the present. "You look miles away."

"Um, yes, I knew Caesar. I mean, I went to one of his concerts a few years ago." She took another sip of her coffee, letting the bitter taste roll around in her mouth. *I know his body*. She wanted to say to Rada. *Every scar, tattoo, and freckle*. "He was nice," Nina said aloud.

"Was he—how you say?—good in the sack?" Rada pointed toward her groin area with an earnest expression on her lined face.

Nina blushed to the roots of her hair, then laughed. "Yes, he was, actually."

Rada patted her shoulder and smiled. "I remember one night with passing peddler man along the riverbank when I was young. Hands so rough, but, ahh..." Her eyes twinkled for a moment. She looked back at Nina. "Is nice to have the memories." She patted Nina's shoulder again and returned to behind the counter.

Nina sunk deeper into her chair, feeling the worn leather enfold her. She knew she should get to work, but her gaze kept going back to Caesar's poster.

When she'd first arrived in the dressing room, she thought he would shout at her to leave or pull her under him, but they'd talked for hours. She couldn't remember all they talked about, but she remembered the moment Caesar reached out a hand to move aside a wisp of Nina's long hair. That small touch had been enough to break what felt like a dam between them, and she'd pounced.

She grabbed Caesar by the collar and pulled him close, reveling in his manly scent of motor oil and musk. She remembered his look of surprise and wonder. Their lips joined with a passion she had never felt before. She let out a low moan, muffled by Caesar's lips. Her hands roamed the wide expanse of his chest, thrilling at the feel of his hard muscles under his shirt.

He was wearing too many clothes. They both were.

Nina pulled, hard. Discarded buttons pinged around the room as she tore open Caesar's shirt, revealing his tattooed chest. She broke away from his lips, kissing his strong jawline, running her tongue down his neck, his pecs, his abs.

Caesar's groan reverberated through the room, buzzing the strings on his now-discarded guitar. His hands found the hemline of Nina's slashed tank top and he whipped it over her head in a single motion. She'd felt a little self-conscious about her curves, but he'd looked at her like she was the most beautiful creature he'd ever seen. Her skin pebbled with goosebumps, exposed to the chilly air of the dressing room. Caesar's warm hands immediately soothed away the cold, moving across her body in ever-widening circles, getting closer and closer to where she wanted him.

His belt clinked as she pulled his leather pants down, revealing boxer briefs patterned with motorcycles. She chuckled before stripping him bare, her eyes widening at the impressive package he'd kept contained in his tight pants. She licked her lips, wanting something more productive to do with her mouth. His breath caught as she licked his thighs, moving closer to her goal.

She kissed the tip of his erection, delighting in how he writhed and reacted under her. His head flew back, his hands gripping onto her long hair as she teased him, gently lapping along his length. When she knew he couldn't take any more, she finally took him in her mouth, massaging him with her tongue. Her hands snaked around to his ass, gripping him tightly as she pulled him deeper and deeper inside her throat.

Caesar's groan reverberated all the way down his body.

He'd stepped away and helped Nina to her feet, kissing every inch of her within reach. But Nina didn't want to wait any longer. She pushed Caesar against the wall, hard, shaking the autographed photos hanging above him. Nina kicked the rest of her clothes off as she pressed against him, nipping at the well-muscled flesh of his chest.

Caesar growled, a low, hungry sound, and spun them around, pressing Nina's bare back against the cold wall. He gripped her thighs, pulling her legs up around him and positioning his length at her core. She'd wanted to protest that she was too heavy for this maneuver, but he held her up like she weighed nothing at all.

Caesar teased her opening with his swollen dick, rubbing it against her soaked folds.

"Caesar...please," Nina begged, trying to pull him closer. "I need you now."

In a single motion, Caesar was inside of her to the hilt, his hands on her waist, his lips on hers. Nina wrapped her arms around his neck and braced herself against the wall as he thrust inside of her. Caesar moving inside gave her such a deliriously perfect feeling, Nina's legs started to shake.

Nina screamed as the orgasm ripped through her body. She gripped onto Caesar's strong shoulders to keep from falling. Wave after wave of pleasure roared through her, so forceful she thought she might pass out.

Caesar smiled proudly as he gently laid her down on the couch. He kissed her forehead with such a gentle kindness, Nina almost teared up.

"It's okay if you're too tired to..." Caesar's throbbing erection was nearly purple with want, but his face was carefully neutral. "We don't have to keep going."

At his words, Nina felt a surge of energy. "Oh yes, we do." She grinned as she propped herself up on all fours. Nina looked over her shoulder, shifting her weight as she slowly began to stroke herself with one hand. "I need you to fuck me, Caesar."

Caesar's smile lit up the room as he positioned himself

behind her. He gripped her hips and thrust inside of her once more.

Nina was still so sensitive, she nearly came again on the spot. Rambling moans and urgings fell from her mouth until she didn't know what she was saying. All she could feel was Caesar, and her desperate urge to be closer to him.

One of Caesar's hands snaked across her body, finding her swollen clit. He thrust rhythmically as he teased her sensitive bud. She gripped the worn fabric of the couch as he slammed into her, sending currents of pleasure through Nina's entire body.

They came together this time, almost harmonizing their screams of delight.

"Neema? Honey? You look very flushed. Are you ill?" Rada's voice cut through Nina's memories. Nina sat up straighter in her chair, pressing her thighs together.

Her face felt hot. "Sorry Rada, I'm okay. I was just thinking about—"

"Ah, your rock star man." Rada's tone was a little too understanding.

"Thanks for the coffee. I better be going."

"Don't forget your things." Rada gestured to the stack of paperwork and yarn Nina had brought in with her and not had the attention to finish.

"Thanks, Rada." Nina scooped up the pile of papers and knitting supplies, stuffing them back into her tote bag. A single orange and neon pink envelope fell onto the floor.

She stooped to pick it up and her breath caught as a familiar name peeked out from a rip in the paper. She tore the envelope open with shaking hands.

It was a VIP ticket to Caesar's show, sent by special invitation.

He must want me to come! She grinned at the thought,

glancing back at the poster. *Well, I suppose it would be rude not to...*

THE ENERGY from the screaming crowd was electric, nearly shaking the walls of the bar as Caesar played. The drinks flowed strong, the local band he'd hired was in top form. Caesar rode the music with the same ease he rode the winds in dragon form.

He was only a few songs in and couples were already dancing in front of the stage. The hall was packed with fans on their feet, swaying to the music. A few were even singing along with all the lyrics, which Caesar loved.

The notes floated around him, the waves of melody and tone sliding and skipping along the walls and around all the listeners. The ebb and flow felt as powerful as tides, one song flowing into another: song about never meeting his older brother, song about living rough on the road before meeting the Iron Claws, love song about the feeling of connection between his new family, song he wrote for Dylan's wedding...

He was in the middle of the musical version of the vows Dylan wrote for his wife, Marie, when Caesar saw Nina. She was standing at the bar, leaning against it with a beer in her hand and a wistful expression.

It felt like a record needle screeched across the world for a second. His fingers flubbed the melody, too fast for anyone but him to notice.

He finished Dylan's song by rote, his fingers playing the chords and his mouth singing the words even as his mind whirled.

She came!

He wouldn't have believed it if he couldn't see her there out of the corner of his eye. He thought he was going to strain his neck staring at her over the excited crowd. The next song in the playlist was the new song he'd finished about life on the road, but his fingers struck up the opening notes to "Knitting Girl" before his mind had a chance to catch up.

"The girl smiled at me and I knew/That fate was over-due/I'd found the girl with the yarn/Who taught me to give a darn."

He inwardly winced at the lyrics even as they tumbled from his mouth. Five years ago felt like yesterday looking at her across the room, but the boy he'd been then felt like someone totally different. *Taught me to give a darn?* Had he really written those lyrics? He hid a wince as he changed chords.

A few fans in the crowd cheered. It had been a while since he'd last played "Knitting Girl", and one couple started to enthusiastically make out against the wall.

"Knitting girl/Knitting girl/You sent me on a whirl/Knitting girl/Knitting girl/You taught me to purl/Knitting girl/Knitting girl/You make my world twirl..."

Did she come here for him? Their time together was imprinted in his memory like the deep grooves of a well-loved record, but he couldn't remember the moment they actually met. Had he seen her across the room and sought her out? Had she found him? There had been so many fans over the years, the parts of his evening with Nina that were like all of the others blended together with other meetings. He vaguely remembered the sex with her being great, but he'd had a lot of great sex. It was that quiet moment, her hands molding his around the needles, the way she smiled, that had stuck with him.

"If I ever find the girl who knits/I'm never calling it quits/Because I have to admit/To her I would submit..."

What if she left? Maybe she was just there to listen to the music. She had to know the "Knitting Girl" song was for her, right? If she hadn't heard it before, she'd have to recognize the reference now. Or did she go around teaching all the guys she met how to knit? He wasn't sure whether he felt jealous, or just amused, at the image of Nina as some sort of sexy, knitting evangelist.

"Knitting girl/Knitting girl/You make my world twirl/Find me again/We'll let dreams unfurl."

He let the last notes of the song float across the bar, lingering until applause and cheers rang out from the crowd. He looked over to where Nina had been standing and felt relief uncoil in his chest that she was taking another beer from the bartender. She was going to stay.

But for how long?

Caesar announced the end of the set, told everyone to stick around because he'd be back soon, and to be generous to their bartenders. He nodded to the band and stepped quickly off stage.

Alec was in the green room as Caesar quickly took off his sweaty shirt and dug in his bag for a clean one. He wiped down his bare chest with a towel. He tried to remember if he had looked much different five years ago. He checked out his rippling six-pack abs in the green room mirror, his flat pecs, the glisten of sweat along his chiseled biceps. *No, it's about the same.* A few more lines around his eyes and forehead, maybe. Alec barely glanced at him, his fingers flying across his keyboard.

"Distribution of Puff in the back is looking really good," Alec said. "Marie found us three cancer patients, a few folks with lupus, and a handful of kids who are going to see a lot more birthdays. A few fans posted pictures of the concert up on social media that showed Iron Claws in the background, but I got them down quickly, so we should be okay. No more incidents like that time the mobster recognized Marie."

Caesar nodded, rubbing the towel across his neck. He'd noticed earlier that the merchandise table was getting enough traffic that the Iron Claws' distribution of Puff inside the "special edition" CD cases wasn't noticeable. Caesar was certainly pleased they were able to provide relief to those beyond the help of traditional medicine, but he wasn't a crusader like Big Joe or Dylan. They'd dedicated their lives to making sure that humans got access to ground dragon scales which could cure them of any illness. But Caesar also didn't agree with the High Council's decree that humans should never be allowed to use it. Caesar was happy that his concerts provided a cover for distribution. It wasn't like people actually bought CDs anymore, and Marie—as a trained nurse with a job at the local hospital—was an excellent screener to find people who really needed help.

"That's good," Caesar said absentmindedly, still rubbing the towel against his skin. "Just give me the signal if any Red Guard goons show up."

Alec coughed. "Something else on your mind?"

"What?"

Alec raised an eyebrow and nodded toward Caesar's chest. Caesar looked down and realized he'd been rubbing the same spot above his heart with the towel for the last minute. He flushed and put down the towel, grabbing the clean shirt and pulling it over his head.

"Nina showed up," Caesar muttered.

"Woo hoo!" Alec whooped. "I knew it would work!"

Caesar eyed his far-too-happy brother. "What did you do, Alec?"

"Nothing really, just hacked around a bit to get her address and sent her a VIP ticket." He didn't look even a little contrite.

"We don't even *have* VIP tickets," Caesar said.

"I know. I made her up a passable fake. 'VIP' just sounded classier." Alec grinned. "Anything for a brother, you know that. It was just a little nudge to get her in the door. You're the one who has to give her a reason to stay." He waved finger guns at Caesar. "Go get her, Mr. Fancy Dragon Rock Star."

"I'm not a rock star," Caesar said under his breath as he exited the green room and headed to the bar area.

Would she be different? He liked to think that he was a different man now than he was back then, but who would she be?

He could remember the softness of her hands like he'd touched them a moment ago. He and Nina were sitting together on the green room sofa. Caesar had been fidgeting, the way he always did when he didn't have a guitar in his hands. The edge of his t-shirt was shredded along the hem where he kept playing with the threads, twisting them into knots and then working the knots free. He hadn't even realized he was doing it until he felt her hands brush across the top of his hands and his fingers stilled.

"Can't stop your fingers from moving?" she had asked, her voice low. "I'm the same when I don't have a keyboard under my fingers."

"You play the piano?" he'd asked, his mind already rushing ahead. They'd travel the world singing and playing and making love in hotel rooms where the silky sheets and extra-fluffy towels smelled like lavender and cash.

She laughed. "No, I meant a computer keyboard. I'm a programmer. Just a lowly grunt at the moment, but I've got big plans to start my own business sometime soon." She nodded to his twitching fingers. "You know what I do when my fingers are itching to move? I knit." She pulled out a ball of yarn and two long, plastic needles from her purse. "It's super helpful when you have to kill time." She nodded toward the worn edge of his shirt. "Easier on the wardrobe too, I bet."

Caesar was drawn into the light of enthusiasm in her eyes. He eyed her lips. He wanted to lean in to kiss them, to see what their plumpness would feel like against his, but he wanted to hear what she had to say more.

"Yeah, knitting is cool. I think I had an aunt that used to knit." Caesar didn't like to think about his biological family. He'd left them when he was fifteen and hadn't looked back. He concentrated on Nina's smiling face.

"I could teach you." Her voice was tentative, her face immediately blushing like she was embarrassed about the offer.

It was the blush that got him. He would have agreed to join a quilting bee if he could make her blush again. "Absolutely. Having something else to do with my hands would probably be a good thing."

He couldn't remember what she'd said next, the exact words she used to explain what to do as she slipped his fingers through the yarn, positioning the needles just so in his fingers. He just remembered the feel of her skin against his, her warm breath against his neck as she leaned in close to correct him when he missed a step, the fluttering in his chest as her finger brushed against the back of his hand. He picked up on the simple knitting pattern quickly, but found himself purposefully dropping stitches so Nina would have to come in close to correct him.

Her shirt was cut low, showing an impressive amount of

cleavage when she bent over his hands. From the curve of her smile as she leaned over, he knew she knew it too. He felt his cock go rigid at her closeness.

"Oops," he said as he dropped the yarn ball on the floor. It rolled to rest under the larger couch on the opposite side of the room.

"I'll get it," Nina said, walking over and then leaning down slowly so that her beautiful, round ass was high in the air toward him.

"No need, I'll get it," Caesar jumped up, resting a hand on her lower back as he knelt down in front of her, reaching a hand under the couch to grab the fugitive yarn. He sat up quickly, the yarn raised in triumph, and he found her face scant inches from his. Her lips were slightly open, her chest rising and falling close enough to his he could feel the warmth of her body. With his shifter hearing, he could hear her heart beat speed up and he reached forward to lace his fingers through her hair. She grabbed his collar and pulled him forward. Her lips were against his, their fullness as perfect as he had imagined.

Caesar shook his head to pull himself back from the memory before he got a hard-on in the middle of the hall-way. He placed a hand against the rough wall, forcing himself to think about the logistics of the week's Puff distrib-ution schedule, contingencies for if the High Council found them again and they had to flee town. Slowly, he felt his breath return to normal.

He was going to play it cool, he decided, treat her like an old friend. She might be with somebody. She might be married. It had been long enough, she might have kids. She didn't owe him anything, and one night of insane passion didn't have to mean anything in the long run.

After the relative quiet of the hallway, the noise in the

bar hit him like plunging into a pool. The flow of conversation swirled around him, some exclaiming happily and shaking his hand when they recognized him, others deep in conversations with friends and not noticing him. He eased his way through the crowd, every dodged fan and shaking hand bringing him a few feet closer to her.

Big Joe waved to him from the merchandise table. Caesar waved back, continuing to push his way toward the bar where he could see the fuzz of Nina's dark hair like an angel's halo against the bar lights. The rest of the Iron Claws were helping out around the table, Dylan and Marie talking with folks who approached while Big Joe handed out items. Emma stood guard behind them, her eyes scanning the crowd for anyone that looked suspicious.

Caesar dodged under the arm of a waitress carrying a tray of shots and stared. Nina stood less than a foot away, looking more beautiful now than she did five years ago. The photo from the top of the magazine had not done her justice. She smiled at him, the curve of her lips a little shy.

"Hey there, Caesar," she said. "It's been a long time. I don't know if you even remember—"

"Nina Alvarez, of course I remember you." He moved closer so he wouldn't have to yell over the din of the bar. "I wrote that last song for you."

"The song about the knitting girl?" She looked confused and Caesar felt his stomach drop. She didn't remember. It really had just been a one-night stand for her.

"Yeah, you, uh, wanted to help me find a way to fix my fidgeting." He felt miserable and awkward. He looked around, hoping he could catch Emma's eye and he could use his club sister as an excuse to get away from the beautiful woman who clearly couldn't remember their past.

"Oh wow, yes!" She laughed. "I had completely forgotten

about that. I was so nervous at the time. I had no idea what to say to you, and I um..." Her voice trailed off and she blushed furiously. Her blush was the same as he remembered. Caesar felt drawn even closer until he was speaking directly into her ear, their cheeks almost touching.

"What is it?"

"Well, at the time I was so focused on what I wanted your hands to be doing to me, I guess I panicked and pushed the yarn into your hands to distract myself." She turned her head slightly so that they were looking deep into each other's eyes and Caesar gulped.

Be cool. Be cool.

"Do you want to have drinks with me tomorrow?" he asked.

Her face stilled. It wasn't a full-fledged retreat, but she drew away from him enough he said in a rush.

"No pressure. It wouldn't have to be a date." His tongue stumbled a little over the last word. When was the last time he had actually been a real *date*? "We'd just be two old friends catching up."

She nodded a little, at first hesitant, then with more resolve. "Yes, drinks as friends sounds fine."

"How about meeting up at eight? I know a great place. I can text you the address if you give me your number," Caesar said.

Without his heightened shifter senses, Caesar wouldn't have seen the slight tremor of nerves in her hands as she punched his number into her phone. She sent him a text of a smiling emoticon a second later so he would have her number as well.

"It was great to see you." She placed her empty drink down on the bar. "You sounded really awesome. Sorry I didn't say that earlier. You sound even better than ever. But I have to get going. I have an early meeting tomorrow morning."

"Of course. I'm really glad you came. And I'll see you tomorrow, right?"

She nodded and smiled. She hesitated. Caesar felt a moment of panic. Should he hug her goodbye? Shake hands? What was the proper farewell to a woman you had a one-night stand with and have dreamed about for five years, but not spoken to at all?

He raised his hand in a half-wave, half-salute and she mirrored the gesture, laughing a little as she turned away. A second later, she was swallowed by the crowd.

Caesar let out a breath and looked at the clock. He still had a few minutes left in his set break and he needed a drink. He felt a hand on his arm and he turned, a smile pulling at his face. *Had Nina decided to stay for the rest of the show?*

The bright red fingernails on his arm weren't Nina's. The woman next to him looked like she had been 3D-printed off a template from Maxim. Her business suit looked painted on her sleek form. Her aggressively-high heels and sharp smile looked as out of place in the dark bar as a crocodile in a dining room.

"My name is Jennifer Wuornos," she said. "Please call me Jenni, with an 'i'. I'm with the Starsound Music Company. I have the deal of a lifetime for you."

"IT'S NOT A DATE. It's just drinks," Nina muttered to herself, pacing in front of the dive bar. She adjusted her shirt for the second time in the last five minutes, pulling the neckline together to cover her bra straps. The pink, neon sign reading

"AUDREY'S" made her shadow dance as it flickered. "It's just a quick drink with an old friend. I'm good at drinking."

Nina pulled out a soft ball of blue yarn from her bag, rolling the threads between her fingers. She couldn't believe she'd forgotten that she taught him to knit. It was exactly the sort of thing she would have done back then. Thank every star she'd gotten past her initial nervousness when he touched her hair, and just went for it.

The knitting needles moved quickly between her fingers, their rhythmic clacking providing a musical cadence to her anxiety as she paced back and forth.

Should I go in? She was a little early, it would make sense to go ahead and wait for him in the bar.

Clack clack clack.

Maybe I should wait outside for him? Too passive.

Clack clack clack.

What if he was already inside? For a second she pictured him waiting at the bar, watching her out the window pacing back and forth, knitting like a crazy person.

Nina took a long, calming breath. She considered herself a fairly confident woman, and had been on plenty of dates. Nobody stirred her up like Caesar. She stuffed her knitting back into her bag.

"I need a drink," she said under her breath.

Nina pushed hard on the distressed wood doors of the bar and stopped short. She'd never been to AUDREY'S before and hadn't known what to expect when Caesar texted her the address. The bar itself was nothing extraordinary— a pretty standard dive setup with one long bar taking up the far wall of the room, surrounded by scattered tables and chairs in various states of disrepair—but the clientele was like nothing she'd ever seen before.

Pixies flitted around a floating table that bumped

against the ceiling supports. A minotaur shared a pitcher of beer with a centaur, both creatures stomping their hooves, laughing at a joke. There was something not-quite-solid, a sticky black ooze in motion, circling a glass of something smoking. An elf walked past Nina carrying a pint of beer the size of his head and she held back a squeal of delight.

The bartender, a buxom woman with a hundred braids snaking around her head, greeted Nina with a wave and pointed her to two empty seats at the bar.

Caesar must have told her we were coming, Nina thought as she slid into the stool. The bartender placed a Manhattan in front of Nina.

"My favorite." Nina happily sipped the strong drink. "How did you know?"

"I'm Lola," the bartender said with a wicked grin.

Lola was impressive to the point of intimidation. Her tight top proudly displayed her tattooed cleavage patterned with thorny rose vines that wound up her chest and around her neck like a collar. The small braids surrounding her face seemed to float, bobbing and weaving rhythmically.

"Hi Lola, I'm Nina." Nina extended a slightly-shaking hand.

"Nervous?" Lola raised a questioning eyebrow at Nina as they shook hands. She gestured toward an enormous troll in the corner arm wrestling a man in a tuxedo. The man in the tux seemed to be holding his own.

Nina let out a shaky breath. "Not about *that*," she nodded toward the troll. "I had a boyfriend who was a fox shifter, so I can see supernaturals just fine."

Lola smiled. "That will make drinking here a lot easier. I always feel a little bad for the humans who haven't gained the Sight yet. This place can be very disorienting without it."

She poured a shot for a sphinx. "So what's making you so nervous?" Lola asked.

Nina sipped her drink and took a moment to enjoy how the whiskey warmed her from the inside. "I'm meeting a guy here. We hooked up ages ago." Nina wasn't sure why she felt compelled to tell Lola about it, but there was something in the woman's knowing smile that invited confidence. "I was a complete mess back then. I have no intention of being that person again. I just hope he's not expecting *her* to show up."

"I'm sure he's changed over time too." Lola handed a sparkling purple drink to a rail-thin woman dressed only in a crimson cape.

"We saw each other yesterday. He seems like he's matured. But that body..." Nina sighed and took another gulp of her Manhattan. "How is it possible for him to look *better* now than five years ago?"

"Witchcraft," Lola said with a wink. "Speaking of, what do you think of AUDREY'S?"

"This place is incredible." She sighed happily. "I've never seen so many supernaturals getting along in one place."

"I'm glad you like it," a familiar voice boomed from behind her. Caesar's familiar musk surrounded her like a lover's embrace. Nina spun to face him, her heart already pounding.

He's here!

She had wanted to play it cool, but she felt a goofy grin stretch across her face before she could stop it. He was wearing a button-down shirt that looked a lot more formal than what she was used to seeing him in. She felt pleased for a second that he'd thought to dress up for her. His hair was still wet from a shower and she thought she could see a bead of water slide down his neck following the same tantalizing path her tongue took all those years ago.

Calm down, she told the warmth growing in her core. *This is just drinks.*

"I heard you knew about—" Caesar gestured at the activity of the supernaturals all around them "—all this. I thought you might like a taste of my world."

"*Your* world?" Nina asked. She looked at him more closely. Even after she gained the Sight, she'd never considered that Caesar might be supernatural. He was so tall and strong, he would have to be something powerful. She licked her lips as she tried to picture what kind of animal waited under his skin. *With those shoulders, he could be a bear...*

"I'm a dragon shifter." Caesar pounded his chest proudly. "It saves so much money on airfare, you have no idea."

Nina chuckled as Caesar laid a gentle kiss on her hand before sitting next to her. She shifted in her seat. She remembered him as kind, but this level of charm was new. She liked it. As he settled on his stool, the opening chords to "Knitting Girl" began to play over the bar's speakers.

"Cute," Caesar said to Lola.

Lola's expression was all innocence. "I can't imagine what you're talking about. It's on shuffle." She placed a whiskey on the rocks in front of Caesar.

Caesar downed the amber liquid in a hearty gulp.

"Whoa there," Nina said. "Is everything okay?" She pointed at the now-empty glass.

"Shit, sorry." Caesar ran his fingers through his long hair. "It's not you. Well..." He shifted on his bar stool. "Honestly I'm a bit nervous, but it's not *just* you."

Caesar's hand was tapping out a quick rhythm on the stained bar top. His nervousness was heartening. Nina slid her hand into his, twining her fingers through Caesar's. "Tell me."

"I think I just got my big break." He fiddled with the thin straw sticking out of his glass. "Well, maybe not *big* break, but big for me."

"Well, that's great!" Nina said. "Why does your face look like that's not great?"

"It *is* great. Someone named Jenni from Starsound Music Company approached me with this insane contract. It kicks off with a huge European tour, and is going to be publicized like crazy. They're initially signing me for a three-record deal so I won't have to worry about money ever again." His forehead furrowed into a deep 'v' between his eyes. "But I'd have to leave my family behind. After everything we've been through, I can't just up and leave."

"Oh." Nina's blood ran cold. "So do you have a wife, or..." *Please no.*

"I meant the Iron Claws." Caesar waved his hands so frantically he nearly fell off his stool. "I don't know if you remember, but they're the motorcycle club I ride with."

"I remember." Nina smiled. The motorcycle thing had been a huge part of Caesar's initial appeal. He sang about them a lot in his songs, making their life on the road sound far more romantic than she suspected it actually was. She felt a moment of gladness that he'd stuck with them. "They seem like a fairly nomadic bunch. Can't they just tag along?"

"The tour hits fourteen countries in fifteen days. I can't ask them to jump on something so hectic. If they traveled with me, they wouldn't be able to follow their mission."

A motorcycle club with a mission? Perhaps they really were so romantic. "What's their mission?"

Caesar looked around, then leaned close to say, "We distribute Puff."

"Puff?" Nina put her drink down on the bar with a heavy clunk. "Are you selling drugs?" She slid a hand into her purse, ready to pay and leave. Caesar might be a sexy badass, but she wanted nothing to do with dealers.

"No! Well...yes." Caesar let out a heavy sigh. "Puff is a powder made from ground-up dragon scales. It has no effect on shifters or other folks like me, but for humans." He smiled proudly. "Honestly, Nina, it's a miracle cure. I've seen things you wouldn't believe: chemo patients up and dancing in weeks."

"If there was a cure for cancer, I'm pretty sure I would have heard about it by now." Nina reached for her coat. First he was a drug dealer and now he was a miracle healer? She wanted to believe him, but this was ridiculous.

"How many people know about dragon shifters? Most people aren't ready for this, so we keep it secret."

Nina sat back down and hung her purse back on the hook under the bar ledge. She glanced at Lola, who nodded almost imperceptibly to back up Caesar's story.

Nina gazed back at Caesar like she was seeing him for the first time. So not only was he an amazing musician, but he also distributed life-saving drugs to people while living on the road. Her stomach fluttered with sparks of admiration.

Caesar took a long drink. "Distributing Puff to humans is against the laws of my people, so that's another reason to keep it quiet."

"Your people? Like your biological family? From your songs, I didn't think they were still in the picture." Nina regretted the words as soon as they came out of her mouth. She always believed being blunt was part of what made her so successful in her career, but sometimes socially a softer touch was needed. "I mean, you don't have to tell me anything." She quickly sipped her drink. "It's honestly none of my business. I shouldn't have asked. Unless you *do* have a wife."

"No, it's fine. For the record, I don't have a wife." He sighed. "I do technically have a biological family. At least I think so. Last I heard, they were all alive and well."

"Last you heard?" Nina asked. She wanted to pinch herself for pushing him but every new piece of information made him more interesting. Piece by piece, he was becoming a full person in her eyes.

"Yeah, we haven't spoken in over ten years." He shifted uncomfortably in his seat. "I grew up in a very traditional dragon clan. The rules were to be followed without question; our Alpha was to be obeyed no matter what. As long as I played their game I was fine, but..." Caesar trailed off. "I have an older brother, Titus, that I've never met. I found out about him when I was fifteen. Before I was born, he was cursed by a witch to be unable to shift to his dragon form. And they just..." Caesar made a pushing motion with one hand. "Cast him out. He was *six* years old. Can you believe that?"

"That's insane." Nina felt her eyes water as she listened. She nodded thanks at Lola as the bartender dropped off another round, then shifted closer to make sure she didn't lose a word over the sound of the bar.

"That's my family. I was already starting to question the clan's rules by then. When I found out what they did to my brother, I just left. Bought a motorcycle and headed out with nothing but my guitar." He sipped his drink. "I've tried to look for Titus over the years, but I never found him. I was on my own for four years until the Iron Claws took me in."

His soft brown eyes drilled into hers. "What do you think? You're a neutral, outside party. Am I crazy for thinking of taking this deal and leaving the Claws?"

How can I be objective about something that will take him far away from me? Nina tried to keep her expression casual as her mind raced.

"I can't decide something huge like that for you." She shredded her cocktail napkin as she spoke. "This is your life. It has to be your choice."

"I knew you were going to say something wise like that." Caesar teased. "But you've always been the smart one. I'll tell ya, teaching me to knit was the greatest idea anybody's had. I was driving people crazy with my fidgety hands. Now I just drive people crazy with hats and scarves." He winked. "Way better."

Nina laughed. "I don't believe you. Rock stars don't knit."

"They don't, do they?" Caesar stood and dropped some money on the bar. He extended his hand to Nina, helping her off the stool. "Let's go to my place. I can prove it to you."

Nina didn't trust her voice to speak—*his place? Holy shit!*—so she just nodded and tried to slow her swiftly beating heart as she followed him out the door.

Caesar gestured for her to follow him past the parking lot, around to the small lawn area behind the bar.

"Do you want me to drive?" she asked, looking around for his bike.

Caesar laughed. "That's not going to be necessary. We're going to travel in style." As he spoke, he unbuttoned his shirt slowly.

"What are you doing?" She couldn't look away from his chest.

"I don't want to shred my clothes when I shift. You may want to turn away." He winked as he continued undressing. "Or not."

He pulled off his pants and she closed her eyes to give him some privacy.

"I hope you're not afraid of heights."

She heard a strange stretching sound and she opened her eyes. Where Caesar had been standing lay a purple dragon, his dark violet scales glistening in the bar's neon lights. He was twice the size of her car, with horns curling from his forehead and spikes trailing all the way down his back. Bat-like wings the color of ripe plums extended out of his back and she longed to stroke their smooth surface. His claws clicked restlessly together and she smiled. Even in dragon form, Caesar couldn't sit still.

"What do you think? Need a lift?" he said. His rich, musical voice was deeper in dragon form, the sound echoing from deep within his larger chest.

Nina approached slowly, looking at his massive back. It looked really high. "How is this even going to work?"

"Just rest your foot on the top of my thigh, grab a horn, and you should be able to hoist yourself up," Caesar said. "I've seen Marie do it with Dylan loads of times."

Nina studied his side and saw he was right. With just a little bit of a jump off of his thigh, she pulled herself up to straddle his back right between two of his spikes. His scales felt cool even through the fabric of her pants.

She paused.

"You said you've *seen* this done before. But have you ever flown with a passenger before?" she asked, eyeing the ground. She was at least fifteen feet off the ground and Caesar hadn't yet taken flight.

"First time for everything." His dragon mouth opened wide in what she assumed was a grin. One eye blinked at her in a wink over a foot across.

She gripped his back tighter, holding onto the spike in front of her as firmly as she could.

"Alright, let's do this." Nina tried to keep her voice steady as she spoke.

"I knew you'd be brave." He beat his wings and the wind buffeted her hair around her face. A leap from his massive legs and they were in the air, the breeze rushing past her heated cheeks. The ground fell away beneath them. AUDREY'S bar diminished to just another brown square in a mass of winding city streets and dotted buildings, their lights blinking and winking like stars beneath Nina's feet.

"What do you think?" Caesar said. His shape felt solid between her legs, his wing beats smoother than she expected.

"This is amazing!" she cried, lifting her hands in the air to feel the gusts under her arms and through her fingertips.

They flew up through clouds fluffed up high like enormous desserts.

"How can you bear to ever come down?" she shouted over the roar of the wind. The exhilaration coursed through her, her heart beating fast in her chest. She felt lighter than she'd felt in a long time.

Caesar laughed and she could feel the rumble roll through his entire body and vibrate under her thighs.

"If I didn't shift to human form sometimes, I wouldn't be able to meet beautiful, intelligent women like you," Caesar said.

She blushed to the roots of her hair. *Beautiful?* She'd had boyfriends tell her she was *striking*, but when was the last time a man called her *beautiful?* More dates like this, and it would be far too easy to fall head over heels for her handsome, dragon rock star.

"How far are we from your place?" she asked.

"It's not far. I'm taking you the scenic route."

She sighed and settled back against his back spine,

letting all the tension flow away as she looked around at the stars.

"I'm okay with the scenic route," she said.

"Don't worry, I'll go slow for you."

CAESAR'S HEART hammered in his chest as he pulled open the door of the Iron Claws' clubhouse. Had he ever brought a girl home to meet his family?

Alec must have said something to them, because everyone was lounging about in the front living room holding books and notebooks in their hands that they clearly weren't reading. They'd even set up a laptop with the camera pointed at the door, Skype projecting Ned's grinning face across the screen. Everyone's eyes turned to Caesar. They all broke out into applause as Nina followed him through the door.

"Caesar brought a girl home!" Alec cried. "See? You all doubted me."

Big Joe laid an enormous hand on Alec's shoulder and squeezed. "You're right. I'll never doubt you again."

"Until the next time you open your mouth," Emma added, laughing. She walked up and held out a hand to Nina. "Hi, I'm Emma. And don't mind everyone. They're lovable monsters once you get to know them."

Marie sat up from where she'd been cuddled in Dylan's arms to shake Nina's hand as well. "Yes, I can attest to that. It will be nice to not be the only human around here. It gets boring when they're all out flying. How do you feel about cocktail movie nights?"

"Hey! Somebody point me a little higher, I can't see!" Ned's voice came through the laptop speakers. Big Joe brought the laptop closer so that Ned could enthusiastically wave at Nina. "Hi! We've been dying to meet the famous Knitting Girl for *ages*."

"Guys, we just had the one date," Caesar said. "Slow down. You're going to scare her away." He gently touched Nina's arm, guiding her toward the stairs that led up to the bedrooms.

"Oh, come on, we're only slightly scary," Dylan said. He stood up, all immense six foot and change of him, his dreadlocks tumbling down his back. "Come hang out with us once you're tired of Caesar talking your ear off about musical theory."

"Yeah, I have some questions for you about Linux," Alec added.

Nina's eyes lit up. "What kind of questions?"

Alec tilted his laptop toward her. "Well, I've been working on this tricky sequence—"

"Nope, don't you dare," Caesar interrupted, pulling Nina toward the stairs. "I just got her here. She can play with you later."

Alec laughed, waving a hand at them. "Yes, yes, you're right. You kids have fun, we'll still be here gossiping about you until you get back."

Caesar wanted to crow with joy. She'd met his family for all of a minute and she fit in beautifully. She didn't seem intimidated at all, even knowing that everyone in the room (except for Marie) were all massive dragons under their skin. *Maybe this is going to work out after all.*

"That's your family?" Nina asked as they headed up the stairs.

"That's them. Outcast misfits all." Caesar sat down on the edge of his bed and began rummaging through a duffel bag. "I wanted to show you this." He pulled out a small photo album and paged through it. Each photo displayed his knitting projects, with a note of who he'd donated it to. Most were to children's hospitals, or Puff patients they'd helped.

As Nina turned the pages, her eyes grew wider. He'd started out with simple scarves and line stitches, then watched enough instructional videos online to graduate up to sweaters and socks.

Nina didn't seem to notice the single tear running down her cheek. Caesar reached out to gently wipe it away.

She looked up at him, her eyes still watery. "You did all of these? They're incredible. I never imagined that my lesson would have made such an impact on you."

He put the album away. "I'd understand it if you don't remember much from that night. I mean, it was probably just a crazy hookup for you."

She dried her eyes with the edge of her sweater and laughed. "Do you think I was the type to hook up with every musician that came through town? Your songs, they always spoke to me." She looked down, turning away so he couldn't see her face. "It seems so stupid to say now, but when I listened to your lyrics, it was like you were talking just to me."

"It's not stupid." Caesar placed his hand on the side of her face to tilt it toward him. "What was it about the songs that spoke to you?" The ball of yarn from his knitting bag had spilled onto the bed when he took out the book. He played with the edge of the string absentmindedly as his other hand caressed the side of her face.

She reached up her hand to cradle his fingers against her face, leaning into him. "The way you talked about the road. Everyone else always talked about traveling as either an adventure, or as this lonely wandering. But you...you understood what it was to carry your home with you." Her fingers intertwined with his in the yarn ball, pulling out one edge of the string. She started to weave the yarn through his fingers like a loom. "I always thought I was so weird for not wanting to settle down anywhere. It was the part I hated most about having a day job. It made me so antsy to be tied down somewhere." She tightened the strings around his fingers and wrapped another row.

He held up his hand, yarn trailing behind him. "Being tied down isn't all bad, under the right circumstances."

She giggled. "Sorry about that, I see yarn and I can't help but play with it." She started to untie the string, but he stopped her, grabbing the trailing end and wrapping it around her wrist. He caressed the smooth skin above her hand and she gasped, her cheeks blushing furiously.

"Now that you have your own business and you're not stuck in one place, do you still love the road?" Caesar took the soft yarn ball and rubbed it along her bare arm back and forth, loving the way she squirmed and adjusted her seat. He could smell the whiff of her arousal, and it took all his willpower to not pull her into his arms. She was too important to scare away by getting impatient.

She shrugged as she continued to weave the string through his fingers. With each pass, her fingers brushed against his. His cock stirred with want.

"I love living someplace new every few months. I've lived on each coast. I got to try out living in a small apartment in a big city, and a house in the Midwest." She pulled out her phone and flipped through pictures of sunsets over a pier, of a quaint Main Street complete with a soda shop like something from another decade. "I spent a couple of months in a small town in Maine where everyone knew my name, then another few months in Los Angeles where I lived sublease to sublease in a different neighborhood every week. It was awesome." She flexed her fingers and wiggled the strings, tying a couple of knots around his fingers.

He thought of his longstanding fantasy of what it'd be like to be a true rock star: the fancy private jet, the insane parties, and the silk sheets of hotel rooms on every continent. Jennifer Wuornos's Starsound Music Company business card suddenly felt like it was digging into his skin through his jeans pocket.

"I've been thinking of what it would be like to do what you did, just strike out on my own away from the Claws," he said, softly enough that his voice wouldn't carry to the room of supernatural-hearing dragons one floor down.

Nina squeezed his hand. "Live your life the way you want to live it. But, just remember that all the moving around isn't perfect." She shifted on the bed so she was sitting right next to him, leaning against his shoulder. "I'm pretty close with my family, but I only see them now and then. They're scattered all over the country, so traveling lets me pop in and visit them as my schedule allows. It's tough to go so long without seeing most of them. When they get together for birthdays and other gatherings and I can't make it, they call me on the phone and I get passed around giving the same thirty-second speech to each of them about how my life is going. I can hear them laughing and having fun in the background, and every time it actually makes me feel more disconnected than if they hadn't called at all."

Caesar rested his head on her hair, smelling her sharp scent of coffee and lavender. He thought of Ned. Ned was living his dream life with his wife, his bakery, and kids on the way, but having to always be the face in the laptop— when Ned was available to call in at all—had to be hard.

If I agree to the record deal, would that be my life?

Nina pulled at the strings around his fingers, lacing a complex pattern with the yarn and then pulling the string taut from his hand to show a perfect cat's cradle. He laughed. "That's amazing," he said, admiring the pattern.

She smiled at him. "Thanks. Some habits are hard to shake." She snuggled closer and Caesar felt a slow burn of awe of how *right* she felt at his side.

"Do you regret it? Not staying closer to home?"

Nina shrugged. "It was a tough call to make. But I love my life, and my family is really supportive. I would never want to live in one place, burdened with a mortgage, gathering stuff I don't need. It must be nice to have what you have, where you can bring your family with you wherever you go."

He wrapped his arms around her. From downstairs, somebody—Caesar thought it was probably Emma—whooped and everyone else laughed. The sound of their merriment coming from downstairs pulled at him to join them. What would it be like, to not have them close?

Caesar leaned forward to kiss her gently. Her lips were just as amazing as he remembered, but he pulled away before he gave into the temptation to deepen the kiss.

She looked a bit dazed.

I've still got it. His insides did a little happy dance.

"I can't do it." Caesar pulled away.

"Oh, that's okay." Nina sounded disappointed. "We don't have to do anything tonight."

Caesar grinned and pulled her in for a crushing kiss. "No, not *that*." His hand gently caressed her curves. "I have every intention of doing *that*. It's the record deal." He reluctantly got off the bed and pulled on his jacket. "It took me nineteen years to build my family. There's no way they're getting rid of me anytime soon. I've gotta go tell the record label 'no', right now, before I start thinking too much and change my mind. Those rock star dreams aren't me anymore. I've already got what's most important." He caressed her cheek, yarn still trailing from his fingertips. "This shouldn't take long. Do you mind waiting? Will you still be here when I get back?"

She smiled. "Yes. It sounds like there's a party going on downstairs. If you're heading out, I was thinking of seeing what they were up to."

"Great!" he cried, overjoyed she wanted to spend time with his family. He grabbed her hand and led her down the stairs.

The Iron Claws were all huddled around the center table, a pile of yarn in between them. Everyone had knitting needles or crochet hooks in their hands, but the knotted messes growing in their hands looked like rats' nests.

"Oh good! You came down!" Marie said.

Emma held up a few inches of what looked like a scarf, the edges weaving in and out as the width of the knotting varied with each row. "Look how far I got!"

Big Joe stood up to gravely hold out his arm to Nina. "My lady, come save us. After you two went upstairs, we got to talking about knitting. What you see is our brave attempts to understand the appeal."

Marie held up a mass of knots that looked like a napkin with a hole in the middle big enough to make it a crown. "Save us, Knitting Girl. You're our only hope."

Nina laughed. "Seems like we came down in the nick of time!" She turned to Caesar, kissing him on the cheek. The contact sent a zing through his body. "Do what you have to do, we'll be fine. And when you get back..." She leaned close to whisper in his year. "I've been having some thoughts about other ways of tying you up."

Caesar's cock was suddenly standing at full attention and he pulled her close for a kiss. Sparks felt like they shot through his body as his lips brushed against hers.

"My cell is up on the charger. If you need me for any reason, I'll be at the offices of Starsound Music Company downtown," he said to the Iron Claws.

He couldn't resist kissing Nina again. He lingered long enough until he felt her pulse speed up under his skin. He opened his mouth to lick along the inside seam of her lips. She groaned, her hands tightening around his arms.

"Either get a room, or get out of here. You have our teacher hostage," Alec called out.

Caesar and Nina broke the kiss, laughing.

"Go quick, so you can come back," she said.

Caesar kissed her swiftly on the forehead before ducking out the door. He swung his leg over his motorcycle, but waited a second, listening, before he gunned the engine.

Laughter, teasing, more laugher.

He smiled. Becoming a famous rock star used to be a fun fantasy, but Nina was the real dream come true. Now he just had to convince her to stay.

IT TOOK LESS than an hour with the Iron Claws for Nina to understand why Caesar would give up his dream for them. They were all so amazingly welcoming and *genuine*, she felt like she'd known them for years.

"Yahtzee!" Alec yelled, raising a triumphant fist in the air. He had been trying to program his handmade drone to deliver packages to specific individuals based off certain attributes—height, hair color, etc.—he entered into his program. Nina had noticed a tiny coding error that Alec overlooked, and now the little drone was flying around the room, flitting from Big Joe to Emma to Marie as Alec commanded.

"Sometimes it just takes another pair of eyes." Nina grinned.

"Or maybe Alec isn't the computer whiz we thought he was," Emma said, hands busy with a rapidly-lengthening scarf.

"Oh...what's this?" Alec pointed at the screen of his laptop. "Is this *your* bank account it just took me less than a minute to hack into?" He tapped experimentally at the keyboard. "I wonder who I should send all this money to..."

Emma put up her knitting needles in surrender. "I take it all back, oh wisest of the computer nerds."

"Damn straight," Alec said with a chuckle.

"Hey, can you hack into the Starsound Music Company's website? I want to see the deal they offered Caesar," Nina said.

"What?" Dylan nearly dropped his beer bottle, fumbling to catch it.

"Caesar got a record deal? When did this happen?" Emma asked.

Shit. Shit shit shit.

Nina had assumed, since the Claws were so close, he would have told them already.

"Oh crap, guys, sorry. I shouldn't have said anything." She wished she could pull the words back into her mouth. "It's not even an issue. He's not going to take them up on it." She pointed vaguely at the door. "That's why he's there right now. He popped out to go tell them 'no' in person."

"Why now?" Alec chuckled. "It's so late, I doubt they're even open."

Big Joe's voice rumbled across the room. "It was only a

matter of time. Caesar's an amazing musician. Somebody was bound to pick up on that." He shrugged. "If he wants us with him, we can ride alongside his tour bus. And if he doesn't." He looked around the room, stopping to give each individual a solid few seconds of eye contact. "We will respect that. Once an Iron Claw..."

"Always an Iron Claw," the group echoed in response. They placed their hands over their hearts and Nina felt her own heart lighten on Caesar's behalf. They believed in him.

"Guys." Alec was frantically typing on his laptop. "That's sweet and all, but I think we've got a bigger problem."

"What is it?" Marie asked. The pretty nurse went over to stand behind Alec's computer.

"I wanted to see what Caesar was giving up for us, so I kind of hacked into the Starsound Music Company's website." Alec gestured at his computer. "It's a shell company. *For* a shell company. I traced everything back to the source, and you guys aren't going to believe it."

"It's the Council, isn't it?" Emma's face was pale.

"Sneaky bastards." Alec slammed his laptop shut. "It's a trap. We've got to get Caesar out of there!"

"Gods, first they kidnap Ned, now they're going after Caesar?" Dylan shook with rage.

Nina looked between all of them, fear creeping up her chest. She beckoned to Marie, who was staring at Alec's computer with something like shock.

"What's the Council?" Nina asked Marie. From their tone, it couldn't be good.

Around them, the other Claws were jumping to action. Big Joe yelled out instructions for Alec to pull blueprints of the office Caesar was heading to, while Emma started pulling a truly impressive arsenal out of crates. Marie picked up a white bag with a medical logo on the side and slung it over her shoulder, then dragged Nina out of the way.

"Did Caesar tell you about what we do, distributing Puff to humans?" Marie asked.

Nina nodded. "He said it's illegal."

Marie's lips pressed thin, her expression grim. "Yes, and it's the Dragon High Council that made it illegal. Their goons, the Red Guard, enforce the law."

I shouldn't have let Caesar go. Nina's hands shook with fear.

"The High Council has been after us for a long time," Marie continued. "They have no problem with killing us, since they know that's the only way to stop us from helping humans." She grasped Nina's shaking hand. "This isn't your fight. You should get out of here before it gets messy."

Nina shook her head. "No. If Caesar is in trouble, it *is* my fight. Just let me know how I can help."

Marie squeezed her hand. "Then Alec was right. You really are one of us." Dylan beckoned Marie over and she ducked away to talk with her husband.

Alec was typing furiously in the corner. Nina strode over and sat next to him.

"What do you need?" she asked him, booting up a spare laptop.

Alec barely glanced at her, his fingers flying so fast across the keyboard they almost blurred. "I'm working on getting those blueprints, but we need staff listings for these shell companies so we can fake up some IDs. It might be a long shot, but we might be able to—"

"Excuse me." An impressively-coiffed woman stepped through the front door. "I'm looking for Caesar de la Vega." Her stiletto heels echoed against the clubhouse floor as she moved. "I'm from Starsound Music Company. I'm sure he's mentioned me."

Everybody froze.

Big Joe spoke a single word, "Council," and the room burst into a flurry of action. He dove over the clubhouse bar and emerged with two huge rolls of duct tape. The woman didn't have time to react before Emma wrestled her into a wooden chair, while Alec helped hold her down. Dylan and Marie worked together to loop the duct tape around the woman's arms and legs, securing her to the chair.

Nina watched with awe as they all worked together, moving as one. In less than a minute, the Starsound Music Company representative—or whoever she really was—was bound tightly in the middle of the room with the Iron Claws surrounding her.

Big Joe didn't look away from Jenni's face. "Dylan, check the perimeter. Make sure she didn't bring company." Dylan nodded and jumped out a back window so he wouldn't be seen by anyone watching the front door.

"You're the one who offered Caesar the record deal," Nina said, approaching the bound woman slowly. Jenni didn't look like a dragon shifter. She was too slight, too fashionably starved. The woman smiled at the room, her expression creepily serene for the circumstances.

"I offered Caesar de la Vega a record deal." She looked down at her bound wrists. "And I must say, this is a very strange reaction."

Big Joe glared down at the woman. As the largest man in the room, he seemed to loom menacing without even trying. The woman barely blinked.

"We know you're with the Dragon High Council, and you're trying to hurt Caesar." Big Joe paced deliberately in front of her. "What happens next is up to you. Either you tell me everything that's planned for Caesar or..." He stopped and looked her in the eye. "...we're going to do exactly what you'd fear a gang of pissed-off dragon shifters would do to somebody like you."

"You don't know as much as you think." The woman stared Big Joe down, never breaking eye contact. "I'm not with anybody. I'm paid to do a job. If you want to make a higher bid than the Council to get your buddy out of danger, that's fine by me." She looked around the room and pursed her lips. "Assuming you lot *have* any money, that is."

Nina's mind raced. The woman was obviously a professional. It would take more money than any of them had to get her to risk her reputation. "Emma's had some banking problems recently." Nina looked pointedly at Alec. "I'm sure Alec can arrange something similar for you."

"You're a genius!" Alec frantically typed on his laptop. He grinned widely and brought his laptop towards Jenni and tilted it so she could see the lines of numbers dancing across the screen.

Nina tried to keep her voice steady as she spoke. "What you're looking at is your bank account."

Jenni's face turned pale, then bright red as she bellowed. "What are you doing?"

"We're bankrupting you," Nina continued. The screen showed a seven-digit number at the top that was dropping every second. "You can either tell us everything, right now, or you can sit there and watch everything you've worked for melt away."

Alec propped the laptop up on a nearby table so it was in Jenni's eye line.

"You might want to decide quickly. You're fast approaching non-millionaire status." Nina spoke slowly, letting as much of Jenni's money drain as possible.

The woman bucked against her restraints. "You son of a bitch!" She stilled and took a long breath. "Okay, stop. You win. I'll tell you everything."

Alec leaned towards the keyboard, but Nina stopped him. "Stop it after she's told us," she said. "We don't have time for her to bullshit us."

"The Dragon High Council hired me to take Caesar away," Jenni said, talking quickly. "They've pissed at you guys for selling Puff. After their more straightforward attacks failed, the Council put a new guy, Sterling, in charge of taking care of the *Iron Claws problem.*" She sneered the words. "He's completely obsessed with you all, and dangerously clever. He decided to pick away at you guys one-by-one. I was meant to get Caesar onto a plane to Paris to kick off his world tour." She squirmed and looked at her feet. "The plane was going to blow up twenty minutes into the flight."

Nina felt the blood drain from her face. When they'd realized the High Council was behind Caesar's offer, she'd known he was in danger. But imagining him blown up over the Atlantic made it feel like there was a boulder in the pit of her stomach.

"Where is Caesar now?" Big Joe bellowed.

"I thought he was here!" The woman screeched. She looked desperately at the computer with the number ticking down. "I was coming right now to convince him to take the deal."

Nina felt an enormous sense of relief wash over her entire body. "Caesar didn't call ahead, he just went to their offices. There's no way they could have known he was coming."

"He should be back by now." Dylan grabbed a backpack

with a shotgun sticking out of the top. "Who knows what could have happened?"

Jenni glared at Nina. "I told you all I know. Turn it off, you crazy bitch!"

Alec struck a key and the countdown stopped.

The sound of a door slamming echoed through the building. They all turned at once, weapons raised for whatever new threat was about to walk through the door.

Nina felt her heart soar as she recognized the familiar outline in the door.

"Hey guys," Caesar called.

A rustling sound came from behind them and Nina spun around. Jenni's chair was empty, covered in wide loops of duct tape and her discarded clothes.

A scorpion scuttled away and disappeared through a hole in the wall before anyone could react.

"So..." Caesar gestured toward the chair. "What'd I miss?"

CAESAR GENTLY WOUND Nina's hair through his fingers, amazed at the softness. He couldn't believe he'd forgotten how much he loved playing with her hair.

"We came so close to losing you," Nina said. She was still dressed, although he hoped that wouldn't be the case for long. Her fingers caressed the side of his face. She leaned forward to kiss him, her lips gentle against his.

"You wouldn't have lost me." He pulled her in close, his tongue tracing the inside of her lip. He felt her pulse race against his skin.

She frowned. "I would have if you'd been blown to bits by a scorpion-shifter assassin."

"Well, there is that." He turned away to lean back and look up at the ceiling. She curled up against his side, her head resting on his shoulder. "We've dealt with High Council goons who broke our Puff distribution stalls, or who tried to run us out of town, but this Sterling character sounds like something new. He really won't stop until he breaks apart the Claws, or kills us all."

"Then it's a good thing you'll have another tech whiz around to stop them. I believe in what you all are doing, distributing Puff to people that need it."

"What?" Caesar cried, turning toward her. "You're going to be traveling with us?" *Why the hell would she throw herself into danger with me?*

"I figured it would be fun to wander with you all for a bit rather than just going along by myself." Nina's fingers traveled across his jaw down to the base of his throat, following the path of his tattoos and leaving a trail of sensitive goosebumps where she touched.

"Well, that's, um, nice." He could hear the tightness in his voice. This close, her smell washed over him and he was hard as iron in his pants. He clenched his fists in the covers.

She withdrew her hand. "Do you not want me to come along? I know it's been really fast."

He reached out to grasp her hand and pull it back to his chest. "We've known each other five years. I wouldn't call that *fast*."

She laughed, but didn't take away her hand. "You know that's not really true."

"Does it count if I've been dreaming of you for five years?" He leaned forward to kiss the side of her mouth. She turned toward him to press her lips more firmly against his. They lingered there for a few seconds, but when he opened his mouth to deepen the kiss, she pulled away. Her eyes danced with laughter.

"No, that actually counts *less*, because it means you've been building up a *fantasy* about me for five years. That fantasy is going to take *even longer* to get past so you can eventually know me for myself." Her tone was light, but he could tell she was serious.

He sat up on one elbow so he was leaning above her in the bed.

Shit, shit, shit. She really thought he didn't see the real her.

Emergency action needed.

He pulled off his shirt, turning his body so that the planes of muscles on his chest showed up well in the light. He watched the irises in her eyes dilate with arousal as she watched him.

Gently, he took her hand and placed it against the naked skin of his chest, reveling in the feeling of her fingers flexing and exploring the tight muscles in his stomach.

"Is it a fantasy that you're a genius programmer who successfully built her own company and international reputation?" he said softly as he unbuttoned his pants and slid them onto the floor so he only wore his whiskey-bottle-print boxers.

She licked her lips as her hands continued to explore, touching all over his waist and sides, then continuing onto the hard muscles in his back and shoulders. He wanted to nudge her hands lower, but he was determined to be patient.

"Is it a fantasy that you're blunt and sarcastic, but also kind and empathetic to the people you care about?"

Seeing her arousal was making his cock so hard he could barely think. Her eyes were latched onto his increasingly hard bulge and she bit her lip. He moaned. She was going to kill him if she didn't say something soon.

"Is it a fantasy that you are so beautiful I can barely stop myself from tearing off your clothes and making love to you until you scream with ecstasy?"

"Then why don't you?" Her voice was breathless. She tossed off her shirt and Caesar stared, words gone, at the perfect roundness of her breasts. Her nipples were hard points, begging to be licked and suckled.

"Because we've been through a lot these last few days." He forced the words out, determined to give her a choice. "I want to be with you, but I don't want you to feel like you're bound to me. You're right that we don't know each other that well—and I can't tell you how much I want the chance to change that—but just because you're now a part of the Claws...it doesn't mean you're obligated to be with me."

She traced the outline of his muscles on his chest in slow strokes until he thought he was going to go mad. Then she closed her eyes and leaned forward. She kissed him hard enough on the neck to leave a bruise.

He groaned, lacing his fingers deeper into her hair and pulling her on top of him until her legs straddled his waist.

She still didn't say anything and he continued, "What I'm saying is that it's okay if you just want to help with the Puff distribution." Caesar's throbbing erection was nearly purple with want, and the feeling of her squirming on his cock was excruciating bliss. "We don't have to keep going."

"Caesar, stop talking." Nina sat up to pull off her pants and underwear in one quick movement, then resettled on top of him. "I want you desperately." She pulled his boxers low to reveal his cock, starting to rock her hips on top of it, slipping the tip in and out of her increasing wetness. "I've dreamed of you too. I've dreamed of *this*."

She sat down, guiding his cock deeper inside. She was so aroused, he sunk into her in one smooth stroke. The pleasure around his cock was so amazing he flexed upward, pushing himself to the hilt.

Memories of the last time they were together flashed through his mind: fucking her hard against the wall, the sight of her eyes looking back at him as he thrust into her from behind, the mind-blowing ecstasy of their mutual orgasm and feeling her clench around his cock.

This was better.

She gazed down at him. Her expression was alive with lust and confidence, and something else, some deeper affection in her eyes that made him catch his breath as he thrust up into her again. She grabbed the back of his thigh, pulling it upward to change the angle slightly. She started to ride him hard, her breasts thumping against her chest like a glorious goddess.

"Oh gods, Nina, you're incredible." He found her rhythm and thrust upward in time with her ride, increasing the pace until it felt like they were flying together again. He placed his finger along her clit and rubbed it in tune with their thrusts, playing her sensitive bud like an instrument.

"Caesar, yes, oh yes! Yes!" She screamed. Her face contorted as she came, gorgeous and amazing. She fell limp on top of him, her silky hair falling into his face. She looked deeply into his eyes. "More," she whispered. "I need so much more."

"Yes, my beautiful darling. That I can do." He rolled her onto her back and grasped her legs up to put them over his shoulders. The new angle of his cock inside her passage made her gasp.

"How...how can that feel so amazing?" she cried.

"Love, you're with a dragon now." He winked. "We're

always amazing." Then he began to thrust into her, pumping his cock into her in increasingly fast strokes until she cried out his name again. As he felt her come around him, he let go, cumming so hard he saw stars dot the front of his eyes.

He reached for her and she curled into his side. Their bodies fit so perfectly together, Caesar wondered how his younger self ever let her leave.

"I must have been an idiot," he said.

"What was that?" she said sleepily.

"Five years ago. I knew I loved you then, but I let you walk away."

"You loved me?" she said, sitting up on one elbow to look at him. "I was just a groupie."

He shook his head. "You were never a groupie. You were the one that got away." He traced a finger down her beautiful face until he touched her lips. "There's only one part of us not staying together back then that I don't regret."

"What's that?" Her eyes were wide.

"It gave me the chance to get to fall in love with you all over again."

"Caesar, I—" Her mouth fell open and she leaned forward to pull him close, smashing her lips against his. He heard the pounding of her heart and desperately hoped that it meant she felt the same.

She finally pulled away, cradling his face between her two palms. "I've never felt about anyone the way I feel about you. I love you so much. I didn't know how much until I thought I might lose you. I'm going to ride with you and the Claws through any battles that are to come. I can't imagine being apart from you again."

He pulled her close. "My Knitting Girl. I'm going to tie you to me for the rest of our lives."

She laughed and kissed him again. "Just don't sing the song again any time soon. Alec has been playing it on a loop, and it's been stuck in my head for ages."

He kissed the top of her nose. "Deal. I'll just have to write you a new song for every way I love you."

"And how many songs is that going to be?" she chuckled.

"All of them."

HER HACKER DRAGON

Dedicated to the transgender community, written with love and respect by two cis women who tried their best.

Two dragon shifters had been following Dr. Penelope O'Hara for blocks. She pulled up the collar of her jacket to hide her vulnerable vampire skin from the sun and ducked under a barbershop's awning.

Penelope prayed to every god she could think of that she was just being paranoid.

She held her breath as the two heavily-built men continued past her. Three steps. Four. The dragon shifters stopped and turned to talk to each other, one pointing at something on the opposite side of the street while the other just stared at her with his beady eyes.

Fuck me with a fairy wand, Penelope cursed to herself. What could they want with *her*? She ran through a quick mental list of the research she was conducting back in her lab. Not a single experiment would impact dragons.

So why the tail? She wondered.

If dragon shifters were after her, she needed somebody to get her the fuck out of here. Fast. She scrolled through the contacts list on her phone and sighed. It was dishearteningly barren. Her family had been dead for centuries now, and the rest of the vampire community tended to think anyone who didn't go clubbing for blood orgies every night was contagiously weird. Penelope tapped on her lab assistant, Bog's, number.

"Sorry, I'm not here right now," Bog's distracted voice sounded after a few rings. "I'm probably asleep. Or working. Or eating. You don't know. I don't know. But I don't check my voicemail, so if you want to talk to me, just send me an email. But I don't check that very often either. So I'll see you at work tomorrow."

Penelope tried calling again, but Bog still didn't pick up.

I need to make more friends. Penelope stuffed her phone back in her bag and assessed. The sun was blazing strong, sapping Penelope's vampiric strength enough that a bunny shifter could probably take her out, let alone two dragons. There were no cabs around, and the closest bus stop was miles away. Most of the shops were closed or closing, and the lab was too far to make it on foot before the dragons would be on top of her.

One of the shifters started to stalk toward her and Penelope tried to casually move away from him, just as a beam of sunlight burst from the clouds. It hit her on the cheek and Penelope gasped from the pain of it. The ray hit the entire side of her face, and she could smell the burning flesh.

Stupid son-of-a-harpy sun. She hastily started moving down the street, pulling out the small vial of blood she always kept with her in case of injury.

She flipped open the cap and downed the lukewarm liquid like a shot, trying to avoid the taste. As quickly as she drank it, she still caught the slight aftertaste of the blood's source: female, human, kind and open-hearted, slightly bored, probably from waiting in a reception area before donating blood. Penelope pushed back the sensations-- easier to do with a blood-bag source than directly from the vein--as she felt her cheek return to smooth, healthy skin. She patted down her jacket, confirming what she already knew: that was the only vial she'd packed that morning.

Fucking ball of fire in the sky dicking with me.

Penelope looked around, reviewing a mental map of the city between here and her apartment. There was a supernatural-friendly bar, AUDREY'S, a few blocks up. Penelope felt a fresh burst of energy as a plan formed. If she could get to the bar, there would be enough vampires, shifters, and whatnot there to keep the dragons busy until the sun set and she was strong enough to fight back.

Penelope tried to walk quicker, but the sun felt like a

heavy weight against her shoulders. From the corner of her eye, she could see the two dragons moving quicker to keep pace. *Of course they don't mind the sun. Fuckers.*

The dragon shifters looked like normal humans at first glance, perhaps a little taller and more muscular than most. One of them had a small cut on the back of his hand. The scent of his blood on the air told Penelope's nose all she needed to know about him: male, dragon, angry, violent...and frightened? The last one was faint, but definitely there.

If it was night, they would have reason to be scared. Dragons and vampires were about equally matched in strength: her scale-piercing fangs opposite their flames meant that everyone tried to get along. Penelope didn't need to glance at her watch to know there were a few hours until nightfall, and she would be back to full strength.

"Hello, there. You'd sure be pretty if you smiled," a rough voice said from so close Penelope nearly stumbled. The shifter without the cut hand had gotten much closer than she'd expected--the fuckers could move a lot faster than her in the daylight--and was walking so near she could smell his blood through his skin: male, dragon, ready for a fight and desperate to prove himself to his superiors.

"Thanks for the valuable life advice," she said, walking quicker. "I'll keep it in mind." There were just a few more blocks before she reached the bar, but fear twisted a knot in Penelope's chest.

She glanced around. There were too many people around; humans and magical beings hurrying home after work or out to one of the restaurants a few blocks away. If they got into a brawl here, a lot of people could get hurt.

What if that's their plan? Dragons weren't famous for their subtlety, and if a fight between a vampire and two dragons took out a city block, Penelope and her lab would come under the kind of close scrutiny from the magical community that she'd been avoiding for years.

Did the covens finally lose patience with my work? Penelope wondered, her sweating hands clenching into fists. She had spent the last three hundred years trying to unlock the scientific foundations of magic. As far as she knew, her lab was the only place on Earth investigating how magic actually worked, rather than blindly accepting that chanting could defy physics.

"Hey lady, my friend just wanted to give you a compliment." The dragon shifter with the cut hand was now on her other side, herding her in the direction of an alley bathed in dangerous sunlight.

"Your friend needs to get better at sweet talk." Penelope tried to move away from the shifters, but the first dragon was now blocking her path whenever she tried to walk around him.

Her pulse quickened. This was not good. The men were closing in on her from two directions, leaving the alley the only path not blocked by a wall of sweaty muscle. She didn't need her four doctorates to know what would happen once she got to that alley.

"Leave me alone, assholes," she shouted, looking around for anyone close enough to hear and intervene. Everyone was either on their phone, or out of earshot.

Fuck this.

Penelope turned on her heel, pushing through the men with every ounce of her strength. They shifted just enough for her to break through and she sprinted down the street. The sun burned the back of her neck as the collar of her coat bounced with each stride. She could smell her own seared skin.

Adrenaline coursed through her and she ignored the pain. Running under the hot sun was like trying to push her way through taffy. Her chest felt tight and her side ached from the effort, but she kept struggling forward.

"Help! Somebody help me!" she cried, her voice coming out in a gasp. She dashed around corners, trying to shake her pursuers, but their footsteps sounded closer and closer.

A strong hand latched around her elbow and swung her whole body around.

"It's nothing personal, sweet cheeks," the man sneered. "Our boss just doesn't want you around."

She lashed out, kicking him square in the nuts. The man let out a pathetic groan as he doubled over. Penelope barely registered the second shifter's presence before he punched her, sending agony pulsing through her face.

The cement roared up toward her as she fell, the world suddenly blurry through the tears and blood streaming over her eyes. A boot appeared out of nowhere and struck her hard in the abdomen. She choked for air as spots fluttered across her vision.

After three hundred years, this is how I go?

"Your blood fucking stinks like goat-dicks, cowards," she wheezed, the worst insult that came to mind.

Her mind raced. If only she'd waited longer before she left the lab, she wouldn't have been so vulnerable. If only she hadn't worked a thirteen hour shift, she would have been less desperate for sleep and she wouldn't have left in the middle of the day.

Penelope tried to get to her feet, her palms scratching against the gritty concrete. The kicks kept coming, from both men now, buffeting her from all sides. The world felt like a distant whirl of pain and color and burning light.

Need...blood...

"Leave her alone!" A deep voice yelled from somewhere nearby, but Penelope was too disoriented to tell the direction any more.

The blows of pain finally stopped as the two dragon shifters moved towards the stranger.

Penelope retched and gasped for air, holding her surely-broken ribs. The crunching of a fist meeting bone made her gasp with alarm as droplets of her attackers' blood sprayed across her face. She licked her lips, capturing a drop on her tongue. It tasted of pure fear.

A familiar jolt coursed through her body as Penelope began to heal. A single thought looped through her mind, over and over. *I need more blood.* She was still too weak to stand; all she could see were blurry forms grappling and punching. Finally a high-pitched squeal rang out like a dying pig.

"Get the fuck out of here if you don't want to end up like your friend," Penelope's savior said.

"You shoulda' stayed out of this," one dragon shifter growled. The two sprinted away as quickly as they could.

"Yeah, you...better run," Penelope managed to groan at their retreating feet. A blurry figure in a leather jacket with skin the warm color of burnished bronze crouched down next to her. Penelope struggled to sit up, but her head swam at the motion.

"Don't move, you got hurt pretty bad. I'll call for an ambulance."

"No," Penelope said. There was no time to be delicate. There was no way a human could have fought off two dragon shifters; her hero had to be someone supernatural. "I'm a vampire. I...just need blood. A little and I'll heal."

A strong arm wrapped around the back of her head and

gently cradled her into a seated position. Warm skin pulsed against her lips.

"Take what you need." The voice seemed to come from miles away. Penelope focused on the skin, savoring its intoxicating scent. Her fangs sprang out instinctively, plunging deep.

The hot blood streamed over her tongue and down her throat, details of her rescuer rolling over Penelope like notes in a fine wine. Her savior was male, another dragon shifter. Confident, strong--*that explains how he was able to take those assholes down*--open-minded, curious, and profoundly intelligent.

Hot damn, this guy is amazing. Her fangs sank in deeper, a part of her keeping track of how much she was drinking. It would be a very poor thank you to drain this guy dry. She could feel her bones healing, and the slight tickle of cuts rapidly closing up. It had been years since she drank directly from a donor's vein. *This is so much better than bagged blood.* She'd almost forgotten the sensation of somebody's personality and emotions splashing against her mind as she consumed them.

The feelings were almost overwhelming. Her savior was kind, living a life surrounded by people he loved, and yet a loneliness permeated every drop of his blood in a way that made Penelope's heart ache. It was like focusing a microscope onto the secret corners of her own heart.

She withdrew her fangs and licked the puncture marks they left behind, her saliva restoring the man's skin to perfection. Her tongue lingered a beat longer than was strictly necessary on his wrist, basking in his scent, savoring the taste of his skin.

Penelope finally had the strength to sit up and wipe her eyes clean. She smiled and looked up.

Penelope blinked.

Her savior was a woman.

"Um, hi. Thanks for saving me," Penelope said too quickly, trying to hide her disorientation.

This doesn't make any sense. Blood doesn't lie. Her savior had tasted distinctly male, and yet...this person had a pair of shapely breasts under their jacket and a lovely, feminine face.

"My name is Dr. Penelope O'Hara," she said, reaching out a shaky hand.

"It's nice to meet you, Doctor. I'm Alec Harper. *Mister* Alec Harper if we're going to be formal about it. How are you feeling?" They shook hands a little awkwardly.

Penelope flexed her fingers and did a quick assessment. Alec's blood had healed her completely, although she knew she'd feel better once she was out of the sun. She snuck another peek at--*his? her?*--face.

"I seem to be okay, thanks to you," Penelope said.

Alec stood, then reached down to help her up. Penelope could feel herself grinning like a moron, her heart pattering in her chest at Alec's touch.

What's happening? Penelope had never been attracted to a woman before, but there was no mistaking the strong attraction she was feeling. He did say 'Mister,' and so did his blood.

She dug into her purse to push a business card into Alec's hand. "Here. I own a lab not far from here. I'm a specialist in the science of spellwork. If you ever need anything, just let me know. I owe you my life." She half-heartedly tried to fix her blonde hair, tousled from the struggle. "Feel free to call on me for whatever you need." She had no idea what kind of a favor a heroic dragon shifter might want from her, but she wanted to ensure that Alec would have a reason to come back into her life.

Alec slipped the card into his jeans' pocket. "Thanks. I'll hold onto it." His mouth curved into a smile that didn't reach his eyes.

He doesn't want to see me again, Penelope decided, feeling a little hurt. She'd heard that being drained by a vampire could be an unsettling experience, sometimes resulting in a euphoric high. It could be a very disorienting experience for first-timers.

"I've got to get back to my family soon. I ride with the Iron Claws." He paused like Penelope would recognize the name, but the name didn't ring a bell. "We're an outlaw motorcycle club. Those guys that attacked you had the scent of the Dragon High Council all over them, probably Red Guards."

"But what would the Dragon High Council want with me?" Penelope asked.

Alec shrugged and turned so he was shading Penelope from most of the sun's rays. "They're bullies. They probably saw a weakened vampire in the daylight and decided to take advantage." He took her hand in his and Penelope's breath hitched.

But what had that one said? Something about his boss wanting me out of the way? She couldn't remember what she'd heard. The feeling of Alec's hand in hers was almost as distracting as the sun still blazing down at them.

"You're an outlaw, eh?" Penelope's flirty tone surprised herself. She rubbed her thumb along the top of his callused hand. "You just saved my life; you don't seem the type."

"The Iron Claws and the High Council don't see eye to eye on...have you heard of Puff?" He laid his other hand on top of hers, his fingers lightly caressing her wrist.

Of course! Penelope realized why Alec thought she'd know the name of his club. The Iron Claws were infamous for distributing healing drugs against the dragon shifters' official rules.

"I've never worked with Puff personally, but it's *fascinating*. How ground dragon scales could work such medical miracles for humans is like nothing I've ever seen."

Alec shifted a little closer. "The old fogies on the Council fear humans would start hunting dragons again if they found out."

The scent of Alec's blood called to her, beckoning her to lean even closer to him. She forced herself to move away, squinting at the sunlight and pressing a finger to her throbbing temple.

"Listen, I really have to get out of the light." She bit her lower lip and looked at him. "You can still call me though, even if you *don't* need a favor."

He patted the side of his pants where a faint outline of the card was visible. "I wish I was sticking around town longer. We're leaving soon on another distribution job. But I can at least see you safely home." He pushed off the wall, holding out his arm like a gentleman in an old movie, and started to walk her down the street.

"You don't have to walk me all the way home. If you can get me to AUDREY'S around the corner, their blood cocktails can hold me over until the sun sets." She sighed, the light making her head throb. She pressed her head into his shoulder, blessing even the small amount of shade his head provided. "I'm sorry, I'm not usually this helpless," Penelope said.

"I believe that. Any woman who can curse at her enemies when she's bleeding on the ground is someone worth getting to know."

Fucking hell, he heard all that? Penelope blushed to the roots of her hair. "I've always had a bit of a mouth on me."

Alec's eyes locked on her lips for a second and Penelope resisted the urge to lick them.

"Yes, you do." He winked.

They chatted happily as they walked the remaining block to AUDREY's blinking neon sign. Through the window, Penelope could see the familiar sight of leprechauns, trolls, shifters, and other supernaturals gearing up for the night's arm wrestling competition.

"Do you want to come in? The least I can do is buy you a drink," Penelope said.

He shook his head. "You have no idea how tempted I am, but I have to be getting back. It was lovely meeting you, Dr. Penelope O'Hara." He touched her shoulder in a light caress that sent electric shocks down her arm. "Get home safe." He turned and walked away.

Part of her wanted to run after him, kiss him senseless and convince him to stay. She sighed as the dark smudge of his jacket rounded the corner and disappeared. If Alec had wanted to be with her, he would have stayed.

I'm never going to see him again.

ALEC WANTED to kick himself for walking away. Penelope was brilliant and gorgeous. He smiled at the memory of how her blonde hair twisted into tiny braids and spiraled buns added extra dimension and character to her face. Her eyes sparkled at him in a way he hadn't seen in a long while. Her curves left him dizzy. She was everything he could ask for in a woman. Part of him longed to run back to the bar, apologize for being an idiot, and kiss her for hours.

He nearly stumbled on the sidewalk remembering what it felt like when she fed on him. The sensation of her fangs penetrating his skin... he couldn't remember being so turned on in all his life. His knees had nearly given out under him, and it had taken all of his willpower not to rip off all of their clothes in middle of the street and bury his face between her thighs.

She said she would owe him a favor. *Would a date count?* Alec felt his pulse race as he considered the idea, before realizing how creepy that could sound. The whole situation was impossible anyway. He'd given up on dating long ago.

The sharp heat of the sun bore down like it was scolding him for being so pessimistic about romance. Penelope had obviously been interested in him. He paused. *Is it too late to go back?*

He turned around, and then back again, pacing a small circle on the sidewalk. He had to admit that he was spectacular at first dates. And second dates. He let out a long breath.

What was the point? He turned back in the direction of the Iron Claws' clubhouse and kept walking. First and second dates were one thing, but once his relationships started to get serious, or started to get physical, that's when things *always* went pear-shaped.

Dating was hard. Dating as a transgender person was playing the game of life set to an expert-level difficulty. The women who wanted his female body were thrown by how much of a guy he was. The women who wanted him based on his masculine personality were thrown by his female body. The confused look in Penelope's eyes when she'd withdrawn her fangs and seen him for the first time was all he'd needed to know that they wouldn't work out.

He clenched and unclenched his fists, trying to draw his

attention away from the longing that throbbed through his chest. A vampire scientist who studied magic? Even if she hadn't looked like a stunning dream he would have wanted to spend time getting to know her.

The cheerful sun seemed to mock his misery. A man and woman walked past, their arms interlocked, so focused on each other the man nearly walked into a tree. The woman pulled him out of the way at the last moment and they fell into each other laughing. Alec looked away.

When Alec joined the Iron Claws years ago, it had just been him, Big Joe, Ned, Caesar, Emma, and later Marie (the human medic). When the former-detective Dylan joined a year ago and promptly fell for Marie, it seemed as if the world suddenly turned into an enormous game of musical chairs with people rushing to claim their mate. Ned was next, finding his mate at a tiger shifter orgy of all places and moving away to run his bakery business. Then Caesar was reunited with a groupie he'd been pining over for years. And everyone knew Big Joe and Emma were in love, once they got over their pride to admit it.

Which left Alec alone when the music stopped.

Alec pulled at the collar of his leather jacket, the fabric too thick for such a warm day. Sweat beaded on the back of his neck, the droplets sliding down beneath his clothes, soaking the tight binding he always wore around his chest.

Stupid breasts. He'd contemplated surgeries in the past. While he respected the hell out of anybody who went that way, he'd decided in the end that surgery just wasn't for him. In the past, girlfriends had pressured him to go under the knife, but Alec knew that anyone who required such a major physical change would never really accept *him*.

He let out a long, slow breath, trying to force a smile to his lips. *Focus on the positive.* Alec scrunched his face up as he tried to remember his mental list of "things to be grateful for".

I'm healthy.

I have found an amazing family.

I save people for a living.

I can fly.

I can't have her, the traitorous thought whispered in his head.

Alec finally arrived at the clubhouse, managing to fake a pleasant expression as he pushed open the door. *No need to worry anybody.*

Alec's blood immediately ran cold. Something was *very* wrong. Emma and Big Joe were whispering furiously by the bar, too low for Alec to hear. Emma's palm kept twisting the hilt of the dagger at her waist, something she only did when truly upset.

Over on the couch, Caesar was furiously yelling into a phone in Spanish. His arm wrapped around his fiancée, Nina, but she was so busy typing on her laptop that she didn't seem to notice. Nina's forehead creased with a deep 'v', and her mouth moved silently as she read from the screen.

Alec's eyes swept the room until he found Marie in tears behind the pool table, rummaging through a box of paper files. Dylan was at her side examining pages with his intense stare.

"What's happened?" Alec called out to the room. Nobody appeared injured, but..."Is it Ned? Did something happen?" Nobody answered and Alec felt his palms begin to sweat. *What the fuck happened?*

"It's my fault." Marie shook as she spoke, her voice so soft that even Alec's shifter hearing could barely make her voice out. "I'm the medical professional. I should have run some tests or put together a trial..." Dylan moved to hold her, his arms encircling her as she cried hysterically. "They're all dead!" Marie's scream cut through the clubhouse like an axe, silencing the room. Caesar hung up the phone.

"Who's dead?" Alec's heart raced.

"Alec, thank fuck you're here," Emma said, leaving Big Joe in mid-sentence at the bar and walking quickly over to Alec. "We need you." She pushed Alec's laptop into his hands.

"Who. Is. Dead?" He repeated, fear and frustration shaking his voice.

"Our Puff patients. Eight so far." Big Joe's rumbling tenor echoed against the clubhouse. "We're still figuring the situation out."

"This is a load of crap," Caesar stood up to pace. Caesar always felt more comfortable when he was moving, but right now, his quick movements just made Alec feel even dizzier. "Puff doesn't hurt people. It heals them. That's the entire point."

"Apparently not." Emma traded a loaded look with Big Joe.

Alec's head swam. "You don't think... I mean it's not like Puff killed..." He sat down on a beer-stained wooden chair. "Fuck." If they'd been mistaken all these years and Puff actually harmed the people they'd been trying to help...the thought made Alec feel sick.

"I was checking in on Mrs. Bernstein from last month," Marie explained. "I spoke to her grandson. She was doing fine, the stomach cancer was in remission and even her arthritis was gone and then..." Marie gripped Dylan's arm like a lifeline. "She suddenly died. It was natural causes--or so the autopsy said--but with her Puff treatment she should have had a least another ten years. It doesn't make sense!"

Alec forced down his sense of rising panic. For so many years they'd been distributing Puff against the laws of the High Council. How many people had they endangered?

Emma's lips tightened. "The eight humans we've found so far all died this month. They were all being treated for different ailments, were all from different towns, and had no places and no people in common." She shifted her weight uncomfortably. "Except the Puff. She pulled a list of names off of the bar and handed it to Alec.

He remembered most of them, could picture their faces. Mothers, grandfathers. His eyes stopped on the last name.

"Bobby Spencer? He was five years old!" Alec cried. "How could this have happened?"

"We don't know a lot about how Puff cures people," Emma said. "We've seen it heal hundreds of humans, and always just assumed..." Her voice faded away and Marie's soft sobs filled the silence.

Alec felt like he couldn't breathe. The years before Alec joined up with the Iron Claws was a dark time he hated to think about. He'd shut the door on his past. Providing Puff to sick humans, saving their lives, that was how he atoned. It felt like a weight had been placed on his chest.

The Dragon High Council had declared Puff a forbidden substance over a millennia ago. An insidious thought wormed its way into Alec's mind and he couldn't shake it loose.

Was the High Council right this whole time?

"Okay, everybody. Listen up." Big Joe clapped his hands together and everyone stopped and looked at him. "We're going to get ahead of this thing," he said. "But first we need to figure out what's actually going on. Until we know for sure that it's safe, nobody is going to distribute or use Puff." He nodded to Emma, who stepped forward.

"We're going to have to split up." Emma's gaze swept across the room, daring somebody to argue. "Marie and Dylan, go through the distribution files and tell everybody currently using Puff to stop. Make sure Ned gets the memo too so he stops using the stuff in his pastries." She threw a small roll of cash at Caesar. "Caesar, you and Nina go to AUDREY'S, chat up the clientele, grease some palms if you need to. Use that charm you're always bragging about. I want to know if anybody or anything has heard of Puff killing humans."

"Got it." Nina set down her laptop.

Emma continued, "Joe and I are going to hit up the morgues of our eight confirmed dead. We're going to need all the information we can get on how these people died. And Alec--"

"Actually I know exactly what I need to do," Alec interrupted. He still felt sick, but an idea was starting to form a small bubble of hope in his chest. "I met a vampire today who specializes in the science behind magical substances. If anybody can determine the true effect of Puff on humans, it's her."

"Fine," Emma said. "But when Joe and I are at the morgue, we may need your remote assistance checking into any electronically-stored records--"

"Yeah, yeah, I should be able to hack into anything you guys need." Alec checked outside. It was still so bright out, Penelope would probably still be at AUDREY'S keeping low until the sun set. *Or would she have gone back to her lab?* His finger caressed the edge of her business card in his back pocket.

The possibility of seeing her again filled him with an

intense longing he didn't want to examine. Life was complex enough without adding in a beautiful, brilliant vampire. But a sly voice in the back of his mind reminded him.

She still owes you a favor.

THE VIALS of synthetic fairy dust hanging from the lab's ceiling were singing louder than usual today. Penelope pinched the bridge of her nose and concentrated on the computer screen in front of her, trying to ignore the music and the rumbling voice of her assistant, Bog.

"The man who saved you was *super* handsome, right? Heroic guys are always insanely hot." Bog adjusted her glasses, pulling awkwardly at the corner of the white lab coat that didn't quite fit around her leafy body. "It's all about confidence, isn't it? I mean, if *I* was going to rescue a damsel in distress, I'd automatically be much more attractive, wouldn't I? I read online that if you stand up super-straight and square your shoulders, you immediately seem more attractive." Bog straightened up, her swamp-being form (she hated the term "swamp monster") sending a mass of reeds and cattails up through the top of her lab coat. She moved her hands to the vague area where her hips would be if a walking mass of moss, vines and leaves with a human-like face at the top had hips. "What do you think, Penelope? Powerful?"

Penelope shrugged. "If the Internet says it, then *obviously* it has to be true." She winced at her harsh tone. It wasn't Bog's fault Penelope couldn't stop thinking about Alec. Flashes of his essence from his blood--hope masked by a growing loneliness--kept distracting her. It annoyed her that she couldn't seem to forget the taste of him, or how much she wished he hadn't walked away.

Bog slumped, green ferns falling from her neck like feathers. "One day you are going to be sarcastic to someone who doesn't know it's how you show you care. And then they'll be hurt, and you'll be very sorry."

"So long as *you* know I don't mean to be mean, that's what matters." Penelope forced herself to smile at her long-suffering assistant. They met years ago when Penelope was investigating the magical properties of certain marsh grasses. Bog had emerged from the water, started asking insightful questions, and Penelope offered Bog a job. The swamp-being had been a valuable asset to the lab ever since, despite her near-constant chatter wearing on Penelope's nerves.

"All I'm saying is not everybody has my infinite patience and magnanimous understanding." Bog brushed up against the dangling string of fairy dust, making them sing louder.

Penelope smiled. Synthesizing singing fairy dust had not been one of her more practical achievements, but it certainly made the lab look more festive.

"Someday, you'll meet someone who'll sweep you off your feet." Bog opened her arms wide and then wrapped them around herself, swaying slightly to the music. "Someone who will feed you grapes while you're relaxing on some chaise lounge. Someone to lay under the stars with--"

"Bog, that only happens in movies. And porn."

--"Someone who sends you boxes of chocolate and life-sized teddy bears." Bog continued unabated. "*Romance*, Penelope. Somebody *romantic*. Like your hero from yesterday." Bog wiggled the sticks above her eyes, an imitation of lifting her 'eyebrows' that always made Penelope laugh.

"I don't know if I'd say what happened yesterday was

romantic. It was more like a blood donation." Penelope didn't want to think about how deeply she'd been attracted to Alec. It was all too confusing. Her impression of Alec from his blood was so different than his physical appearance...*Maybe if I got another hit of his blood, everything will make sense...* She shook her head. That train of thought was dangerous.

"Right, it was just a *blood donation*." Bog leaned forward, her neck ferns fluttering with amusement. "So why are you blushing?"

"He didn't even want to have a drink with me at AUDREY'S. I'll probably never see him again," Penelope said.

The obnoxious buzz of the main entrance's doorbell cut off Bog's response.

"Are you expecting someone?" Bog asked nervously. Her neck ferns lay flat against her collar and she eyed the fire axe they kept installed on the wall.

"No." Penelope switched the view on the computer to show the feed from the security cameras installed around the perimeter of the building.

Her breath caught when she saw Alec standing outside the door. His motorcycle was neatly parked behind him. His hands dug deep into his pockets and he was shifting his weight anxiously. Alec didn't seem the type to be nervous. *Something's wrong.*

Penelope hit the door release and heard the distant buzzing of the door unlocking.

"Who is it?" Bog asked.

"It's the dragon shifter from yesterday. The good one." Penelope sighed. "Is there any chance I can get you to run downtown to pick up those griffon samples we need?"

"No chance. I want to see him!" Bog crowded up to the

computer screen, looking at Alec walking through the lobby towards the elevator. "Is that...him? That doesn't look like a him..."

"Yup, that's him. Please give us some time alone? You beautiful, brilliant, *stunning* thing you." Penelope looked at Bog with a pleading look and Bog finally nodded.

"Fine, flattery will get you everywhere. This swampy gal is heading out." Bog backed away towards the side door. "But don't think I won't be demanding *all* of the details when I get back." She flashed Penelope a bright, green smile as the door slid shut behind her.

Penelope tried to stay calm as she waited for Alec. Just the thought of him near her again...it made her heart beat harder than she thought was possible.

She quickly checked her reflection in the glass front of one of the cabinets. She fussed with her blonde hair, re-twisting a pinwheel that had come loose and tucking a braid behind her ear. Her skin was unavoidably vampire pale, but she still had a healthy glow from Alec's blood.

Could be worse.

She almost jumped at the knock at the door.

"Pen-- I mean, Dr. O'Hara? I need to talk to you," Alec's voice called from the other side of the door.

Just hearing his voice made Penelope's hormones roar with want, but she pushed them down and focused on schooling her expression as she opened the door.

She couldn't stop herself from looking Alec up and down. Now that she was away from the pain and the heat of the sun, she could see him more clearly. Alec stood confident and tall, his legs spread shoulder width, and his head held high. Penelope had seen kings with a less commanding presence.

"Uh, um, come in," she stammered. *What is wrong with me?* Penelope was never this inarticulate.

"Thanks for seeing me," Alec said. "There's an emergency and I hope you'll...whoa." His eyes went wide as he looked around. "This place isn't what I was picturing."

Penelope glanced around the lab and grinned. Most human labs she knew were sterile and white to the point of austerity. But she researched *magic*. And magic was as much about context and emotion as it was chemical. She had long ago discovered that making her lab as homey as possible made the magical components more likely to cooperate with her experiments. Colorful, lush rugs covered the floor. Paintings from friends she'd met over the years filled the wall: landscapes of swirling colors, geometric shapes, and portraits of long-dead collaborators and co-workers. The light from the fairy dust was bright enough to work by, and didn't have the harshness of fluorescents.

"I'll take that as a compliment," Penelope smiled. "Although, I doubt you came here to check out my interior decorating."

Alec nodded. "I need your help."

"What's going on?" she asked.

His hands skimmed over a variety of proof-of-concept gadgets and half-finished experiments littering the top of the main work table.

"Remember how my club distributes Puff to humans? Some of our patients are dead and we don't know why." His hands shook a little as he spoke. "I remembered you were an expert at this kind of stuff and..." He paused, looking down. "Are we killing them? Is there any possibility that the Council might have been right to ban Puff?"

He looked so low, Penelope fought the urge to embrace

him. *He's here for your professional expertise,* she reprimanded herself.

"I've never had much reason to study Puff in detail, but I've only ever heard rumors of its healing properties." Penelope pulled up her files from a large cabinet, scanning through her notes. "In prioritizing my studies, I've mostly researched how to duplicate magical substances which cause harm to their recipients." Her eyes scanned through the notes in the nearly-empty file on Puff, trying to keep her expression carefully professional. Alec's presence in her lab was distracting.

Alec picked up a tiny spinning wheel and held it up to the light. "What kind of stuff do you study?"

"Put that down." She stood up and gently took the wheel from him. "That's an aerosol dispenser that sprays a chemically-recreated sleeping curse."

Alec stepped away from the wheel. "What would happen if I sprayed that?"

Penelope chuckled. "A small dose would just make you drowsy, but what's *really* fascinating is what happens when you spray this on an eye-of-newt solution that's been taken down to zero degrees Kelvin. In isolation, it would make you stink bad enough to make a skunk jealous, but mixed with other solutions, the molecules can actually merge to—" She stopped short, blushing. "Sorry, when I get going on the properties of magical reactions, I can get carried away in the science."

"I'm an expert programmer, I know something about nerding out on topics I'm passionate about." He leaned in close and Penelope could smell the hot pulse of Alec's blood calling to her. "It's hot."

Penelope pulled at the collar of her lab coat, which

suddenly felt a little too tight. It took all of her willpower to not turn and kiss him. *He's not here for that.*

"I haven't heard of Puff harming humans." Penelope shrugged. "But, before yesterday I'd never heard of a computer-hacking dragon shifter motorcycle-riding rebel."

"Well, I've never heard of a vampire scientist fascinated by magic. Were you a witch before you were turned?" He shifted his weight. "Sorry for being so nosy. It's a personality flaw: when something interests me, I want to know every-thing about it."

She smiled. "That doesn't sound like a flaw." Penelope shuffled the papers around on her desk so they perfectly aligned with the edge of the table. "I was never a witch, just a merchant's daughter fascinated by the supernatural. I wanted to become part of that world, but my options were limited since witchcraft and shifting are passed down through family lines. I spent years searching for a real vampire to turn me. I've never regretted the decision, although I know a lot of vamps who do." It was one of the reasons she tended to avoid their blood clubs. Too much brooding. "After I was turned and I'd gotten control of my blood lust, I stayed close to my brother and father. This was back in the seventeenth century, much more dangerous times. I figured with my supernatural strength I could help look after them. Then my brother got sick."

Penelope took a deep breath. The lights blurred in front of her eyes as she blinked away tears. She hadn't thought about Frederick in years, always pushing away the memory of his expression of pure hatred when she'd first walked in the door, vampire pale.

Alec held out a hand and she grasped it, happy for the warmth of his skin against her cold palm. She forced a smile.

"It was a long time ago. No one knew what was wrong with him, the doctors—such as they were—threw around words like vapors and imbalanced humours. If he had let me turn him, he would have healed, immune to all human disease." She tried to blink away a tear before it rolled down her cheek. "He...refused."

Alec didn't need to know about how Frederick threw around words like "demon" and "unnatural animal" on his deathbed. Penelope still felt the frustration of trying to explain things to him, trying to get the man to save his own life.

"I was still determined to save him." Penelope fiddled with a handheld interdimensional portal device she'd been working on the last month. "I found a coven and demanded that they use their magic to cure him. I knew of a spell that could bring someone back from even the brink of death, but they turned me down."

Alec stepped forward to move his hand around her shoulders, the weight of his arm comforting across her back. "Why wouldn't they use it?"

"Apparently the spell heals by transferring energy, transferring *life* from the surrounding environment. Hundreds would have starved from crops drying up and livestock falling ill. That is why witches are so secretive; people really don't want to know how huge the consequences of some spells can be."

"What did you do?"

"I didn't know about the consequences of healing him, so I stole the spell. I figured that I could gather the ingredients and say the incantation the same as any witch. By the time I had everything prepared, my brother was on death's door." The memory still stung. "I'm not a witch, so the spell didn't work. I've spent the last three hundred years trying to figure out what makes a witch able to interact with magical components in a way others can't."

Alec was silent for a moment, his lips tightly pressed together. "That's one of the most selfless things I've ever heard. How many other people are studying this stuff?"

"I have my assistant, and I've run into a few tinkering humans and historians over the years, but most people take magic at face value. I'm the only one I know of who has made this an intensive study." She sniffed and grabbed a tissue to wipe her eyes. *No more thinking about the past.* "Being immortal gives me plenty of time to learn."

Alec walked back to the table, picking up a metal tube with blinking lights on the end. "Immortal, huh? You looked in pretty rough shape when I saw you yesterday. Were you just biding your time before you took out those two Red Guard dicks?" He spun the tube in his fingers, his touch both light and sure.

Penelope stood, appreciating how Alec picked up on how she was ready to change the topic. She reached for the tube, very aware of the brief contact with his skin as she took it from his fingers. "Careful with that. It's an EMP curse. Get zapped with this thing, and any electronic device you touch shorts out."

Rather than putting the curse device down, she let the smooth metal slide in and out of her fingers. Alec's eyes followed the movement, his gaze almost hungry.

"As for those goons, I could have easily taken them if it was night. At my full strength, two dragon shifters would have been easy enough." She raised an eyebrow at him to see if he was going to challenge her assertion, but his smile was only filled with respect. "But I definitely needed the save yesterday. The sun weakens vampires, especially direct rays. Once we feed, all of those wounds can heal. The worse the wound, the more blood we need. The only thing that even blood won't cure is decapitation." She took a deep breath. "Whoever sent them was trying to send a very violent complaint about my research."

He stepped closer, his expression suddenly concerned. "I thought it was just a random mugging. You think someone *sent* them to hurt you?"

Penelope nodded. "One of them mentioned a boss who wanted me out of the way. I also got a good sense of their essence from their blood. They were terrified of whoever sent them." She placed the EMP curse tube down. "I thought at first it might be the local covens finally coming after me, but it may be too big a coincidence that goons attacked me at the same time that your Puff patients are dying. Something fishy's going on; I should still start examining the Puff right away."

Alec dug out a small packet of white powder from his back pocket and handed it to her. "Thank you so much, Penelope. I really appreciate you putting your other research on hold for this." He ran his hands through his short hair. "Should I stick around? Or will I be distracting? I'd love to watch you work, if you don't mind."

"I'll take *that* as a compliment, too." Penelope grinned. She held the packet up to the light, watching the powder sparkle.

"It is." Alec looked beyond her at her computer. "If the High Council is really behind this, there will be some digital evidence. Do you mind if I use your computer to check something?"

"Go ahead." Penelope was already separating the Puff into different petri dishes, planning out a series of tests for each sample.

His fingers flew across the keys as various screens

opened and closed, shifting to scrolling code that Penelope barely understood. The surety of his movements, the grace and power he radiated just sitting in a chair, was enough to make her mouth go dry.

You're a professional. Concentrate. She reluctantly turned away from Alec and stepped back to her workbench. She dropped a few grains of Puff onto a slide and slid it under her modified microscope. If a human had put the same grains under a microscope, they would see innocuous dust. It was one of the many reasons Puff had never been noticed by the human world. But Penelope was no human. Under the lens, the Puff glowed with magic, grains sliding and shifting across the surface of the glass. She prepared another slide, this one with burned skin cells, and watched in the microscope as the Puff attached to the cells, repairing the burned tissue.

The possibilities this substance could have for humanity, Penelope thought, pulling out a sample of cancerous human cells. *I wonder--*

"Found it!" Alec's voice cried out from the other side of the lab.

Penelope looked up at the clock, amazed that two hours had already passed.

"What is it?"

"Someone hacked into these hospital records before me." He gestured at the screen. "These are the patient records of the last five hospitals where we found people who needed Puff. Somebody embedded a program that would send information on patients who had rapid, unexplained recoveries to a highly-encrypted web address. They tried to erase the digital footprints, but left the program in there." Alec's eyes gleamed. "I recognize this hacker's style."

Penelope looked over his shoulder at the computer. The

lines of numbers and letters looked like gibberish to her. He pulled up another screen and started typing frantically.

"There's a style signature in all that?" she asked, her admiration for Alec growing even more.

His fingers didn't miss a beat as the words flowed across the screen. "We worked together a long time ago before I joined up with the Iron Claws." His mouth twitched downward for a half a second. "She calls herself Roxanne, although it's probably an alias."

"Is she dangerous?"

Alec stood up and, for a second, their faces were so close together Penelope could see the slight dilation of Alec's pupils as he looked at her.

"I'm about to find out. I set up a meeting with her in thirty minutes." He leaned forward and Penelope was sure he was going to kiss her. Her heart sped up and she felt her torso lean forward expectantly, but he turned on his heel and left.

The lab door swung shut behind him and Penelope sank into her lab chair.

Hackers? Murderous dragon goons? What am I getting myself into?

She pulled up the security cameras and watched Alec swing his leg over his motorcycle, gun it, and spin in a tight curve to roar out of the drive.

"Please be safe."

"MEDIUM LATTE FOR ALEC SUCKS?" Alec could feel his face turn bright red as the barista's voice rang out. "Alec Sucks?"

Seriously?

"I'll take that." A silky voice responded, grabbing the cup

labeled "Alek Suchs" in black marker. The dark-haired woman with cold, golden skin wore a red, leather jacket unzipped to just below her breasts. A hint of leopard-print bra peeked out from the edges of her black shirt which read "Turn it Off and On Again" in red letters across her chest. Laced boots slid above her knees, their tops caressing the lower edge of her thighs.

The poor barista was staring at her so distractedly, he'd been pouring coffee onto the floor for the last five seconds. Alec hid a grin, looking around. The eyes of almost all of the men, and a large percentage of the women, were on Roxanne as she glided towards Alec's café table. The succubus knew how to make an entrance, he had to give her that.

Roxanne's grin was more baring teeth than actually smiling as she approached. Sometimes, Alec wondered how they'd managed to work together for so long before he joined the Iron Claws.

"Real mature, Roxanne." Alec frowned at her from his seat before gesturing for her to join him. "I thought we patched things up after I helped you with that hack in Barcelona."

"Hardly." Roxanne took a slow sip of her latte. "Barcelona was bullshit and you know it. You left me hanging with the job half-done" She crossed her legs, her miniskirt riding up dangerously high. "Besides, I'm just having a little fun."

"That's your problem, Rox." Alec shifted his laptop towards himself as Roxanne placed hers on the small table. "You always do whatever the hell you want, consequences be damned. As long as you're having fun."

Roxanne moved to stand. "Do you want my help, or did you want to lecture me about my life choices?" Her eyes briefly glowed, a reminder of the raw power hidden beneath the succubus's pleasing exterior. "I don't have to explain myself to anybody, least of all you. You were more than happy to hack for hire right alongside me until you grew that disgusting conscience."

"You're right, Rox," Alec said with a sigh. "You can do whatever the fuck you want." Before he'd joined the Iron Claws and learned what real friendship looked like, he'd imagined he and Roxanne were friends. He knew better now. "I need your help. You've hacked into the patient files at a dozen different hospitals. I need to know why." It was a long shot that she would ever tell him, but the worm he had tearing through the coffee shop's Wi-Fi needed a few more minutes to finish downloading all of the information he needed from her computer.

"You can go on wondering, dragon-boy. You know I don't discuss my jobs."

"What's a little intel between old friends?" Alec gave her his patented little brother look that always worked so well when Emma or Caesar were annoyed with him. He didn't dare look at his screen, where the download bar was mostly green. *Just a few more seconds...*

She rolled her eyes. "Don't give me that face. I'm a succubus; I'm immune to cute." She leaned low, her breasts popping out of her shirt and more lace from her bra peeking through. "Just like you've always somehow been immune to *these*."

"Survival instinct," Alec muttered, while daring to glance at his laptop. *99% downloaded. 100% Ha!* "Well, according to this," Alec turned his laptop around so Roxanne could see. "You created a program to identify patients at those hospitals who have suddenly recovered from life-threatening illnesses. All of the evidence to tie you to the crime is right here on my hard drive and saved on the cloud. You've been very naughty, Rox, even for you. Messing with the Iron Claws, you had to know that would be dangerous for you." Alec smirked. "You really shouldn't use the public Wi-Fi at places like this. It was almost too easy to get inside your system."

"Oh, please." Roxanne spun her laptop around so Alec could see her screen. "If I wanted you locked out of my computer, you'd be locked out. I decided to focus on something else." The entire screen was covered in surveillance footage blinking "LIVE" in the bottom corner.

Alec felt cold sweat bead on the back of his neck. Emma and Big Joe's familiar faces were questioning a receptionist in what looked like a hospital. Caesar and Nina were tossing back shots with a pixie at AUDREY'S; Alec would recognize the hovering braids of their main bartender, Lola, anywhere. Roxanne had found all of them, even hacking into a security camera feed in the bakery where Ned lived with his wife.

Alec felt like he'd been slapped. She'd never gone to this level of vicious for a simple job.

Roxanne flashed her teeth and waved. Alec's eye was drawn to the movement in the bottom left corner of her screen: she'd hacked the camera in the coffee shop as well, the image showing the two of them, but at an angle that didn't display Roxanne's face.

"I knew you goody two-shoes would get your scales all ruffled if I helped find your clients. If you want the people you love to stay safe, you'll back off." She clenched her teeth. "Now."

It's almost like she's scared. Roxanne was one of the toughest people he'd ever worked with. The Iron Claws alone wouldn't be enough to make her so defensive. The list of people who could scare her and who wanted the Iron Claws hurt was a very short list.

"How much did Sterling pay you?" Alec asked in a low voice. The High Council's head goon had been circling closer these last few months. Although Alec had never seen his face, the man's reputation was enough to make even somebody like Roxanne quiver in her stilettos.

Roxanne let out a low chuckle. "Oh honey, more than you could ever afford."

I can't believe that worked. Alec grabbed his things, stuffing his laptop into his bag before she realized how much she'd revealed.

"Next time you need a favor, don't call me." He gave Roxanne a hard glare. "Enjoy being a soulless bitch."

"I always do, darling." Roxanne swooped up her laptop in a smooth motion and rose from the table. Her hips swayed as she walked out, men and women swooning in her wake. "I always do," she called as the door swished behind her.

Alec sat back hard against his chair. His mind raced. He didn't realize how horrified he'd been about Puff killing humans until this spark of hope ignited in his chest. There was no way Sterling was identifying Puff users for anything good. *Would the High Council go this far? Murdering humans?*

It all made a terrible kind of sense. Last year the High Council attacked the Claws' clubhouse straight on and the motorcycle club had beaten them back. Then Sterling's goons kidnapped one of the Claws' members, Ned, and they also hired an assassin who attempted to murder Caesar in a fiery plane crash. But the Iron Claws were too strong when they worked together. It made sense this would be his next move: the only way the Iron Claws would stop distributing

Puff was if they believed they were killing the people they'd wanted to help.

Alec couldn't help but be impressed at the mind game. Even hiring Roxanne to do his dirty work was a respectful piece of villainy. Her trick hacking into all of those security cameras was masterful.

Alec felt the blood drain from his face.

She couldn't have hacked all those cameras while they were sitting there. Which meant she'd been watching them all for a while. And she'd let him know as a warning.

"Shit!" Alec grabbed his bag and sprinted out the door. If Sterling had been watching all of them, then he had seen Alec save Penelope, the one person who could prove Puff isn't poison.

Sterling was going to murder Penelope.

PENELOPE STOPPED herself before she pulled up the security footage from the previous day. Again. She didn't need to look at the grainy black-and-white images of Alec to remember what he looked like. She remembered Bog's reaction to seeing Alec for the first time. *Umm, that doesn't look like a him...*

No, he didn't.

If Alec hadn't told her differently, Penelope would think Alec was a truly stunning woman. Those curves, the smooth skin of the chin, the intense intelligence in the eyes. He was beautiful; even his bulky jackets and short haircut couldn't hide that.

When Penelope concentrated on Alec's breasts, his female features, she could almost convince herself she didn't feel anything for him. But then when she remembered the glimpse into his heart she'd tasted in his blood, her longing for Alec was so strong it scared her.

Penelope was too old to believe in love at first sight. That only happened in those movies Bog liked to watch so much. In three hundred years, Penelope had never met someone who understood so completely her drive for knowledge. His intelligence, his kindness...

What chance do I have of not falling for a man like that?

Alarms blared. Red lights on the ceiling started to pulse.

"Warning: Unauthorized Breach Attempt. Warning: Unauthorized Breach Attempt." Bog's recorded voice bellowed from the speakers. "Warning: Unauthorized Breach Attempt."

A deep roar echoed from outside the building, followed by a hot blast that Penelope could feel even in the lab. The lights on the ceiling swung back and forth, their song all minor chords.

"Fucking goat lickers!" Penelope cursed.

Of course the High Dragon Council wasn't going to stop at a few goons roughing her up in the street.

Penelope checked the security cameras. Two dragons in their full monstrous forms were blasting fireballs at the front door. Another was sending waves of fire at the rear entrance. The doors were already starting to buckle under their raw force.

She yelped in surprise as her phone started ringing. She hit the speaker button and yelled.

"Whoever this is, my lab is under attack. Hang up and call the police right now." She left the line open and ran to the emergency fire axe, averting her eyes as she smashed through the surrounding glass box with her elbow. The wail of the alarms drowned out the voice on the other side of the line, but Penelope heard the caller respond quickly before hanging up.

Three dragon shifters against one vampire, even at night when she was at her strongest, was going to be rough. She gave the axe a few experimental swings. The balance wasn't great, but it would have to do. Even if the cops arrived, the most they could contribute against dragons would be a distraction.

Penelope grabbed her notes on Puff and the last bit of the sample Alec gave her and stuck it deep into her bag. Her purse was one of her own inventions, designed to tap into fifth dimensional space to have a near-infinite storage capacity without taking on weight. As she stuffed as many gadgets, files, hard drives, blood bags, and tools in as she could reach, Penelope assessed her options.

There was an escape hatch on the roof, but dragons could fly and they had excellent hearing. They would hear the roof's squeaky latch, fly up, and roast her like Texas barbeque. The lab's building was built on bedrock without a basement, so she couldn't escape by going down. She tightened her grip on the axe. Her best bet would be to fight her way out of the back door with the one dragon on it and hope that she could get away before the other two dragons joined in the fight.

An enormous crash roared out from outside.

"Warning: Unauthorized Breach of Front Entrance."

Oh, fuck.

"Warning: Unauthorized Breach of Hallway. Warning: Unauthorized Breach of Lab in 3... 2..."

Penelope sprinted out the lab and down the hallway toward the back door. Heat pushed at her from behind and she could smell plastic and wood burning. Crashing echoed from the lab and she could picture all too easily the two enormous dragons smashing into walls and destroying all of her precious equipment. Tears and panic welled against her eyes.

My work!

She kept running, brandishing the axe in front of her.

The bastards are going to pay.

The back door disappeared just as she was about to reach it, the hinges giving a mighty crack as it flew like a flaming Frisbee down the hall. Penelope rolled underneath it, feeling the heat singe the top of her head. A purple dragon filled the space, blocking her way out.

Penelope held up the axe. "Want iron in your jugular? Get out of my way. Don't make me axe you again!"

The bottom of the dragon's throat glowed orange as the fire brewed in his chest. Penelope managed to dodge to the side just as a giant fireball roared past her. It crashed into the wall, which immediately caught fire. Smoke started to fill the hallway and Penelope knelt low to keep away from the choking fumes.

"I'm not afraid of puns, little vampire. You won't get close enough to use that toothpick." The dragon chuckled, his voice deep and rumbling.

"Oh yeah? Then let's take this outside!"

The dragon's throat was already turning orange again with stored heat. Penelope forced down her panic. The hallway was too narrow to effectively dodge any more fireballs. Even if she didn't get roasted, the smoke was weakening her.

This won't kill me, this won't kill me, Penelope repeated to herself. She coughed and gulped down a vial of blood she had stashed in her coat. Her throat cleared, but she could still feel her grip on the axe weakening. If she couldn't get out of here, the fire and smoke could incapacitate her.

"Penelope!" Alec's voice, deeper than she remembered, bellowed from above.

"I'm here!" she screamed. The roar of the flames was so loud, she called out again. "Alec! I'm by the back door!"

The purple dragon roared another fireball and Penelope stumbled away as fast as she could. Not fast enough. Her lab coat caught the edge of the flames and started to burn. Penelope threw off the coat and hurled it as far as she could down the hallway. A rumbling sound came from above and she screamed as the weakened ceiling collapsed, spraying burning debris and raining ceiling tiles.

Adrenaline coursed through her veins as she faced the only way out: directly behind the sneering purple dragon. She gripped her axe and let out a roar.

"This is for destroying my home, assholes!" she bellowed as she rushed him.

The dragon suddenly disappeared from the entrance. Penelope sprinted out of the burning building, coughing the smoke out of her lungs. Beside the parking lot, a dragon the color of fresh blood had the purple dragon's neck in his powerful jaws.

"Alec?" Penelope's feet slowed as she looked closer at her dragon defender. Alec's dragon form was male. It explained so much about why his blood had been so unquestionably a man's. A shifter's animal form was a reflection of their true self.

Alec's tail lashed out, spearing the delicate film of the purple dragon's wing and causing the purple dragon to cry out in pain. The dragons still in the building called out in response and Penelope heard more loud crashing and roaring inside.

"Alec!" Penelope cried. "They're coming!"

He dropped the unconscious purple dragon and was at her side with two flaps of his wings.

"Get in your car!" he cried.

Penelope ran through the parking lot to her car, jumping inside. A second later, the passenger door opened and a noticeably naked Alec jumped into the seat. The smell of his blood filled the cabin and Penelope inhaled deep.

"Drive!" he yelled. "They won't be able to follow us as well when I'm in human form."

Penelope stomped on the accelerator and zoomed down the familiar street. She glanced at the rearview window as they turned the corner and felt a pain in her gut like she'd been stabbed. The entire building was in flames, fire spurting out of the windows and the side walls already beginning to list and lean inward.

"Do you have a first aid kit?" Alec asked.

"I think in the glove compartment," Penelope said. She glanced over at him and gaped. She hadn't really appreciated just how *naked* Alec was after shifting back from his dragon form. And how much of his skin was covered in bruises, cuts, and lines of scars. "Are you okay?"

The smell of his blood was so tangible she could taste it in the back of her throat: courage and fear for her beat through his heart.

"I will be in a few minutes, shifters heal quickly," he said. He found some bandages and Penelope forced herself to concentrate on driving as she heard the sound of ripping fabric and the slight swish of cloth sliding across skin. The smell of the blood decreased and she swallowed hard.

"There's a blanket in the back if you need it," Penelope said.

"Thanks."

Penelope had a good look at his back as he leaned

between the two front seats to grab the blanket. Overlapping scars painted a horrifying grid across his back.

"I guess this wasn't your first fight," Penelope said softly.

"Nor the last, I suspect," he said.

"You get those scars riding with the Iron Claws?"

"Some of them. There are always folks after us, even if we try to avoid fights when we can. Others are from before I started riding with the Claws. And some are just from people who get...upset," he said the word through gritted teeth, "when someone who looks like me *claims* to be a man."

There were few other cars on the road this late, although a wail of sirens in the distance sounded like the police and fire departments had finally arrived to investigate the destruction.

"For what it's worth," Penelope said, "I knew you were a man before I ever actually saw your face."

Alec was silent for a long moment. The night road stretched empty in front and behind them and Penelope allowed herself to relax her grip on the wheel. If the dragons were following them, there wasn't any sign.

"I don't know why I find that comforting, but I do," he said. "When I called and you said you were being attacked, I thought I was going to lose my mind."

"You're a good person. You heard I was in danger and you rushed to help. I'm sure you'd have done it for anyone." Penelope's heart was beating so loud she was sure he could hear it on the other side of the car.

"Maybe. But I came because it was you."

The air inside the car felt suddenly charged and Penelope felt her chest tighten.

"Thank you."

A motel sign beckoned and Penelope pulled in, killing

the engine. She knew better than to head home where others from the High Council would probably be waiting for her.

The events of the evening came crashing down all at once: her lab's destruction, dragon goons trying to kill her, Alec saving her. She had no idea when she would be able to go home, or if her apartment was even still standing. She would have to call Bog to let her know what happened and to go into hiding for the time being. So many details to figure out. Penelope wanted to curl up in a ball in her car and sleep forever.

"Are you okay? Do you need blood?" Alec leaned toward her.

She wanted to say yes, but even the brief smell of it when he entered the car was enough to remind her of what would happen if she drank directly from his vein again: she wouldn't be able to stop until she was naked on top of him.

"I have some bags in my purse, and I have contacts I trust where I can get more. I'll be okay until we can get all of this sorted out."

"I'm so sorry that you got pulled into this. This conflict is between the Claws and the High Council. Now your lab is destroyed and you're on the run--"

"Alec, stop." She pressed her hand across his lips, silencing him. "If someone is harming your Puff patients, then I want to help. And if all of this meant that I got to meet you then..." She couldn't quite meet his eyes. "Then it might not be so bad for life to be more interesting for a little while." She climbed out of the car, grabbing her bag. Alec followed her out of the car, stepping back to transform into his dragon.

"I know the timing is really shitty," he said, stretching his wings behind him. Penelope noticed with pleasure that all of his wounds appeared to be completely healed now. "But I'm going to regret it if I don't ask."

"What is it?"

"Do you want to go on a date with me? A real one?" It was hard to read the facial expression on his reptilian face in dragon form, but Penelope thought she detected a hint of nervousness.

"Absolutely." The words popped from her mouth before she had time to overthink.

"Great!" he cried, launching himself into the air with mighty flaps of his wings and disappearing into the night sky.

Penelope let out a deep breath. Life was certainly going to be more interesting.

THE SHEER MASS of Roxanne's files to decrypt and go through was overwhelming, but Alec could barely resist the urge to whistle as he sifted through the stolen data. *Penelope said yes!* The delight on her face when she'd accepted his offer was going to warm his insides for a long time.

Print-outs littered the kitchen table of the Iron Claws' clubhouse, along with six networked laptops. Big Joe had initially grumbled about Alec and Nina taking up so much space with their equipment, but backed off once Alec pointed out that the key to catching Sterling was probably hidden in Roxanne's files. They just needed to find something concrete.

They'd had a breakthrough earlier in the day when he'd finally located the list of Puff patients Roxanne sent Sterling. There were a lot more than eight names on it, and the rest of the team had rushed out to protect the surviving people.

Only a few of the Claws remained at the clubhouse to look through the files. The silence was chilling. Alec hated how their good intentions had turned people in need into Sterling's targets.

We're going to make this right.

Alec pulled up a new set of files and let his decryption program run, changing the view so he could look at the code directly. Diving into code to distract himself from the negativity of his reality was an old trick he'd perfected since he was a kid. Concentrating on coding helped him hide from his family's disapproval. Later, reading about code in stolen library books distracted him from hunger pangs as a homeless, transgender teen on the run. As a black hat hacker, he dove into code to distance himself from thinking too deeply about the impact of the hacking jobs he took to survive. It was so easy in those years to be like Roxanne, to view each job as inevitable. Somebody was going to be hired to get the job done, so why shouldn't he profit? He'd hack into a system, pull some data, leave a virus, or simply cause enough mischief and mockery that Alec's client could do... whatever they wanted to do. Roxanne taught Alec not to ask questions, so he stuck to the coding and tried not to think about the horrors his clients could wreck with the information he'd stolen.

Until he couldn't ignore it anymore. Too many nights he woke up screaming at the imagined blood dripping from his hands. He knew he had to disappear and find a different life. He hacked into the High Council's computers on a whim and discovered the thorn in their side: The Iron Claws. Alec searched surveillance footage from bank CCTVs to ATM cameras, and in less than a month, he found Big Joe. Every day since was wiping away a little bit more of that blood.

The program in front of him beeped that it had completed the decryption. He jumped.

Time to focus, he thought.

It took him a long moment to realize what he was looking at: schematics for Penelope's EMP curse device. Roxanne had hacked Penelope's computer before the Council burned all the hard drives. Alec felt rage bubble in his chest. The succubus should know better than to come after somebody he cared about.

The schematics to Penelope's invention beckoned to him from the screen, making him forget about Roxanne. The EMP curse was a beautiful combination of hardware and magic that he hadn't believed could exist together until he saw it for himself.

The woman was a genius.

He rubbed between his eyes. Tonight's date needed to be perfect. He'd already flown over gifts to her motel: a bouquet of flowers, and special blood-filled chocolates he'd commissioned from Ned. It had been tricky to keep the cargo intact, clutched in his dragon claws, but he couldn't help himself.

"Hey, space cadet." Nina elbowed Alec. "Wanna help me out here?"

Alec jumped. He'd been so deep in his own thoughts he'd nearly forgotten she was there. "Yep, yep, I'm working." He unplugged the drive of EMP schematics and placed it in the discard pile. "Nothing about Puff or Sterling on this one."

Nina handed him another of the drives she'd cleaned up. "Uh huh," she said in a doubting tone. "Where's your head at, today?" She loaded up more of Roxanne's files on her computer projecting the images onto the wall behind her for the other Claws to look over. Alec was eternally grateful Nina had been one of Caesar's groupies back in the day and the two managed to reconnect last year and fall in love. As the club's resident hardware genius, if anyone could recover hidden data in Roxanne's files, it would be Nina.

The sound of motorcycles roared up from outside and Alec grinned. The rest of the Claws were coming back from arranging the protective details for their remaining Puff patients. Caesar, Dylan, and Marie entered first, Caesar immediately walking over to Nina to kiss her.

He murmured something low in her ear and she blushed, pushing him away playfully.

"Well, maybe I'll have a chance," she said to Caesar, "if *somebody*," Nina mock-glared at Alec, "would get his head in the game."

"Go easy on him, mi amor." Caesar wrapped a tattooed arm around his fiancée. "Can't you see he's distracted by his girlfriend?" Caesar sang the last word out in a perfect schoolyard taunt.

"Oooooo," Dylan chimed in from where he was rifling through some print outs.

Marie stood next to Dylan, her arm linked around his waist. She sang, "Alec and Penelope sittin' in a tree."

Alec beamed. "Oh, yes, please continue teasing me for dating a smokin' hot vampire." He sighed sarcastically. "You cut me deep."

Chuckles broke out across the room. Alec grinned. Everyone being able to joke again gave Alec hope that perhaps they'd actually get away from Sterling in one piece.

Big Joe swung open both doors of the Iron Claws' clubhouse as he entered, slamming the doors against the walls with a bang. Emma walked at his side holding a stack of folders.

"Listen up, Claws," Emma said. "We...borrowed these

from the morgue." Emma handed the files to Dylan. "Take a look at these. See if there's anything fishy going on."

Dylan thumbed through a stack of files, pulling out the pictures of the deceased for himself and handing the medical records to his wife. "From what Alec learned from the succubus, we're pretty sure Sterling is behind all this. If he's a professional..." Dylan rummaged through the first aid kit and pulled out a magnifying glass. "Yup. Injection site under the fingernail." He held the photo up, pointing to a tiny, red pinprick on the corpse's hand. "The medical examiner wouldn't have spotted this unless she was looking for it."

"Between that and Roxanne hacking into the hospital records for Sterling, I think it's pretty safe to say that Puff isn't harming anybody," Alec said. The wave of relief he'd been holding back ever since he began to suspect the truth in the coffee shop washed over him.

"That's it!" Nina said. She pointed at a file on her screen and a second later it projected onto the wall behind her. "Roxanne has been sending a ton of information--patient records, streaming surveillance feeds--over to Sterling. She's still in contact with him, right?"

Excitement zinged through him like electricity.

"Nina, you're a genius!" Alec bounded back over to his computer.

"This I have often been told," Nina said with a grin.

"Alec, fill me in." Big Joe looked at the laptop over Alec's shoulder, squinting his eyes at the fast-moving keystrokes.

"I hacked Roxanne's computer earlier today. If I can exploit that connection, I should be able to view all incoming *and* outgoing traffic, and I can drop in a nice virus that will stop her from helping Sterling."

Big Joe stared.

"I can find Sterling's computer by tracking the information sent from Roxanne's computer. Once I find it, I can hack into Sterling's system which should give us access to..." Alec could feel the corners of his mouth ache from smiling so wide. "...*everything.* Joe, we can see all the shady crap the Red Guard is doing: what they've done, what they're planning to do. If this works, we *own them.*"

Big Joe's mouth hung open. "Shit." He finally spoke. "Yeah, let's do that."

PENELOPE DISMOUNTED from the back of Alec's bike, looking up at where he'd stopped. "Don't tell me a *planetarium* is making you so excited."

The domed building was dark at this hour, the employees and visitors long gone. Alec pulled off his helmet, grinning wildly.

"I'm stoked about tonight, but I'm more excited about Sterling."

"What could possibly be exciting about that murderous creep?" Alec had filled her in on what Sterling had been up to during the drive over. It made her skin crawl to think of how anyone would go so far as to enforce such an outdated High Council rule. *Kill people? Just to keep Puff away from humans?* She was almost happy Sterling had come after her: it gave Penelope a chance to be part of taking him down. After she published her findings on the restorative effects of Puff on humans, the covens and clans would all be clamoring for it for their human friends. The High Council was going to have a much bigger problem than the Iron Claws.

She followed Alec to the front door, which opened easily

under his hand. She raised an eyebrow at him as he held the door open for her.

"Electric locks." He followed her inside. "I *may* have hacked their security and unlocked the door before we showed up." He shrugged, his smile a little smug.

She punched his arm lightly. "Don't get cocky, it's not attractive."

"No danger of that." Alec took her arm, leading her down the dark hallway. "Not only am I *extremely* attractive, I don't have a cock." Penelope knew a test when she heard one. *How many other dates couldn't deal with the difference between his appearance and the man inside?*

"So?" Something in her casual tone must have mollified him because he stood up a little straighter. Penelope waved her arm across the shadowy hallway. "I thought this was a date. I figured you'd take me a nice restaurant or something."

"Nervous? I thought vampires had perfect night vision."

"We do, but after what happened back at the lab, I gotta say I'm developing a fear of hallways."

"Just a little farther." He gave her arm a reassuring squeeze, as he pushed open the doors to the auditorium.

Penelope's breath caught.

The lights in the planetarium were already lit, projecting a swirling array of stars across the ceiling in dizzying patterns. Lasers played through the air, lighting up constellations and crisscrossing into mesmerizing shapes. Soft music played an instrumental cover of OneRepublic's "Counting Stars" over the speakers. A wide platform divided the upper and lower stadium-style seating, and in the center Alec had set up a picnic blanket and pillows. He'd even included a vase of roses to complete the romantic setting.

"Do you like it?" he asked.

It was like something out of a fairy tale. "Fuck me with a fairy wand." She sighed.

"Is that an invitation?" Alec chuckled.

Penelope blushed. "I just meant that this is all amazing. I curse elaborately when I'm overwhelmed. Bog says it's one of my--" She made finger quotes. "'Coping mechanisms'."

Alec chuckled. "My coping mechanism usually involves hacking into someone's computer to discover all of their secrets."

"When mine is fixed, feel free to hack whatever you like." Penelope turned to him. "Is that how you found out about Sterling?"

"I got to him by hacking one of his minions, but same difference." He led her to the blanket and sat down.

Penelope sank down beside him. His smile was so joyous, she wanted to capture it and hold it like a firefly in a jar.

"But I don't want to talk about Sterling and murder," he said. "I want to talk about you." He reached into a basket and brought out a bottle. "Dinner for you: A Negative." He pulled out a wine glass, filled it with the rich, dark liquid, and handed it to her. She sniffed it: it was fresh enough to still have a lingering sense of the source (male, wolf shifter, loyal and overwhelmingly in love with his mate), but not so old that it tasted metallic. She drank deep.

He reached into the basket and brought out a sandwich. "I wanted to make a fancy, romantic-looking meal for you, but I'm not the cook in the clan. I hope you're not disappointed."

"I'm glad that there's one thing you can't do. And I don't eat food so this works out great." Penelope lifted her glass and tapped it against the side of his sandwich. "Cheers. My A Negative is perfect." The warm blood worked its way through her body, making her feel energized and alive. Alec was wearing a button-down shirt over his jeans. He looked *good*.

"How did you know A Negative is my favorite?" She licked her lips. The scent of the blood filled her nostrils and the back of her throat, overpowering the enticing smell of Alec's blood pulsing under his neck.

Alec tapped his nose. "A guy never reveals his sources. Takes away his entire air of mystery."

Penelope smiled. "Which means that Bog told you. I swear my assistant wants me to date more than I do."

"You don't want to date?"

"It's not something I have much time for." Penelope shrugged. "I spend twelve to thirteen hours a day in the lab, and when I'm not there, I'm usually thinking about my experiments."

"That's not a *bad* thing. You care about your work," he said.

"It's not great for my social life. You'd be surprised how many guys suddenly have someplace else to be when I start lecturing about the chemical components of gryphon feathers versus fairy dust."

He lounged along the blanket, resting his weight on his elbow. "And what are the chemical components of gryphon feathers versus fairy dust?"

"Well, gryphon feathers aren't actually feathers; they're elemental particles that can break down solid matter on a quantum level once they're disconnected from a gryphon's body. They just happen to bond together into the shape of feathers, while fairy dust..."

Penelope looked back at Alec and he was much closer than she remembered. His nose was a few inches from hers, his enticing lips barely a breath away. She could see each pulse of blood through his veins, calling to her, sending a flush of heat from her chest all the way down to between her legs.

"But you're just being polite." Penelope looked away, blushing. "Nobody actually cares about this stuff."

Alec tilted his head to the side. "You have obviously been hanging out around the wrong people. I think you're fascinating. In fact, I think you're the most fascinating person I've ever met." He leaned forward and Penelope felt her pulse speed up. "You're extraordinary." Penelope's body inched forward, drawn to him like a magnet. "Beautiful." His lips were so close, the heat so palpable, Penelope thought her whole body might catch on fire if he didn't kiss her. "A light I never expected in my life."

"Fucking hell." Penelope grabbed the back of Alec's head and pulled him on top of her, loving the feel of his weight pressing her into the blanket. His hands slid up and down her waist, lifting her legs up to wrap around his hips. His lips covered hers, his tongue probing into her mouth. The feeling of him was perfect. His hands expertly found every sensitive spot, making her squirm under him, wanting more.

Penelope fangs started to descend, their sharp points longing to drill into his flesh. She forced them back, pulling away slightly from Alec's intoxicating smell.

"What? Too fast?" Alec asked. He pushed a strand of her hair away from her face, the gesture so touching Penelope almost cried. He started to sit up, but Penelope grabbed him, holding him close.

"No! Not too fast. I was just about to bite you, and I wasn't sure how you'd react." She looked away. "It's a vampire thing. Sex and blood...I tend to drink when I'm, um, aroused."

Alec grinned. "Aroused you already, have I?" He kissed her, his tongue playing along the top of her teeth. "It's okay to bite me. I'm glad I'm not the only one going crazy." His hand slipped under Penelope's shirt, his fingers playing across her skin. She pulled off her shirt, throwing her bra across the room. He stared at her breasts hungrily for a second before diving down to play along her nipples with his tongue. Penelope writhed under his touch. His mouth was amazing.

"Holy crap, they're even better than I imagined," he said, his lips firmly around her breast.

"Think about my rack a lot?" Penelope asked, arching her back to bring her chest closer to his lips. His tongue played against the tip, sucking and then gently nibbling, teasing her until her whole body thrummed to the rhythm of his mouth.

"Maybe. Sometimes." His tone was too innocent and Penelope laughed. "You're distracting," he said, his fingers tickling the soft skin beneath her breasts and along the sides. She squirmed against him, needing to feel more of his skin against hers.

She pulled at his shirt, vampiric strength making short work of his buttons as the fabric ripped open. Some kind of binding held his breasts tight against his body, the fabric unsuccessfully hiding his curves. She reached for the laces and he grabbed her hands, holding them above her head.

"Let's keep that on, shall we?" he said, leaning down to kiss the side of her neck. It felt amazing, but Penelope shifted until she could turn her head to look up into his face.

"Why don't you want me to look at you?"

"It's not the real me," he said.

"It's your body." She leaned up to slide her face against

his, feeling the soft hairs rubbing against her skin. Her hands flexed against his shoulders. "It might not reflect your soul, but it's how I can be...physically...closer to you." She wasn't going to touch anywhere he didn't want her to, but all of her ached to have Alec naked with her, unbound and free.

"There are other ways for us to be close," Alec whispered into her skin. "But I would need some things I don't have here."

"Like a strap-on?" Penelope said excitedly, leaning up quickly and reaching for her purse. "I did some reading up before our date, and then went to visit the sex shop downtown to get us some options." Her hand fished deep into the near bottomless recesses of her magical bag, pulling out a couple of different harness styles in leather, and then five different dildos, two realistic models of a penis (one including an anatomically-accurate scrotum), another a vibrating rod with rotating beads inside, another a ribbed plastic pillar, and lastly--in case they were feeling whimsical--a bright green, thick cock the woman at the store had called "The Hulk".

"Wow, you really went all out." Alec picked up the vibrating dildo and pressed a button. A small attachment flipped up from either side for dual clit stimulation. "These are awesome."

"Do you have a preference?" Penelope gestured to the harness and dildos.

Alec lifted the one that looked like a purple banana with smooth, plastic ridges all along the sides. Penelope noted with disappointment it wasn't the one with the rotating beads, but she eyed the ridges on Alec's selection with a wetness already growing between her legs. She could easily imagine each ridge's effect as it entered her over and over. Alec lifted it up with one hand and the realistic penis-shaped dildo with the other. He leaned close and kissed her.

"Which turns you on?" Alec whispered, running the two dildos across Penelope's stomach. Penelope didn't think she could be more aroused, but her hips unconsciously thrust up toward him. She grabbed the ridged dildo and pressed it to Alec's chest. She eyed the harness still laying on the blanket.

"Have you worn one of these before?" she asked.

Alec nodded. "I left it at home. Didn't seem gentlemanly to assume you'd want to go that far on the first date." He kissed her again, licking along her lips and then leaning down to lock his lips around her breast again. "Not that I'm complaining."

Penelope moaned. Her canines had extended far enough down to prick her bottom lip, but she knew she wouldn't be able to retract now. She needed Alec inside her too badly.

"So what were you thinking you'd do if things started to get physical?" she gasped. Her whole body ached for release.

"That's easy," Alec said, lifting his head from her breast to grin at her widely. "I would have eaten your pussy until you came so hard you couldn't walk."

"For the love of all fucks," Penelope panted. "Fuck me now." She was beyond all foreplay. She clawed at Alec's clothes, pushing the harness and dildo into his hands as she threw off her pants.

By the time she'd pulled off her underwear, Alec had gotten his pants off and positioned the dildo into the harness. He still wore the binding across his chest, but Penelope no longer cared.

She lay on her back, spreading her legs wide for Alec to

bend over her. His fingers gently probed into her wetness, licking the moisture off of his fingers.

"You're already so wet," he said, his voice filled with wonder. He flexed his hips, the tip of the dildo sliding between Penelope's wet lips. She lifted her waist to take it deeper, the length sliding against her clit, her cunt sucking at it. Penelope reached up to grab Alec's ass to pull him deeper, lifting her legs higher on his back. He slid in deep and she cried out at the marvelous feeling of the ridges rubbing her most sensitive places.

"Yes! Yes!" she screamed.

Alec pressed down, rocking her body until they found a rhythm. Just when Penelope thought she was going to crest, she leaned up and bit down hard into Alec's shoulder, sucking his blood, letting his essence wash over her: male, dragon, strong, open and kind, aroused with a passion that made Penelope's heart pound. Beneath it all was something more, a deeper feeling Penelope recognized as a mirror to the love growing in her own heart. She came screaming his name, followed seconds later by Alec.

Penelope came back to herself slowly. Above them, the domed screen dazzled with planets and stars swirling in a majestic dance. She turned over to see Alec looking at her.

"What is it?" Penelope asked, tucking her hair behind her ear. "Do I have something on my face?"

"I was just thinking..." He hesitated. "You were the last thing I ever expected." Alec's voice was low.

"What do you mean?" Penelope leaned forward, resting her head against his shoulder.

"Before I met you, I'd accepted that I was always going to be alone. I was going to be the last solo Iron Claw riding around distributing Puff after everyone else paired off and left. I never thought I could find somebody like you."

Penelope kissed him gently. "Me neither. I figured I didn't have time for both a profession and passion."

Alec sat up onto one elbow, looking down. "It's still not going to be easy. We both have intense lives, with a lot of demands and loyalties."

"I know," Penelope said. "I think I'm falling in love with you." Her voice was almost a whisper. "That's something worth prioritizing."

Alec smiled into her hair and kissed her. "I'm falling in love with you too. But the rest of the world isn't going to wait for us." He sat up, reaching for his shirt and handing her the clothing closest at hand. "We should get dressed. There's Sterling to take down, and the High Council goons will be after us and--"

"Yeah, yeah, you don't have to be right *all* the time." Penelope grabbed her pants from him. Her underwear was somewhere under the chairs and she didn't feel like searching for them. "It might be your only major personality flaw."

Alec grinned, finishing buckling up his belt. "Well, that's one flaw I'm sorry to say that is never going to change. Being told I'm right fuels my superpower, you know. Every time someone says it, I become five times stronger."

Penelope laughed.

A crash and a bang echoed through the planetarium and the front doors to the auditorium ripped open.

Roxanne stood between the doors, the gun in her hand pointed directly at Alec's chest.

"What the fuck did you do to my computer, Alec?" she cried.

∾

THE LIGHTS SWIRLING around the planetarium sparkled off the silver plating of Roxanne's gun. Alec pulled Penelope behind him, broadening his stance to be as effective a shield as possible.

"You're going to shoot me for messing with your computer? You were helping the Red Guard *murder* innocent people!" He shouted. "Did you honestly think I was just going to sit by and let that happen?" Alec tried to subtly maneuver Penelope towards the emergency exit, careful to keep himself between Penelope and the gun.

"Stop right there." The click of the pistol being cocked sent a shockwave of adrenaline through Alec's system.

"Stop this," Penelope said from behind Alec. "Shooting Alec isn't going to fix your computer."

"But it will sure as hell will make me feel better." Roxanne held the gun steadily pointed at Alec's chest, supported with both hands, feet placed in a wide stance. "Now tell me what happened to my files, or I start redecorating this place in arterial red."

Alec's breath caught. The Roxanne he had known all those years ago hadn't been a killer. But from her stance, she was clearly an experienced shooter.

Alec swiftly catalogued his abilities. Speed, strength, fire. The planetarium was too small for him to fully shift into a dragon without hurting Penelope, but that didn't mean he was powerless. In an instant, red scales rippled across his neck, his face stretched and morphed, transforming into a dragon from the top of his chest, just enough to include the well of fire in his lungs. He pushed Penelope further behind him and breathed a fireball at Roxanne before the succubus could pull the trigger. She rolled out of the way at the last second, avoiding the flame by mere inches.

"You asshole!" Roxanne shouted, lifting the gun once more.

Alec let loose another fireball, burning Roxanne's outstretched hands. The gun clattered to the floor, and Penelope ran forward to kick it far down the planetarium's stadium seating.

Roxanne dove at the vampire, grabbing Penelope by the arm and pulling her close. "Watch it with those fireballs, lizard." Roxanne sneered. "You wouldn't want to hurt your girlfriend." A cool, blue mist started to emerge from Roxanne's skin as she stroked Penelope's arms. The succubus's magic rose like an aura from Roxanne's skin to float along Penelope's shoulders, making the vampire moan and lean into Roxanne's touch. An excited blush overtook Penelope's torso. Where the blue mist touched, Alec could see little goosebumps form on Penelope's skin.

"Good girl," Roxanne purred. She spun Penelope around and captured her mouth with her own. Roxanne's tongue visibly darted into Penelope's welcoming mouth. Roxanne broke away, hatefully glaring at Alec. "Penelope, smack yourself in the face."

Like she was in a trance, Penelope's hand swung back to connect with her own cheek. The slap echoed off the starry walls of the planetarium, making Alec jump. He lurched forward on instinct, knowing he couldn't cover the fifteen yards between them before Roxanne commanded Penelope to hurt herself again.

"Penelope!" Alec's heart raced as panic began to set in. A succubus's touch was almost unbeatable. "You have to fight it!" He ran forward, but Roxanne grabbed a dagger from her boot and handed it to Penelope. Penelope was shaking, fangs protruding.

"Slice yourself if he comes a step closer," Roxanne commanded.

Momentum made Alec's foot fall another step before he stopped and Penelope sliced a long cut along her chin, blood dripping onto the floor.

"No!" he yelled.

"Stay back!" Roxanne shouted. "Unless you want her to start carving limericks into her neck."

"Leave her out of this!" Alec's voice rumbled out darkly, his head and neck still shifted to dragon form. "What do you want?"

"When you dropped that virus on my computer, you destroyed some very important files." She glared at Alec. "I need those back. Now."

"Back off and we can talk."

"You're no fun anymore." Roxanne shoved Penelope to the ground, taking her dagger back. Penelope started to crawl away, but Roxanne smashed down a stiletto heel onto Penelope's back. "Don't go anywhere, sweets. Your boyfriend and I aren't done talking." Penelope stilled, but out of the corner of his eye, Alec could see Penelope's fingers twitch. When Roxanne dropped her, she'd freed Penelope's hands from her control.

"What's so important about these files?" Alec asked.

He forced himself to back up slowly, drawing Roxanne's eyes away from Penelope's subtle exploration of the depths of her bag. *I've got to keep Roxanne distracted,* Alec thought. He walked backward until he was near the planetarium room controls.

"I made copies of everything before I dropped that virus. I can grab whatever you need, there's no reason to bring a gun into this. We can talk this through like old friends," Alec said.

"As if that means anything," Roxanne spat.

"What's all this about?" He was so close to the panel, he just needed to keep her distracted for a few more seconds. "What does Sterling have on you?"

There! He flipped the switch, killing the laser show and bringing up the house lights to full strength. Roxanne blinked, stumbling back a second in the sudden glare. Penelope swung into action, pulling a black cylinder with blinking lights out of her bag and pressing it against the exposed skin of the succubus's midriff. The smell of ozone filled the room as it burned against Roxanne's skin, and Roxanne flailed, knocking Penelope away. Penelope quickly grabbed a vial of blood from her bag and downed it fast.

"Bitch!" Roxanne spat. "Go throw yourself down the stairs."

The blood was already working. Blue smoke dissipated from beneath Penelope's skin as she stood in defiance of the succubus's command. "You can't control me anymore!" Penelope shouted. The cuts on her face started to close up like they were never there.

The lights overhead sputtered and shut off. Even the emergency track lighting and exits signs flickered off.

Penelope grinned wildly. "Actually, you're not going to be controlling anything for a long time."

Roxanne brandished her dagger at Alec and Penelope. "I hate to break it to you, sweetheart, but it takes a lot more than a taser to take me down."

Penelope smiled. "That was no taser. Look at your phone."

Roxanne raised a suspicious eyebrow, but kept her weapon in a firm grip. "Okay, I'll play." She pulled her cell phone from the inside pocket of her jacket. Roxanne jumped back as the phone sparked in her hand, shooting out blue flares of electricity into the air. "What the fuck?" She tossed the phone to the ground. "You broke my phone? Seriously? Do you really think that's going to stop me?"

"Actually, that's just a little preview of what will happen every time you get near anything electronic for the rest of your life," Penelope said. "I just hit you with an EMP curse. No more hacking, no more texting. Heck, no more TV."

"I'm sensing a 'but'," Roxanne said, her lips pressed thin.

"You have information we need, we have information you need," Penelope said. "Tell us everything you know about Sterling, and we'll tell you the counter curse."

"Alec has copies of everything. I've done my part already. Now give me the damn counter curse!" Roxanne yelled.

"Come on, Rox. You always dig up dirt on your clients in case you need the leverage and we both know information like that isn't going to be just sitting on your laptop. You've got it stashed somewhere," Alec said.

Roxanne experimentally touched the track lighting along the planetarium's steep stairs. It sparked in response to her touch. "Fuck, you guys weren't messing around." She sighed, pulling a small notebook with a tiny pencil from her pocket. "Fine. Since we're such *good friends*. There's a jump drive hidden in a book in the municipal library. This--" She handed the paper to Penelope. "Is the title and the Dewey Decimal number. It's all in there." Roxanne quickly pocketed the notebook. "Are we done now? Can you get this damn curse off of me?"

"It's going to be a little more difficult than that." Penelope gently took the dagger from Roxanne's hand, exchanging it for a small stack of papers she'd pulled from her purse. "Here's all my research on the counter curse. With some time, you should be able to figure it out."

"Pleasure doing business with you," Roxanne said

through gritted teeth. She backed toward the door, taking a moment to run her hand along Alec's laptop bag next to the toppled picnic basket. Smoke rose from the small sack, wafting up towards where the stars once shone.

"Oh, come on!" Alec yelled after her.

"Something to remember me by," She flipped him the bird as she sashayed out the door.

Alec and Penelope let out long breaths of relief. The lights flickered back on as soon as Roxanne was out the door.

"That actually went way better than I expected," Penelope said.

ALEC'S SCALES felt warm under Penelope's hands as they flew. He'd taken the scenic route back to the Iron Claws' clubhouse. Far below, all Penelope could see was rolling hills with little spots of light from cabins and flickering glows from campfires. Misty clouds floated all around them, turning the night into a surreal painting of spirals and refracted shapes.

"I called my assistant, Bog, before we left. She said 'hi.'"

Alec chuckled, the rumbling sound sending vibrations through his body and between Penelope's thighs. "From my brief conversation with Bog setting up our date, I bet she said a lot more than 'hi'."

"She had a question or two." After Bog's initial shock about hearing what happened to their lab, she had plenty to say. Bog's exact questions had been, "How big is his dragon dong? Dinosaur porn big? Sperm whale big? When can I see him?" Penelope wasn't going to ask him the last. She wasn't sure when *she* was going to see him again. "Bog hasn't met many dragon shifters, so she's curious."

"I'd be happy to answer any questions she has when I meet her," he said.

"You say that like you're not leaving to fight the High Council," Penelope said in a low voice, half afraid how he was going to reply. After what Sterling and the Council did, the Iron Claws would have to fight or flee. From how Alec described them, they didn't seem like the running kind.

"I've been thinking about that," he said. "Hold on."

Penelope tightened her grip and squeezed hard around his back with her thighs as he tilted down and to the right, descending toward the top of a hill peeking out from the clouds.

Alec was silent as they landed. A thick carpet of grass and wildflowers covered the top of the hill before the ground swiftly dropped off a steep cliff. A lone tree grew along the edge, strong roots anchoring it to the side. Penelope swung her leg over to dismount from Alec's back and he raised one of his front feet to help her down. She smiled.

"Always so chivalrous." Penelope untied the bag secured around one of Alec's dragon legs and handed it to him.

Alec shrugged and walked over to the tree. "Give me one second, I'd rather not have this conversation as a quadruped." The tree was too small to actually give him much privacy, so Penelope turned away as she heard the squish and crackle of Alec transforming back to his human form, and the swish of clothes as he got dressed.

The clouds below the cliffs shifted and she could see a clump of lights from a campsite. At least five groups were all camping within a few feet of each other. Penelope had never gone camping--she couldn't quite get over her seventeenth-century mindset that sleeping outdoors was for outlaws and the hygienically insane--but being outside surrounded by friends looked like fun.

She blinked away tears. She didn't blame Alec for being part of the events that destroyed her lab: her second home. Having him in her life had opened her eyes to how isolated she had become. She has assumed that it would be enough to have work to provide purpose, and her assistant for companionship. But there was a source of additional joy she had been avoiding for these last centuries since her brother rejected her: love.

And he was leaving.

She wasn't sure she'd be able to be content again now that she'd tasted what it felt like to have so much more.

"It's okay, you can turn around now," his voice said from behind her.

He was wearing the same outfit he wore when they first met. His battered leather jacket, blue shirt, and jeans were so very *him* that Penelope felt her heart breaking all over again at the thought that she might never see him again.

She crossed her arms tight across her chest. If this was when he told her he had to leave her forever, she wasn't going to embarrass herself by running into his arms. Penelope *hated* feeling so uncertain.

"What did you want to talk about, Alec?" she asked.

"I wanted to tell you how sorry I am about what happened to your lab," he said, stepping toward her. "And at the planetarium. I never wanted to put you in danger like that."

Penelope shook her head. "That wasn't your fault. That was Sterling, Roxanne, and the dicks in the High Council. I'm only sorry that I wasn't able to help more."

"That's one of the other things I wanted to talk to you about." He took another step closer. "You are the most brilliant person I've ever met. I know you've been through a lot already, but I *also* know how tough you are. If you're still interested in helping, then I have a lot of ideas for how your knowledge and gadgets could give us the upper hand against the Council."

Penelope uncrossed her arms, hope beginning to stir in her chest. He wanted her to keep helping, which would mean he would have to stay in touch. "Those sons-of-a-mergoat burned down my lab. I will do whatever it takes to stop them."

Alec chuckled. "That's another thing I'd stick around for: nobody can curse quite like you."

Did I hear him right? "You're staying?"

"If you don't mind having me around," he said. "The last few days showed me the kind of connection that was possible between two people. I don't want to walk away from that." He closed the space between them, his hands gently rubbing her shoulders. "I can't walk away from you."

"Technically, I think you were going to *fly* away from me." Penelope felt like fairy dust was blinking and singing inside her chest. *He wants to stay!*

She wrapped her arms around his shoulders, pulling him tight. His arms slid around her waist, roaming lower to cup her ass and draw her closer. Penelope felt a zing of need flow through her and she moaned, pressing herself closer and turning her head to inhale the sweet smell of his blood pulsing in his neck. What a difference from the fake lust from Roxanne's magic. Just thinking about the woman made Penelope's skin crawl.

"I thought about asking you to ride with me and the Iron Claws," he said, his hands reaching up to caress her hair and the base of her neck. "But it's really difficult to conduct delicate scientific research from the seat of a motorcycle.

Besides, I can pull intel and hack for the Claws from anywhere. If they get into trouble, that's what wings are for."

Penelope snuggled closer. "I guess I can stand to have you underfoot."

He leaned back to look at her face. "I love you, Dr. Penelope O'Hara. I know we've only known each other a few days, but I already know that I want to spend the rest of my life with you."

"I love you too, Mister Alec Harker," she said, her voice breaking with the amount of emotion pushing against her tongue. "And I want you at my side for however long fate gives us."

Penelope wasn't sure who moved first, but Alec's lips were on hers, his tongue probing the inside of her mouth as Penelope felt her body open to his. His body felt so *right* against hers, the smell of his blood washing over her and through her like a healing and calming balm. She gripped his shoulders hard, her skin beginning to prickle and warm.

"I still have the dildos in my purse," she said. Her canines were beginning to descend as her arousal grew, their delicate prick pressing against the soft skin of Alec's neck. He groaned, his hips grinding against hers.

"I want to, love." He moaned again, his hands reaching down to squeeze her ass. "You have no idea how much I want to just lay you down on this grass and spread your legs wide." He licked the tip of her earlobe and she gasped. "I want to lick your sweet pussy until you lose control and scream my name hoarse." His fingers reached up under her shirt to play with the skin on her stomach, his hands moving upward so slowly she wanted to rip off all of her clothes and demand he get on with it.

"Then do it," she moaned, her hands already unbuckling his pants. He reached down to stop her.

"Not yet. The Iron Claws are waiting for us. If we take much longer, they're going to come searching for us." He kissed her swiftly and stepped back. "And you don't know how fast a romantic mood dies until Caesar flies up and starts singing One Hundred Bottles of Beer at the top of his lungs."

"I guess," Penelope grumbled. She still ached for him. "We could mess around at least a little..."

Alec jumped back, his eyes laughing. "You have no idea how aroused and gorgeous you look like right now. Trust me, if I wasn't sure we'd be interrupted, I wouldn't take my hands off of you. But the second we get to the clubhouse and we've checked in, we're locking the door and celebrating our future *many times*." He grabbed his bag of clothes and disappeared around the tree to transform back into his dragon form.

As soon as his large, red form appeared, Penelope ran forward to launch herself onto his back.

"The sooner we get to the clubhouse, the sooner we can bone. So leg it," she said.

Alec laughed. "Yes, ma'am." He kicked off hard and the ground fell away beneath them. "Hold on tight. We're going full speed."

Penelope hadn't realized how slowly he'd been flying before until he zoomed forward with the force of a rocket. The scientist in her immediately started calculating speed and distance compared to his wing to body ratio. She leaned forward until her entire body was flush with the top of his back, turning her head away from the roar of the wind. From the speed of the ground below them, they had to be going hundreds of miles an hour, but the ride was so smooth it was like a bubble of cushioned air around him cradled and protected her. Penelope smiled. She loved magic.

It felt like just a few minutes before Penelope felt a change in Alec's wing beats. They were slowing down.

"What's wrong?" she asked.

"I smell smoke."

Penelope craned her head around, looking for a source, but the clouds still blocked her view of the ground.

"Alec! Thank the gods you're okay!" A whoosh of wind and a grey dragon appeared flying next to them. The scent from a cut along the dragon's side told Penelope all she needed to know about her: female, caring, trained warrior, scared.

Alec changed course to fly beside her. "Emma, what happened? Is everyone okay?"

Penelope remembered Alec mentioning Emma: the only female dragon shifter in the Iron Claws. She was the strongest fighter in the bunch. If she was scared, then something terrible had happened.

Emma's reptilian mouth twisted into a frown. "Dylan is wounded, but Marie is patching him up. It's the clubhouse. Follow me." She turned and Alec followed behind her, the two dragons descending toward the ground. Once they got closer, Penelope could smell burning wood, followed a second later by the bright blaze of a two-story building in flames.

The memory of her burning lab struck her like a blow. She felt Alec still under her and she knew exactly the kind of sorrow he had to be feeling. Men and women covered in soot were pacing and shouting angrily. One man with long dreadlocks was lying on the ground, his entire side was covered in a large burn, while a curvy dark-haired woman poured disinfectant on his wound. Motorcycles in various states of damage lay behind them. The largest man there, his deep, brown skin covered in layers of sweat and ash, stepped toward them.

"Alec, I'm so glad you're safe." He lay a hand against Alec's shoulder and took a deep breath. "When we couldn't get in touch with you, we feared the worst. Ned and his family are flying in now. We need to stick together."

Alec nodded. "We're going to be okay, Big Joe." He lifted his voice to the group. "Everyone, this is Dr. Penelope O'Hara. My mate."

Penelope felt a blush pool in her cheeks. She nodded to the rest of the Iron Claws as everyone suddenly turned to look her over. "It's nice to meet all of you." She glanced at the burning club house. "I wish it was under better circumstances."

A heavily tattooed man walked forward to help her off of Alec's back. "I'm Caesar. I'm sure Alec has told you about my handsomeness and excellent singing voice."

Penelope smiled. "He's told me many things about you, but somehow never mentioned any of those things."

Big Joe stepped forward to pull Caesar away from her. "We have more important things to discuss." He walked over to the wounded man, Dylan, and gestured for everyone else to gather around. "By poisoning the humans we have helped, burning Dr. O'Hara's lab, and then attacking our home, Sterling and the High Dragon Council have declared war. There is no line they won't cross, and they are willing to throw all of their resources into wiping us off the map. We have two options: run or fight. And I'm done running."

Emma, still in her grey dragon form, moved forward. "So am I."

The rest of the Iron Claws stepped up, pledging the same, until only Alec was left. He turned to Penelope.

"You pledged that you wanted to be with me, but I won't hold you to that promise. Whatever comes next is going to be dangerous, worse than anything we've faced together in the last few days. You should leave. This isn't your fight."

Penelope pressed a hand to the bright, red scales of his face. "This was my fight from the moment those fuckers came after me. But even if they hadn't, you're my family now. I'm going to stick by you no matter what."

Alec said nothing, just leaned forward to press the smooth scales of his cheek against her for a long moment. Then he stepped forward toward Big Joe and the assembled Iron Claws.

"We will fight. The High Council must be stopped before it destroys any more lives. "

Big Joe nodded. He stood straight, but his expression looked sad as his eyes fixed on their burning home.

"The Iron Claws are at war."

The Iron Claws face down the Dragon High Council once and for all in the final installment of the _Her Biker Dragon_ series: _Her Alpha Dragon_. Big Joe and Emma, meanwhile, face an even more terrifying challenge: their love for each other.

HER ALPHA DRAGON

The wedding was a blur of joyful faces, but Joe Silver, called Big Joe by his friends, kept feeling his smile slip. He was thrilled that his fellow Iron Claw, Caesar, was finally marrying the woman of his dreams, grateful that all of the members of the motorcycle club had survived so many battles against the Dragon High Council, and happy that almost all of the Iron Claws had found their life-long mates despite the omnipresent danger.

Caesar's wedding celebrated the deep love Caesar found with Nina after so many years of pining. But Joe also saw it as a testament to the team's good fortune that they were all still together, continuing to pursue their mission to distribute Puff, the healing drug made from ground dragon scales, to humans against all opposition.

Yet Joe still couldn't shake off the melancholy that clung onto his shoulders like a misty rain. He hated weddings.

"Come on," a husky voice broke him from the haze. "Caesar will think you're not dancing because you hate his music." Emma Hernandez, his fellow Iron Claw, held out a hand, nodding toward the packed dance floor. The wedding wasn't very large, only about fifty of Caesar's friends, mostly various musicians he'd worked with throughout the years on the road. Colorful lights swirled around the increasingly-intoxicated crowd all grooving to the music of Caesar's band.

Joe didn't have to force the smile that always appeared when Emma was around. Just having her nearby helped shrug off his wedding blues.

"He already knows I don't like his music," Joe said in his grumpiest voice. "A third grader could write better lyrics."

Emma laughed. "Fine. Don't do it for Caesar, do it for me. You're my best partner." She coughed. "Dance partner. Obviously, is what I meant."

The wet weight of melancholy slammed back down on his shoulders. Emma and he both knew damn well *dance* partner wasn't what she meant. But they also knew that they couldn't have the real, romantic partnership they craved.

He grasped her hand and led her out onto the floor. "Then a dance partner you shall have." Her palm felt warm and right inside his, her grip was strong, her skin calloused from years of handling weapons. If he was free to do so, Joe knew he'd hold her hand for the rest of his life.

At least I can dance with her, he thought.

Caesar's band played fast and rocking. Joe danced carefully, keeping enough distance so he and Emma didn't touch, but moving close enough that he could feel the heat from her body. Her hips swayed rhythmically back and forth, her strength showing in her lithe movements. The defined muscles in her arms flexed as she raised them above her head and punched the air to the beat of the drums. After years of living side-by-side on the road, dancing with Emma felt as natural as unfolding his wings and soaring in his dragon form. His body moved to mirror hers, their rhythms synchronizing so they danced as one creature, flexing and reacting to one another in harmony.

The song ended suddenly and a new tune started, a slow ballad which had couples all around them stepping into each other's arms and swaying slowly as they held each other. The switch from fun dance music to a love song was so abrupt Joe looked at the stage. His suspicions were confirmed as Caesar grinned at him with a mischievous smile, pointed to him and Emma, and made a kissy face.

Joe shot him a nasty look, then saw in the corner of his eye that Emma was sending Caesar an identical expression. It was little wonder the Iron Claws kept trying to push them together. Even Joe knew that he and Emma were perfect for each other.

"Shall we?" he asked, opening his arms. She hesitated for a second, and then moved forward so that her body was flush against his, her curves fitting against the hard lines of his body like she was made to be there. "You know Caesar will ridicule us forever if we flee from a slow song."

"You could just tell the others you're married; they'd stop with the matchmaking." Her voice was low enough not to carry. The hot breath of her whisper tickled his ear and he resisted the urge to pull her closer.

Joe shook his head. When Emma first joined the Iron Claws, the attraction between them had been so immediate and so strong, he had confided in her right away why nothing romantic could happen between them. But just because Emma knew about his failed marriage didn't mean he wanted it to be gossiped about by the whole club.

"It's been over five years. Do you ever think you'll move on?" Emma tilted her head to look up at him. Her gorgeous, brown eyes had tiny flecks of gold in them. He wanted to say yes to them, to her, but he knew he couldn't.

"I made a vow to be loyal to Rachel for the rest of my life." Vows mattered. They were important. His mother had never understood that, and her infidelity destroyed his entire family. He would never be like her, *could* never be like her. Loyalty and duty were as much a part of him as his dragon.

Emma nodded solemnly. She raised her hand like she was going to touch his cheek, but lowered it to rest platonically on his arm. "I understand. I wouldn't care so much about you if you were the type to cheat." She raised her chin. "Just know that I have no plans on waiting around for you."

Joe leaned forward so that his forehead rested against hers. He could feel her pulse speed up, feel the echoing tempo in his own chest as his heart raced to match hers. No, she wouldn't wait for him. She deserved a life. It wasn't her fault he'd already made the vows that ruined his.

"We should get something to eat," she said in a low voice.

Joe stepped away from her, already feeling bereft from the loss. "You go ahead, I'm not hungry."

He forced himself not to watch her walk away, turning to where a few of the Claws were sipping drinks around one of the tables.

Marie, the Iron Claws' human medic and Dylan's wife, was chatting excitedly with Penelope, a vampire and the newest addition to the Claws. Having a vampire scientist in the club was infinitely useful, but Joe was most grateful for the effect Penelope had on his hacker extraordinaire, Alec. Now that Alec had found his true mate, he was transformed: truly happy and at peace. Joe chided himself for the twinge of jealousy he felt as he thought about how the Iron Claws had all paired off in the last few months. *All but Emma and me.* He shook the thought away.

Joe wrinkled his nose at the pungent scent of blood and vodka in Alec's hand as the hacker sauntered past Joe to Penelope's side. Alec kissed her cheek as he deposited the beverage in front of her.

"Bloody Mary, just the way you like it," Alec said as he waved Joe over.

"Here, see this." Marie pointed to her phone.

Joe pulled up a chair, happy for the distraction. "What is it?"

"Peace in our time," Alec said. "All because of my favorite genius." He looped his arm around Penelope's shoulders and a faint blush overtook her pale cheeks as she leaned into him.

Joe read the headline on Marie's phone: "Dragon High Council Summit Considers Radical Proposal in Light of Scientific Achievements". Joe handed the phone back to her, frowning.

"That hardly looks like peace in our time. Sounds like more political bullshit," Joe said.

Marie shook her head. "The study Penelope published proving the medical benefits of Puff on humans had a huge impact. I've been getting calls from all over from people asking how they can get some."

"There's been a ton of chatter online," Alec added. "Lots of shifters and covens are clamoring for it. They want the Dragon High Council to make it legal so they can have easier access."

"But Puff doesn't work on shifters," Joe said. "Why would it be such a big deal to them?" After distributing Puff from the shadows for so many years, constantly looking over his shoulder to keep it secret, the idea that other clans might actually help felt inconceivable.

Alec huffed. "We're not the only ones with human friends. They know this stuff is legit. Penelope's been around for over three hundred years; that's long enough to get a pretty solid rep." He added with a whisper loud enough to carry, "And to look super hot while doing it."

Penelope blushed. "It was a good article, I'm proud of the work I did. But credit also goes to Alec and Nina for all their technical know-how. They were the ones who made sure the results were published all over the shifter blogs and the news sites."

Marie grinned. "Pretty soon, the Dragon High Council is going to have to get their heads out of their asses and—"

Screams echoed from outside the reception hall. The screech of breaking glass and twisting metal cut across the room, followed by a ground-shaking explosion. Everyone jumped to their feet and Caesar and his band threw their instruments aside, sprinting towards the falling rubble.

Across the room, Emma jumped onto a table and called out, "Listen! Dylan, you, Caesar and me are going outside to investigate. Alec and Nina, you check online to see what the fuck is going on. Marie and Penelope set up a triage area in case anyone is injured. Big Joe," he felt a zing of heat through him as she caught his eye, "you stay in here and keep the civilians safe."

Emma didn't bother checking if everyone was complying with her orders. The Iron Claws all knew Emma was the team's best strategist. She led the charge outside with Dylan and Caesar close behind. Big Joe quickly assessed the room, herding the guests to the area of the room furthest from the commotion outside.

Ned and his wife Maya rushed up to him in the crowd. Ned was smaller and slightly younger than most of the Iron Claws, so it was hard for Joe to not think of him as the baby of the group.

"What about us? What should we do?" Ned asked Joe, pointing to himself and his extremely-pregnant wife, Maya.

"Is it the Red Guard? Do you think the High Council would attack us at a *wedding*?" Maya was a tiger shifter and been the head of security for her clan before she married Ned and started up her own security company. If her instincts said this could be the Council's Red Guard, then Joe was tempted to believe her.

"You both need to get out of here." Joe looked toward the entrance. He could see flames and the flash of sunlight off of metal through the door. He pointed toward the back door.

"Run!" They looked like they were going to protest, but Joe locked eyes with them both. "I don't play the Alpha card often, but I'm playing it now. You have to protect that baby, and as your leader I'm ordering you two to get the fuck out of here."

Maya gave a small salute and grabbed Ned's arm. "Fine. But we'll be back as soon as it's safe."

He felt a small ball of relief uncoil in his chest when he saw them get safely out the door. He wasn't sure if it was safe yet to herd the rest of the wedding guests outside into possible danger, but at least Ned and Maya had made it out.

A groaning sound above him was the only warning Joe got before a wooden beam split off from the ceiling, crashing down on top of him. His arms shot up reflexively, grunting as he bore the weight of the rough wood.

"Fucking hell." Joe felt his body straining as his knees began to buckle under him, his entire body bowing under the beam. Debris rained down around him as the air filled with screams.

Penelope appeared at his elbow, grabbing a trapped woman caught under one edge of the beam and pulling her to safety.

"Just keep that steady," she said. As Joe held up the beam, Penelope reached under him and guided shaking bruised people out, carrying the wounded over to the tables surrounding Marie. Those that could walk fled out the back door.

The beam holding up the crumbling roof felt like it was slowly flattening Joe, and he ground his teeth as he struggled to stay upright. He could taste blood in the back of his throat. His muscles screamed for release. Once the last civilian got to safety, he let go with a roar. He barely managed to sprint away before his half of the hall finally imploded like a house of cards.

The echoing crash subsided and the swirling cloud of dust gradually settled, revealing the battlefield outside. Wounded members of the Red Guard were fleeing the scene, leaving trails of blood behind them. Emma sat talking with a woman turned away from him near the parking lot. He couldn't tell if either of them was injured, the woman's t-shirt was torn across the back revealing her smooth, dark skin, and she sat bowed and shaking.

"Is everybody okay? What happened?" Joe called, walking towards Emma and the woman.

Emma stood, her expression stormy. "High Council goons. They were attacking her for distributing Puff." Emma turned to the woman. "Don't worry, you're safe now. We can help you." Emma reached down to help the woman stand and she turned.

Joe felt all of the blood drain from his face. He wobbled on his feet and he saw his own shock mirrored on the woman's familiar face.

"Rachel."

He could hear the other Iron Claws begin to crowd around, yet everything but Rachel seemed far away and out of focus. She was older, new lines had formed around the edges of her eyes, her cheeks were a little more taut, but it was definitely Rachel and she still looked beautiful. His heart pounded as he looked down at her left hand. She still wore her wedding band.

"Rachel?" Emma's confused voice seemed to come from a million miles away. "As in…" She didn't finish the sentence.

This can't be happening, he thought.

"This is my wife," he heard himself say.

Exclamations of surprise and questions surrounded him

as the rest of the Claws reacted with their usual lack of restraint. Marie and Penelope had handed their patients off to the arriving paramedics and dashed over upon hearing the din. Even Ned and Maya had returned while Joe wasn't looking. Joe couldn't seem to move his mouth to answer their questions.

"Rachel Silver," Rachel said, her eyes barely leaving Joe's face as she reached out to shake Emma's hand. She turned back to Joe. "Please Joe, I need your protection. The High Council is going to kill me."

EMMA CLOSED HER EYES, squeezing the lids tightly together as she tried to stop the world from spinning.

After all this time.

Rachel.

She's here.

Since Big Joe had never described his wife, Emma had mentally cast her as a stereotypical villain: somebody bone-thin, with a perpetual sneer, draped in a full-length fur coat. Somebody who wore sunglasses indoors and only ate salad. Somebody *evil.*

Emma felt almost disappointed that Rachel looked like a normal person. She was around Emma's height with a skin tone only slightly lighter than Joe's, dressed in a t-shirt and jeans, with big, honest eyes that sparkled as she thanked her rescuers.

Fuck, she's gorgeous.

Emma tried to nod supportively as the other Claws reeled at the revelation.

"Congrats, big man!" Caesar slapped Joe on the back, grinning like a madman.

"You're married?" Ned looked hurt. "You're married and you never told us?"

"There wasn't any reason to tell you. Rachel and I got married right out of high school." Joe stood near Rachel, but Emma noted with satisfaction their lack of physical contact. "We separated almost six years ago, before the Claws came together."

"Still, though," Marie said. "You know so much about all of us. I can't believe you'd keep something so huge from us."

Rachel stepped between the crowd and Joe. "It's actually my fault. We broke up because I didn't understand why Joe wanted to give Puff to humans. I was young and afraid of the Dragon High Council." She shifted uncomfortably. "I know better now. That's why the Red Guard was after me. I've dedicated my life to distributing Puff, like all of you."

"She's going to need our protection." Maya stepped forward, one hand gently balanced on her pregnant stomach. "The Red Guard doesn't mess around."

"No, they don't," Alec frowned at Rachel thoughtfully. "We might not actually be the safest place for you. The High Council has a guy named Sterling who's been targeting us for months. He's obsessed with stopping us from distributing Puff."

"But you've stayed safe, right?" Rachel asked, looking around at their concerned faces. "If you've all survived this Sterling guy and the Red Guard so long, then I'm sure I'm safer with you than on my own."

Joe stood up a little straighter and Emma's chest tightened. She knew Joe: now that Rachel had declared herself under the protection of the Claws, Joe was going to do everything in his power to keep her safe. Once a Claw, always a Claw. *Damn it.*

"If you all are going to run off on another exciting adventure, I'm going to have to skip this time, mis amigos." Caesar pulled Nina close. Yards of white tulle pooled at her feet and she smiled at him. "I have to whisk this beautiful bride away for the honeymoon of a lifetime." He raised his eyebrows suggestively. "I'll try to get her back in one piece, but no guarantees."

"Get outta here, you two." Big Joe winked at Caesar as he lifted his wife off her feet and towards a car decorated with shaving cream and tin cans.

Joe turned back to the rest of the Iron Claws. "We've got a lot of ground to cover. I'll be on Rachel's protection detail." He turned to Emma expectantly. "Emma? Plans for everyone else?"

Emma enjoyed a private moment of pride at being the obvious choice for tactical assignments. She had been Joe's right-hand man for four years now, and still thrilled at how effortlessly her chiseled Adonis trusted her. She quickly did some calculations about the outstanding tasks and the team's skills.

"We're going to have to split up to take care of everything," she said to the group. "Penelope and Marie, you need to be at the shifter clan summit for the High Council's decision. You both have more understanding of how Puff interacts with human biology than anybody else. We need your expertise on hand if there's even a *chance* of the Council legalizing Puff." Emma grinned. "Take Alec and Dylan along if you must."

"But they're *such* a terrible inconvenience," Penelope elbowed Alec with a giggle before pecking him gently on the cheek.

"The worst. Very distracting." Marie agreed. She rested her hand on Dylan's chest. "I guess we'll have our hands full, educating the Council and keeping these boys out of trouble." Dylan snaked an arm around Marie's waist and pulled her tight against him.

Emma pushed down a pulse of jealousy as she saw the happy couples interact. *No time for that now,* Emma reprimanded herself.

"Ned and Maya, I need you to keep an eye on our Puff patients, and make sure Sterling doesn't try any more shit. I'm not going to let anybody else die on our watch." Emma eyed Maya's baby bump. "If you think you're up to it."

"No shifting during the third trimester, so Ned'll have to be our muscle." Maya leaned into Ned and squeezed his arm. "I'll coordinate with my security team to make sure all the patients are covered. No problem."

"Perfect." Emma braced herself before continuing. "And I'll be joining Joe for Rachel's protection detail." She looked over at Joe's response, but he only nodded.

"What? Why?" Rachel's screech echoed across the partially-destroyed reception hall.

"It's for your protection, and for Joe's," Emma said.

"Oh, look at the time," Ned muttered. His face had turned an embarrassed pink and he kept his arm around Maya as they hurried away, quickly followed by the rest of the Iron Claws.

Rachel looked around at the departing Claws, her expression increasingly indignant. "I don't understand why you have to come with us. The big one with the dreadlocks looked like he could handle himself."

Joe placed a calming hand on Rachel's arm. "Dylan is a fine investigator and fighter, but Emma was in the military. She is the best fighter in the Claws. And if the Red Guard catches up with you again, you'll be glad to have her at your back."

"Unless she's *stabbing* me in the back," Rachel muttered

so low Emma decided to ignore it, partially because it was true. There was something about Rachel that rubbed Emma the wrong way.

Although I'm hardly the most objective judge, Emma reminded herself. "I'm coming because of the potential security risks," she said. *Including you.*

Rachel turned to Joe, her brown eyes brimming with tears. "Joe, I don't like this. I'm scared and being *hunted*, and you want me to go to a cabin with some *stranger*?"

"I'll be there too," Joe said. He stared at the tears rolling down Rachel's face and Emma could see him starting to wilt. The man had never been able to resist a crying woman. "If she really makes you that--"

Emma cut him off before he could finish his sentence. "You're a stranger to me too, and I need to protect everyone in the Iron Claws, including my Alpha."

Something in Emma's expression must have hinted at her feelings, because Rachel immediately turned into Joe and started pawing at his chest. "But you know me, Joe. Tell me at least *you* trust me," Rachel cooed.

Joe looked down at where Rachel's nails curled in his shirt and didn't pull away. "Umm-"

"Okay, I'll admit it, I was a bitch back in the day." Rachel took Joe's hand in hers. "I'll even say the thing I *never* say: I was wrong. You were right."

"Wow." Joe looked stunned. "I never thought I'd hear you say that." His hand closed around Rachel's, their fingers intertwined. Emma felt like her heart was being squeezed in a vise.

"I understand now that Puff should be available to humans." A slight pink colored Rachel's cheeks. "I was hoping someday I'd find you while I was distributing Puff. You're the love of my life. Always were, always will be. Will you try to make us work again?" Rachel traced her perfectly-manicured fingers down Joe's strong jawline.

The sound of Emma's grinding teeth was so loud in her own ears she was sure it could be heard all the way to the parking lot.

Joe cleared his throat and pulled away from Rachel, his hand slipping away from hers. "We can figure that all out later. First thing's first. Emma and I need to get you to one of our safe houses. Someplace off the grid."

Shit. She hadn't wanted Joe going off alone with the woman, but now it looked she was going to be stuck in a small space with Rachel hanging all over Joe. There was only one place far enough off the grid for this mission.

"Pack your shit." Emma forced a smile. "We're going to the cabin."

JOE LET out a gusty sigh of relief as the car's headlights washed over the cabin. They could finally escape the awkward silence that hung in the car like a bad smell. Driving instead of flying sounded like a great plan at the time; the Council couldn't track a single, nondescript car the way it could track three massive dragons. But the car ride had been two hours of uncomfortable attempts at conversation, punctuated by efforts to get the ancient radio to pick up a decent signal.

The sun had set about an hour earlier, plunging the cabin and surrounding woods into layers of shadows. Joe unlocked the door and fumbled for the light switch. It was tricky enough to find it in the dark, and Rachel crowding him was no help. She gripped his bicep as he struggled, standing so close her perfume was like a fog surrounding him.

"Is this place going to be safe?" Rachel asked in a soft voice. "It looks like the set of a horror movie."

Emma chuckled behind him, but didn't say anything.

"It's going to be fine. This place is great," he said with more gusto than he felt.

Joe finally hit the light and they all stepped inside. The two-bedroom cabin wasn't glamorous, but it would do until they could find a more permanent place for Rachel to hide out. The main doorway opened up into a large living room with a long couch, a fireplace, two comfortable reading chairs, and a wall of old books. An archway on the opposite side of the room led to the kitchen and the back porch. The two bedroom doors were on the right, a shared bathroom in between.

Rachel moved toward the kitchen, dropping her bags onto the couch.

"Joe, you look like you need a drink," Rachel said, her hips swaying as she made her way to the kitchen and switched on the lights. She started to open cabinets, pulling down two glasses and shaking them in his direction. "I have some emergency tequila in my bag."

Joe chuckled. "Emergency tequila sounds perfect." He turned to Emma. "What about you, Emma? You up for a drink?"

Emma shrugged, smiling toward Rachel, but Joe could hear her teeth grinding. "I wouldn't want to intrude."

"Who's intruding? It's just the three of us here, we might as well have a drink," Joe said.

"Of course you're welcome to join us." Rachel took down a third glass, closing the cabinet door a little stronger than was strictly necessary. "I'm glad to share." She smiled thinly as she poured two fingers of tequila into the three glasses and brought them out.

Emma sipped at her drink, seated on a reading chair while Joe collapsed onto one end of the couch. He took a long gulp of his drink and tried to let the adrenaline rush of the day—the fight, fleeing to safety—drain away. *The others will be okay*, he told himself. The rest of the Iron Claws would watch each other's backs. They'd all lived on the run from the High Council long enough that one more fight against their goons was just another Tuesday.

Rachel settled close to Joe on the couch, holding out her arm toward him so that the back of her hand brushed the nape of his neck. He wanted to shift his seat so that they weren't touching, but stopped himself. *She's my wife*. She was the woman he had been loyal to for the last five years. He had to get used to her touch.

"So..." Rachel said, taking a long sip of her drink and then flicking her tongue across her lips. "You two are the experts on Puff. Tell me, how do you get it to the humans that need it? I've been having the *hardest* time." She moved so that she sat a little closer, her leg now pressed against Joe's. "I know now how worthwhile it is to help humans, baby. I want to do better."

"You've been having trouble getting Puff to humans?" Emma asked, sitting forward. "You know, we—" she gestured to herself and Joe, "--had a similar problem in the beginning. We could find sick people easy enough, but didn't know how to offer our magical cure without sounding insane."

Joe chuckled. "Yeah, those early days were really awkward. Remember the time we tried to slip Puff into that old woman's tea?"

Emma started to laugh so hard she nearly spilled her

drink. "Yes! She beat you over the head with her umbrella! She was screaming like a banshee that you were trying to roofie her, and—what did she keep saying?—that you wanted to 'have your way' with her."

"Oh man, she got me good, too." Joe rubbed the top of his head. "Don't mess with old ladies, they mean business."

Emma's eyes danced with mirth. "We were such a *mess* back then."

"It was so embarrassing," Joe said to Rachel, whose lips were pressed so thin they looked like a single line. "The old broad had me apologizing for hours, before she made me buy her dinner *and* a new rocking chair to make up for giving her such a fright."

"Thank goodness Marie joined us," Emma said, turning to Rachel. "Marie's a human nurse. If you want to get Puff to the people who need it, recruit somebody already embedded in the human medical community."

Joe nodded. "When we move around, Marie gets a job at whatever hospital or clinic we want to distribute Puff out of."

"And then once you have an in at the hospitals..." Emma raised her glass to clink against Joe's. "Everything becomes much simpler. Marie adds legitimacy to what we're offering, and then all we have to worry about is finding a way to get the Puff to them in a way that won't bring any extra attention from the High Council."

"Of course we tend to draw attention anyway, having to fight our way out of whatever ridiculous trap Sterling and the Council have come up with."

"Haha, remember that time when—"

Rachel yawned loudly enough to interrupt Emma, stretching her arms out wide. Rachel's hand brushed against Joe's shoulder as if by accident, and then settled on his arm.

She squeezed his bicep, smiling at him as she curled against his side.

"Baby, today has been really exhausting. I'm too tired to talk shop with you guys. Don't you think it's about time we head to bed? We have a lot of time to catch up on."

What? Joe's mind skidded to a halt for a second before grinding back up again like a stalled car. *She's my wife. She's my wife*, he told himself. She was beautiful, sexy, and the one woman on earth that he was free to make love to.

Out of the corner of his eye, he could see Emma playing with the dagger sheathed at her waist. She always wore it, and the rest of the club gave her shit for the fact that she fiddled with it whenever she was upset.

Rachel curled up closer to him and he fought the urge to push her away. He couldn't turn his eyes away from Emma. She didn't say anything and stayed resolutely looking down at her glass, but her fingers twirled back and forth along the hilt in small, agitated jerks.

"You're right. It's been a really long day." Joe scooted away from Rachel to stand up. "You ladies should take the bedrooms. I'll take the couch."

"But—" Rachel started to say, but he waved his hand.

"Rachel, you're right that we have a lot of time to make up for, but the High Council is after you. You were nearly killed today. Tonight isn't the right time."

She narrowed her eyes for a split second, then she smiled at him, teeth flashing. "You're probably right. Of course, baby. I'll see you in the morning." She caressed the side of his face and then sashayed back to her room. She looked over her shoulder, her hand on the door knob. "But if you change your mind, you know where I am." She flipped her hair and closed the door behind her.

"Laying it on a bit thick, isn't she?" Emma said the words

so softly to herself, Joe wouldn't have been able to hear it without his enhanced shifter senses. "Good night, Joe." She turned on her heel and closed her bedroom door firmly behind her.

"Night, Emma," he said, falling back against the couch cushions.

It was going to be a long night.

When the dream started, he wasn't sure he was still asleep. Blankets covered his naked body and a fire roared in the fireplace. The ceiling was gone and a full moon bathed down soft light all around him.

A soft sigh from behind the couch made him turn. Emma was there, naked except for her leather belt and dagger resting against her hip. Her full breasts glowed in the moonlight and the swell of her thighs were strong and lean. Her hips didn't sway like Rachel's when she walked toward him, rather she stalked forward like a lioness approaching prey. Joe's pulse raced with arousal.

The couch and blankets disappeared, and the walls of the cabin faded away until it was just him and Emma alone and bare in the grassy clearing behind the cabin. She moved toward him with the grace of a hawk, and he leaned forward with his hands outstretched to grab at her. His cock was so erect it ached, pointing toward her like an arrow.

"You're my best partner," she said.

Emma barreled into him and he cradled her body as they fell onto the grass. Their limbs tangled together, his arms wrapped around her soft skin, his cock nestled in between her thighs. He grabbed at her hair, pulling her face towards his, desperate for her kiss, but she turned her head at the last moment to nip at his neck. He moaned, pulling her closer and bucking below her until her hips were positioned directly above his straining cock.

Her smell surrounded him, familiar and warm. He grabbed hold of her hips and rolled her under him, looking down at her beloved face. She smiled up at him, but her eyes looked sad.

Then he remembered.

He was married.

Emma melted away beneath him and he cried out, trying to grab at her, keep her there.

"Emma!" His hands slipped through her like water. "No!" She was gone, his hands digging at the dirt, tearing up the grass.

"It's okay, baby, you still have me."

He turned toward the voice and Rachel stood there in a red, lace teddy that hugged her breasts and ended just below the curved edge of her ass. She sank to her knees next to him in the grass, her hands caressing his chest. Her fingernails were painted red, and longer than he remembered. They curled into tight points and left long lines across his pecs as she lightly scratched across them. She moved closer, pulling each strap of her teddy slowly off her shoulders in a tantalizing strip tease like she used to do when they were first married.

"My Big Joe," she purred, her eyes at his cock, not his face. She pulled the teddy off completely, leaning forward to press her breasts against his chest. Her nipples were hard points against his chest and she grabbed his hands to cup them. Her breasts filled his hands just as he remembered. She moaned.

"Rachel, it's been so long. We're not the same people we were..."

She leaned forward and kissed him, silencing his protests. She leaned back, licking her lips. "I know."

The light changed, the soft rays from the giant moon

suddenly red and pulsing. Rachel shifted in front of his eyes, not into her familiar dragon shape, but into a demon with enormous horns curling from her hair. He cried out and tried to scramble away from her, but Rachel's fingernails were now six-inch metal blades, which she dug into his chest. Scales erupted along her skin, and her legs fused together into a long snake tail with venomous spines.

"I need your protection." She hissed the words, a long tongue flicking across his face.

Joe sat up on the couch, the blanket falling off of him onto the floor. He was drenched in sweat, his heart pounding in his chest. The pajamas he'd put on the night before stuck to his skin.

It was a dream. Only a dream. He clenched and unclenched his fists, trying to force his heart back to a normal rhythm.

He looked back at the two bedrooms behind him. Emma's door was still firmly closed, but Rachel's door was open a few inches, wide enough for him to see the rumpled sheets of the empty bed inside. He fell back against the couch.

Ugh. He hadn't had a nightmare that vivid in ages.

He grabbed his bag and headed to the bathroom, letting the water from the shower wash away his lingering unease from the dream. By the time he'd wiped a cursory bar of soap across his skin, he'd forgotten the nightmare's details entirely. He made a mental note not to drink hard alcohol right before bed again.

He put on his clothes and followed the sounds of opening and closing cabinets to the kitchen. The sight of Rachel rooting around the refrigerator hit him with a profound sense of déjà vu. How many mornings had he woken up to see her like this?

"Oh good, you're up!" Rachel called as soon as she saw him. A bright smile lit across her face and he felt himself returning it. "I'm making toast!"

He laughed. "You can make toast now? I see you really *have* changed over all these years."

"Very funny," she deadpanned. She grabbed a dish towel and swatted him on the arm. "Just you watch, Mr. Doubty McDoubty-Pants."

They'd only stopped for a few basic groceries on the road up; the food in the cabin was all canned and nonperishables. Joe knew for a fact that they didn't have any bread, but he watched with growing amusement as Rachel pulled out a can of beans, a can of mushroom soup, and a banana from yesterday's grocery run.

"You do know what toast is, right?" he said, smiling.

She shushed him, opening the refrigerator and pulling out a cucumber, and – with a flourish – a box of crackers which Joe couldn't imagine why they were in the refrigerator to begin with. She got down a cutting board, peeled the banana, and then cut up the banana and cucumber into thin slices. Putting the slices in between the crackers like tiny sandwiches, she arranged them on a plate.

"Ta da!" she cried, presenting the plate to Joe with a dramatic flourish. "Toast!"

"That's not what—" Joe stopped talking and he smiled, remembering. "Our first house," he said slowly, the memory coming back in small fits and starts. "We had that banana tree in the back yard and there was that neighbor who was always trying to unload her produce. She gave us a sack of cucumbers. You wanted to make toast, but the bread had gone moldy so I made you cracker sandwiches instead, and we just called it toast."

She picked up one of the small sandwiches and took a

bite. "Never thought these flavors would work well together, but even after all these years...it's still my favorite."

Joe rolled one of the sandwiches between his fingers, the cucumber beginning to slip out the side. "We had some good days. Even if that first apartment was a bit of a disaster."

"Yes!" Rachel cried, pulling out the kitchen chair next to him and sitting down. "With that shower head that never quite worked."

"Water everywhere." He laughed. "And the radiator that hissed so loud—"

"We couldn't *sleep* for the first few weeks. But as soon as I heard it, I knew I was home." She moved her chair a little bit closer until the tips of her knees brushed his. "With us together, there was nothing we couldn't do."

"Except have a honeymoon," he said, pointing his sandwich at her.

"We completely had a honeymoon!" she cried. "We went to that all-inclusive resort! It was gorgeous! Don't you *dare* say we didn't have a honeymoon."

"Yeah, we were able to fly into the resort as dragons, sleep out on the beach, and then barely managed to sneak into the resort for about an hour before they realized we didn't have the proper bracelets and they kicked us out." He got up to get a glass of water and sat back at the table. "Hardly a fairytale honeymoon."

"Do you remember the look on the manager's face when he realized we were dragon shifters? A pitiful, little rabbit shifter telling us we could finish our drinks but," her voice shifted to a high-pitched falsetto. "Then you will have to leave these *hallowed* premises."

Joe laughed, popping one of the sandwiches into his mouth. The banana and cucumber tasted strange together, but the flavors washed over his tongue like a familiar song. How had he forgotten this? So many mornings in the kitchen, just like this, with Rachel, laughing and talking. They would have breakfast for hours, dreaming about what they were going to do with their lives. He felt younger, lighter, like for a second he'd been transported back to his twenty year-old self.

He reached across the kitchen table to cover Rachel's hand.

"We had a fun life, Rach."

She looked down at their hands, sniffed, and bolted out the back door. He thought he saw tears on her face as she rounded the corner of the cabin and he sprung to his feet to follow her.

With each step, the last five years came back. Years wandering alone, trying to distribute Puff, but unsure how to do it. Meeting Caesar and Ned, forming the Iron Claws as a balm to seal the shattered glass of his heart. Meeting Emma, realizing that there was someone so much more aligned with his hopes and dreams than Rachel had ever been, but it was too late.

Riding with the Iron Claws had been a dream come true, picking up Marie and Dylan, then Maya, Nina and Penelope along the way. They never had money, but they were a family. But now it was time for Joe to care for his old family, whether he liked it or not.

He found Rachel crying by the wood pile. She was slumped over her knees, her head in her hands as her shoulders shook in heaving sobs. She held up a hand, stopping Joe in his tracks.

"I don't want you to see me like this," Rachel said, her voice cracking.

In all the years he'd known her, he'd rarely seen Rachel

so emotional. Seeing her cry after the Red Guard attack was the first time he'd seen tears on her face. Even when they were just teenagers, she was always so controlled, so poised. The only real emotion he could ever remember seeing in her was anger. She'd blown up so badly at the little rabbit manager at the resort he'd comped them two more rounds of drinks before the security of wolf and bear shifters had insisted it was time for them to move on.

"I'm sorry, Rach. What's wrong?" He couldn't leave her like this, not when tears were pooling in the dip of her collarbone before dripping down onto her high-heel-patterned pajama bottoms.

"It's just..." She took a deep breath, hiccupped, and started to sob again. "I'd forgotten how good a man you are." She reached out a hand to him and he stepped forward. Her palm was shaking, but he held on. "All those years, I tried to convince myself I'd been right to push you away, but being back with you, it just feels so *right*." She used his hand as leverage to stand up, shifting her weight closer so that she was just a few inches away. "We've lost so much time."

She grabbed the back of his head and pulled him down, mashing her lips against his. He wanted to push away, but forced himself to stay.

She's my wife. I have to try to make this work.

Her lips moved against his, forcing his mouth open with her tongue and all he felt was the taste of banana and crumbs from the crackers. He couldn't really remember what their kisses had felt like before, but this was different.

He felt nothing.

Joe heard a sound from behind Rachel, like the pebbles along the gravel path clicking together. He pulled away from Rachel's wet face and saw Emma. She held a coffee mug in one hand, probably coming out to catch some air, or to investigate where everyone had gone. He saw a dozen emotions flash on her face, from shock to devastation to resigned resignation, and everything in between. She turned and was gone before he could say anything.

He wanted to call out to her, scream that the kiss hadn't meant anything, that it had been the most unpleasant kiss since his first grade dare to smooch a hermit crab. But Rachel was there, looking at him with storms in her eyes.

"Rachel, I think we're moving a little fast. We're still getting to know each other after so long apart. It's just going to take a little time."

"Time." Her dark eyes flashed back and forth between him and where Emma had been standing. "You think this is going to just take *time*?"

Joe put his hands on her shoulders, trying to calm her, but he could feel the tenseness in her muscles. She had the same expression on her face as when she threatened the resort's manager that she was going to eat him and his clan if he didn't pony up the cost of their drinks.

"I want to make our marriage work," he said. "You're my wife and I made a vow to honor you for the rest of my life. We had a few really good years. I believe if we can just talk some things through, get to know each other again, we can come back together." He had to believe it. He wouldn't be like his mother, destroying a family out of selfishness. Rachel was a good person, they'd find a way to make it work.

"But no kissing. No sleeping in the same bed. What kind of marriage is that? You say you *honored* me all these years. What have you been doing with *her*?" She pointed at where Emma had been standing, her expression murderous. "You just want to go slow because you don't want your *girlfriend* to see."

"No, it's not like that. Emma and I aren't together. She's

my club si--" He stopped himself from saying "sister." There was no way he could call Emma his sister. "Friend." He felt the word in his mouth, turned it over. She was his friend. His best friend. And that was all she was ever going to be.

"Uh huh. *Friend.* Is that what the kids are calling it, these days?" Rachel poked at his chest. "Don't kid yourself. You and that *woman* are not friends. She is bad news, baby. Just you wait." She stomped away and Joe sank down to sit on the wood pile, watching his wife disappear into the trees.

"Fuck."

"OKAY, OKAY, OKAY," Emma muttered to herself as she paced around the tiny bedroom, trying to calm herself down. "Okay, o-" Pain shot up through her leg as she stubbed her toe against the bed's wooden frame. "FUCK!"

She plopped down onto the saggy mattress, sending a shower of dust flying off of the long-neglected comforter. Emma dug her elbows into her knees, holding her head in her hands.

"Fuck." She swore again. This time it was a whisper.

Emma took a moment to be grateful that she and Joe had never crossed the line, never moved their relationship from a flirty partnership to a true romance. Seeing Joe and Rachel together would hurt even worse if Emma had been *with* Joe.

And damn, this hurts, Emma thought.

She was so used to having a tangible enemy, to have something to strike at when she was wounded. Emma clung to her last shred of self-respect like a security blanket. *I will not be the crazy jealous girl who beats up her crush's wife.* She could just imagine it, like a clip from a bad reality TV show.

She'd burst in on Rachel and Joe necking on the couch, and pull Rachel off of him by her hair, maybe throwing a drink in Rachel's face for good measure before beating the living crap out of her.

Emma sighed. Reality was much less fun. With great effort, she pushed aside thoughts of pummeling Rachel and decided to focus on the *real* enemy. She slid her phone out of her pocket and scrolled down her contacts until she reached the one labeled 'Nerd'.

Alec picked up on the second ring.

"Emma!" Alec's voice rang out loudly with excitement. "How's the cabin? Is it haunted? Have any axe murderers swung by yet?"

Despite her sullen mood, Emma chuckled. "It's boring so far, exactly what you'd hope for on a protection detail."

"Bummer," Alec said.

"Major bummer," Emma agreed. "I was actually calling to see if you could email me everything we've got on Sterling. I know you and Nina have been gathering information on him like crazy, and I've got some time to kill. Somebody's got to comb through it all, and it might as well be me." Emma loved solving puzzles; unraveling the secrets of this mysterious Sterling figure would definitely brighten up her time in the cabin.

"Sure thing, but it's a huge file and it'll take some time to download. I'll put it together now, but don't expect it for a few minutes," Alec said.

"Thanks Alec. You're the best nerd a girl could hope for," Emma said. "Speaking of, you haven't been looking into Rachel, have you? Do you have any actionable intelligence?" She felt her face turn hot. "For the protection detail, I mean."

"Emma, I would never hack into the accounts of Big Joe's wife. I'm almost insulted you would suggest such a thing."

"Alec." Emma growled through the phone.

"Okay, ya' got me!" Emma could hear the clicking of Alec's keyboard as he spoke. "I *may* have hacked into a few records. She was a bit of a wild child in high school, but her records show she turned away from the juvenile delinquent lifestyle around the time she got together with Big Joe."

"He tends to have that effect on people." Emma couldn't help but smile.

"Says the fugitive," Alec quipped. "I found their marriage certificate, the lease for their first apartment, stuff like that. And just like she says, she went off the grid after they separated." Alec actually sounded impressed. "There is nothing on Rachel for the past five years: no bank accounts, no credit cards, no car loans. I couldn't find so much as a library card."

"Well, that sounds a little fishy." Emma chewed her lip as she thought.

"Do *you* have a library card, Emma?"

"Fair point," Emma said. "Good luck with the Council and text me if there's an update."

"Will do. Later, gator."

Emma ended the call and laid her phone on the bedside table, making sure the volume for email notifications was turned all the way up. She couldn't wait for the info on Sterling to distract her from obsessing over Rachel and Joe. She pushed back onto the squeaky bed, her back bouncing as it struck the ancient mattress.

Rachel and Joe. The thought ricocheted around her mind like a pinball, striking her most vulnerable parts. *What if she sticks around?* Emma's heart pounded in her chest as she contemplated the likely scenario she'd been avoiding contemplating since Rachel arrived: Rachel and Joe together on the road.

The images bit at her brain like mosquitoes, irritating and impossible to ignore: Rachel and Joe snuggling together in the clubhouse, Joe buying Rachel flowers and writing her dorky poetry for Valentine's Day, Rachel giving birth to Joe's children. All while Emma stood by them, always on the outside, brokenhearted.

Of course, Emma thought, *I wouldn't have to stay.* She turned the thought around in her head. She'd done just fine before the Iron Claws, she could be on her own again. She'd been a proud member of the Air Force, for fuck's sake. Kicking everyone's asses from boot camp to her first deployment had been some of the best times in her life. Back then, she was the golden child of her clan, her family sending her so many care packages she was nearly buried in them.

There were downsides to being a shifter in a human army. Although she was naturally stronger and faster than everybody else in her unit, even in non-dragon form, she was forbidden from shifting while deployed. World governments were aware of shifters and other supernaturals, and there were very serious treaties in place to prevent them from using their advantages in the field.

Those first few weeks without being able to shift felt like somebody was constantly rubbing sandpaper along her skin. Emma itched to sneak out for a quick shift to her natural form; piloting jets was nothing compared to the thrill of gliding on her own wings. But her superior officer (also a shifter, a greying old wolf named Sergeant Jones) warned Emma that if he saw as much as a scale, she would be in big trouble.

As difficult as her training and deployments were, Emma loved her time in the military. She learned about battle strategies, designing defenses, and assessing dangerous situations. There was something about the camaraderie of being part of a team that fulfilled her in a way she hadn't thought possible. She would do anything for her unit, and she knew they all had her back.

Which is how everything went so wrong.

A new squad was joining them on base, flying into the desert headquarters on a small-capacity plane. Everyone on base was thrilled for the fresh reinforcements. Emma remembered almost all the off-duty personnel came outside to welcome the new recruits, all shading their eyes as the small aircraft made its descent.

Nobody saw the origin of the rocket that struck the plane, tearing through the metal hull like butter. The entire left wing ripped off on impact, a jagged gash running down the plane's fuselage. Debris rained down upon the airfield. Soldiers ran for cover as the commanders shouted orders.

"We have to do something," Emma cried out. "They're too low to parachute out!" Before Emma could move in to help, a strong hand gripped around her arm.

"Don't even think about it." Sergeant Jones spun Emma around, staring her in the eye. His growled order stank of chewing tobacco. "Let this happen."

Emma's heart pounded in her chest as she pulled away. "There's at least twenty people up there!" The sound of the plummeting plane roared in her ears. She eyed the Sergeant's holstered sidearm. "Shoot me, or get out of my way."

Jones's grip released and Emma pushed forward, running towards the nosediving craft as she shifted. Feet turned to talons, skin to scales as she ran, pushing off the ground as soon as her wings were fully formed.

Emma could hear the panicked screams of the soldiers

onboard as she approached the flaming plane. Whether they were panicking over the plane being shot down, the gray dragon approaching, or both, she didn't know.

She shouted over the din, "Get on my back! Now."

Nobody moved. She heard one of the soldiers scream, "What in the holy fuck is *that*?"

Emma flew even closer to the plane, her scales scraping against metal as she kept pace with the descending craft. Clearly none of this human crew had ever seen anything like her before. She knew she had to explain the situation in a familiar way.

"Soldiers!" She ordered. "Evac off this plane onto this rescue vehicle ASAP." She paused as some of the soldiers started to crawl towards her back. "That means *now*, goddammit!"

She counted as pairs of boots hit her back without hesitation.

The sloping dunes of sand were getting uncomfortably close when the twentieth pair of boots landed.

"Hang on!" Emma bellowed as she broke away from the plane, pulling up with every fiber of her being. Carrying twenty humans was difficult under the best circumstances. Pulling out of a nosedive with twenty *panicked* humans on her back was damned near impossible.

With a roar, she finally lifted away, flapping her wings with all her might to escape the shredded debris. Cheers erupted from her back, quickly morphing into screams as she felt the weight of one of those twenty fall away.

Emma saw him, a figure in desert camouflage hurtling away, almost impossible to see against the backdrop of sand.

"Everybody hold on!" She hollered again, diving. She tried to keep her back as level as possible while shooting down, reaching out with her talons. The man's screams pierced her ears as she came closer, reaching as far as she could.

Something warm landed in her claws and she could hear a muffled, "Thanks," croaked out by the soldier. Emma resisted the urge to giggle from exhaustion and relief as she landed carefully a short distance from the base.

Once safely on the ground, the soldiers cheered and hugged, unabashed in their celebration. "Dragon! Dragon! Dragon!" They chanted, their voices echoing along the dunes.

Emma relished that moment, savoring it because, even then, she'd known what would happen next.

She was dishonorably discharged within days. She'd saved twenty lives, but broke several major laws to do so. Sergeant Jones and the Air Force sent her home in disgrace to her clan, who immediately disowned her for her "foolish and irresponsible" actions.

Emma wandered from town to town in search of work, her motorcycle and the clothes on her back her only possessions. She eventually started making her way working in private security. It was a crap job, night shifts spent intently watching nothing happen on tiny monitors, but at least she had a partner most nights. Having somebody to complain with was Emma's favorite part of the job.

Her last partner was a guy named Rodney, a dragon shifter with bad breath and so many freckles they looked like auburn blotches all over his face. Rodney worked days for the Dragon High Council's private security: the Red Guard. Emma figured he was a nice enough guy, moonlighting at the security firm to save up for an engagement ring for his girlfriend. The only thing Emma couldn't stand was his obsessive hatred of some group of motorcycle outlaws called the Iron Claws.

Emma used to love winding Rodney up, mentioning the Iron Claws casually and waiting for the man to explode. But the more he ranted, the more the club piqued her interest. They sounded like they had everything she'd loved about being in the military: fraternity, discipline, a mission, but none of the red tape. After Rodney started complaining about having to get up early for a Red Guard raid on the Iron Claws, Emma encouraged his complaints until she had every last detail of the planned ambush. Emma knew what she had to do.

The Iron Claws was a much smaller club back then, and she found them in a run-down biker bar having an intense argument about 1980's movies. Emma grinned at the memory. Joe had been standing next to a pool table with a cue in hand, shouting about *Pretty in Pink* when she arrived. They locked eyes as she entered the bar and it felt like a jolt of lightning coursed through her body. Emma warned the Claws of the oncoming ambush and asked to join them in the same breath. Joe welcomed her with a mile-wide grin. She knew then she would never want another man as much as she wanted him.

Emma stared at the knotted wood of the cabin's ceiling. Being with the Iron Claws wasn't just her job, they were her family. Caesar, Alec, Ned, all of them, keeping them safe was what got her out of bed in the morning. Finding them had been like finding the solution to a riddle she hadn't known she'd been looking for her entire life.

She sat up and dusted herself off. It had taken way too long for her to find them, there was no way she was going to let her family go without a fight.

Her phone beeped and she clicked on the email icon. The files on Sterling from Alec had finally arrived. She smiled. Alec always came through. She scrolled through the first dozen files, jotting down notes as she read. After a while, she peered down at her notepad.

-First recorded activity ~5 years ago

-No information on appearance. IDENTITY = SECRET

-Working outside of Council jurisdiction. Vendetta must be personal.

- "Sterling" probably code name. Most likely obliquely related to actual name.

-No conclusive mention of gender. Might be female.

Emma sprung to her feet. Her heart beat wildly in her chest as the pieces came together. She felt wildly victorious and terrified at the same time. *Of course!* She knew something was off with Rachel. It all made a crazy kind of sense. The timing lined up for when Rachel went off the grid and Sterling arrived on record. Rachel would definitely have the kind of personal vendetta against Joe that would explain why Sterling had continued to come after them even after the High Council started to move toward legalizing Puff. Rachel's married name was *Silver*, for goodness sake.

Rachel is Sterling!

JOE LAY ON THE COUCH, squeezing his eyes shut to keep the world at bay. He knew he wasn't in a relationship with Emma, but kissing Rachel still felt like a betrayal. He wanted to explain things to Emma, to convince her the kiss meant nothing, but how could he? Rachel was his wife.

He sighed and finally opened his eyes, sitting up slightly to look at the closed door of Emma's room. She'd been holed up in her bedroom since she saw the kiss, and Joe knew when it was best to let Emma have her space. If

Rachel was sticking around, he was going to have to get used to not having Emma always at his side.

Joe stretched and made himself face the rest of the day. He shifted to dragon form and spent the afternoon flying in wide loops above the woods, checking the skies and grounds for any signs of the Red Guard coming after them. He tried to push down the feeling that he was fleeing the cabin.

The open skies helped clear his head. He'd been wrong to push Rachel away at the woodpile. She was his wife, and if he was going to give their marriage a real try, he was going to have to let her in. Joe could tell he hurt Rachel by being so distant; she'd been watching YouTube videos on her laptop and avoiding eye contact ever since she came back inside. It seemed that no matter what he did, somebody was going to end up hurt.

Joe landed in the clearing behind the cabin and shifted out of dragon form. There was no sign of the Red Guard, but he hadn't been expecting any. It would be very strange for the Dragon High Council to actively pursue people for breaking a law that might not exist in a few days. He thought back to the ferocity of the raid at the wedding reception. *I wonder what Rachel could have done to warrant an attack like that?*

He let out a long sigh as he headed back to the cabin. *Just another thing to stress about.* He knew he was going to have to broker some kind of mutual understanding so that they could work together. He, Rachel, and Emma were all on the same team now, and his job as leader was to make sure that they were all able to move forward with the mission.

But it was sure easier to avoid the cabin and its inhabitants for just a few minutes longer. He didn't know what was wrong with him the last few days. He'd been chosen as the Iron Claws' Alpha for his calm under pressure, his courage, and assurance. But ever since Rachel came back into his life, he felt like he was out of step, second-guessing his every move. Joe hefted another sigh and pushed his way through the front door.

"Joe! You have to help me, she's a maniac!" Rachel nearly leapt at him as he entered the cabin.

Joe could feel his temper rising as he took in the damage to Rachel's face. The skin surrounding her right eye was swollen and darkened from an hours-old bruise.

"Did the Red Guard show up?" Joe was ready to kick himself for being so lost in thought while on patrol. His stomach churned as he contemplated how his carelessness might have resulted in Rachel being hurt. *But if they were here, where's Emma?* "What happened?" he asked. *Caffeine, I need caffeine.*

"Emma. That crazy bitch hit me!" Rachel pointed to her eye. "She saw us kissing and she just lost it. She kept screaming about how you were *hers* and how I needed to back off. I told her I'm your wife and that's forever and..." Rachel winced as she prodded carefully at the wound. "She just lost control!"

"That's not possible." He strode towards the kitchen, desperately hoping there was coffee. "Emma would never hit you." The pot was empty and he started opening cabinets looking for the grounds they'd bought at the store the day before. He'd chew them if he had to.

"She clearly wants you to think that. She told me that I was getting in the way of her plans. I told her that I wasn't going to let her corrupt you."

"Corrupt me?" Joe scoffed. "I'm hardly corrupted."

"Of course you are." She grabbed his hands, forcing him

to look at her. "You're a married man in love with someone who is not his wife."

Her statement felt like a kick to the gut because it was true. He'd fallen in love with Emma almost as soon as he met her. Their connection was stronger than anything he'd ever felt with Rachel. The feelings Joe had for Emma weren't just love at first sight, but based on years of protecting each other, working toward the same goal. They'd laughed together, built a life for themselves and the other Iron Claws together. He loved her like the second half of himself. And he'd let himself continue to fall head over heels for her, knowing he wasn't free to do so.

"We've never—" He took a deep breath. "I never cheated on you."

"But you wanted to, didn't you." She said the question as a statement, her eyes drilling into him. "She tempted you. She's been tempting you for *years*. Tell me she's never asked you to forget you're a married man. Never asked you to just move on?"

"Emma never tempted me—" *It hadn't felt like temptation at the time, but hadn't she said nearly those exact words at the wedding?*

"You're *still* defending her?" Rachel screeched. She pointed to her swollen eye. "She attacked me. She wants to turn you into a cheating scumbag and break my heart."

Joe's head was swimming. This couldn't be happening. "I never cheated," he repeated, but with less conviction this time. Hadn't he? He and Emma had never acted on their attraction, but he'd danced with her, flirted with her, kept her close all these years. He didn't resist her, not truly. He had become a cheater like his mother without even realizing it.

He pressed his hand to his forehead. "Gods, this is a nightmare. I don't know what to do."

"You know exactly what to do," Rachel said, pressing closer. "Come away with me. We can build our life up again, pick up where we left off. We can start a family, have all those kids we used to talk about."

Pain laced through him. Kids. He'd always wanted a rowdy bunch of kids running underfoot. Rachel had wanted to wait, and he'd agreed. Then when they separated, Joe had convinced himself that his dream of being a father would have to translate into being an amazing uncle to Ned's kids, or the gaggle of rambunctious children Caesar and Nina were inevitably going to have.

"You're saying you're ready for kids?" he asked.

"I want us to be together. I want to feel your baby growing inside of me." She traced her fingers behind his neck, drawing him closer. "I don't want our children to have a father who leaves them for some biker chick. I need to know I can trust you." Her fingers stroked his neck, tracing the line of his pulse, "Please, baby, we can go far away where she can never tempt you to destroy our family like your mother destroyed yours."

Joe felt like he couldn't breathe. Leave Emma? Leave everyone? But he would have the family he'd always wanted. Kids. He caught her hand, squeezing it.

He heard running feet sprinting through the living room and turned to see Emma barreling toward them. She pulled Rachel away from his arms.

"Get away from him!" she yelled. She thrust a paper cup of coffee into Joe's hands. "Drink this, I need you awake." She pushed Joe toward the living room. "Come on, we need to talk alone for a second."

Joe sipped at the coffee, his mind whirling. The second

he'd seen Emma, his entire body had come alive, his heart racing and a wild joy surging through his chest. Everything in him yearned to hold her, kiss her. And wasn't that the problem? He had no right to feel that way. His feet dragged as he followed her into the living room.

"I'm going to be right here!" Rachel called from the kitchen. "So don't think you're going to get away with manipulating him again."

Joe shook his head. Emma wasn't manipulating him. It was his own weakness he despised.

"Joe, I was going over the Sterling files." She pitched her voice low so the sound wouldn't carry.

Joe perked up, thanking all the gods this wasn't more about Rachel.

"You're not going to want to hear this, but Rachel is Sterling."

He studied her face, looking for the telltale curve of her lips or the twitch of her left eyebrow that always gave away a prank. "You have to be joking. That's impossible."

"Is it? Think about it. She comes back into your life just when the High Council was beginning to back off of us. This has to be her last-ditch attempt to stop us from distributing Puff."

"That doesn't make any sense. The Council was *attacking* Rachel, don't you remember? Besides, Sterling is a man, all of his minions have been very clear about that." Joe could feel his shoulders tense and rise as he spoke. "Sterling is a murderer. He killed humans just to make us think Puff was poisonous. He sent assassins after us. Rachel could never do something like that. She's a good person." He eyed Emma's empty hands. "Is that all you have to go on? Where's your proof to back this up?"

He walked away from her, needing distance from

Emma's tantalizing scent, the seriousness of her eyes. She had to be lying, trying to draw him away from his wife. Maybe Emma really had punched Rachel.

He cracked his knuckles, frustration surging through his skin. His feelings for Emma were clouding his judgment. If Emma had some husband come back into the picture, he would probably be jealous to his toes, looking for any excuse to hate the guy. Joe couldn't judge Emma for wanting to think the worst of Rachel, but that didn't mean he had to believe her.

"You have to listen to me," Emma said. She tried to move closer, but he backed up, keeping their distance. "The timing lines up. Rachel went off the grid at the same time that Sterling first started showing up. Even the names are similar. Her married name is Silver. She must have chosen Sterling as a giant 'fuck you' to you."

"You need help, Emma," Joe said. "You're just making up crazy stories because you don't like Rachel."

"No! You're the one who needs help. Rachel is going to kill you, kill all of us—"

"Then why hasn't she done it already? We've been alone in this cabin for days, and all she's done is prove that she's committed to trying to make our marriage work."

"She's manipulating you, talking about your mom, playing on your deepest fears—"

"Funny, that's exactly what she said about you. No, Emma, these are dangerous accusations. I will not let you slander my wife like this. We obviously cannot work together any longer. You're out of the Claws."

Emma gaped at him, her jaw falling open for a second before she clicked it shut. "Fine." Her teeth ground together loud enough he could hear it from three paces away. "I am going to go pack up my things. Just watch your back with that crazy wife of yours."

She slammed her bedroom door behind her and he could hear the hum of her starting up her laptop. He grabbed his cell phone from beside the couch and punched in Dylan's number. The former investigator was the informal third in Command in the club; Dylan would be able to help spread the word before Joe changed his mind.

"Listen up. Emma is no longer a member of the Claws. Tell everyone." He clicked the phone shut before Dylan managed to get out more than a surprised noise. Joe felt sick to his stomach.

What did I just do?

He hadn't heard Rachel come closer, but she ran her hand soothingly up and down his arm. "It's going to be okay, baby. You made the right choice, the *strong* choice."

It didn't feel like the right choice. It felt like the worst mistake of his life. He stared at Emma's bedroom door. Rachel grabbed his chin and moved his head to look at her.

"I don't feel safe here anymore, baby. First thing in the morning, the second there's enough light to fly, we need to go."

He felt himself nodding, a sense of numbness spreading through his body. Every muscle felt like it weighed a hundred pounds. Rachel kissed his cheek.

"Will you stay with me tonight?" she asked, the hand stroking his arm stretching up to massage the back of his neck.

He shook his head. "No, the Red Guard might still be after you. I'll be better off protecting you from out here."

"You did the right thing," she said again. "It's why I've always loved you." She kissed him again, gently on the lips, but Joe didn't move. When he didn't react, she pursed her lips and returned to her bedroom.

Joe looked around the living room; it suddenly felt smaller than ever. He grabbed his bag of clothes and made sure that everything was packed. If Rachel really wanted to head out first thing, he wanted to be ready. He stowed everything in the car and stalked out into the night. He'd sleep under the stars if he had to. Maybe then he wouldn't feel like his whole world was falling apart.

EMMA'S BLOOD BOILED. She balled her hands into fists, trying to restrain her rage. She wanted nothing more than to destroy everything in the room: throw the shitty lamp and listen to it shatter, kick the shitty bedside table until it was nothing but splinters. She would have been devastated that Joe kicked her out of the Iron Claws, if it wasn't for how furious she was. Anger was familiar. Anger, Emma could work with.

Rachel was clearly a master manipulator. *Not unlike Sterling.* Emma bit her lip. Joe was too far gone to listen to reason. *I need backup.*

Her laptop came to life with a dull whir as she stabbed at the keys. Alec was always online; he would be able to rally the other Claws. She was halfway through writing him a message when her video chat icon chirped for her attention. Emma clicked the icon and the sight was so welcome, she had to quickly blink away tears before her teammates saw.

Dylan, Ned, Maya, Caesar, Nina, Alec and Penelope's faces all looked out at her from the computer, each logging on from their own computers across the country, but all there for her. Everyone was talking at once, the occasional

"Joe's lost his mind!" and concerned "What's going on?" she could make out amidst the chatter filling her with hope. The Iron Claws weren't going to let her go without a fight. Once a Claw, always a Claw.

"Okay you guys, not all at once." Emma tried to strike a balance between being loud enough to be heard by her team, but quiet enough that Rachel couldn't eavesdrop from her room. "As you probably heard, Rachel has convinced Joe to kick me out of the Iron Claws."

"How is that even possible?" Ned asked, leaning so closely towards the camera he gave Emma a close-up view of his nose hairs. "Big Joe would never kick you out!"

"Something's got to be wrong with him." Alec's forehead was creased in a deep "v" as he spoke. "Do you think it could be a magic spell or something?"

"Or maybe some type of chemical reaction?" Penelope chimed in. "Could she be drugging him?"

Emma sighed. "It's possible, but honestly I think she's just tapping into the enormous guilt he's been carrying around this whole time."

"You can't give up!" Caesar's voice was a little slurred. He was holding a coconut with two straws and an orange umbrella sticking out the top. Emma couldn't help but smile seeing Caesar had jumped on the call even in the middle of his honeymoon. "Once a Claw..."

"Always a Claw!" The rest of the Iron Claws chimed in.

A happy warmth flooded Emma's chest. The military had kicked her out, she'd been exiled from her clan, but dammit, the Claws were sticking by her. She turned away from the screen, staring hard at a shitty unicorn painting on the wall to keep from getting choked up.

"Big Joe's a sensible guy. Maybe let him cool down a little, and then try talking to him reasonably," Dylan said.

"Thanks guys, maybe I will." Emma heaved a sigh. "Now tell me, any news from the Council?"

Alec breathlessly chimed in. "Things are getting pretty exciting here. Penelope gave this huge presentation to the Council and they actually seemed to understand like twenty percent of what she was saying. There were a lot of nodding and affirmative grunts. I think they might seriously consider making Puff legal!"

"Holy shit." Emma wanted to kick herself for moping about personal shit when there was something so amazing on the horizon. "I thought we wouldn't have a yeti's chance in hell. This could change *everything*."

"Marie's about to go in now, but I think Penelope really nailed it. Of course, I'm a bit biased..." Emma didn't need to look at the monitor to know Alec was grinning goofily

"Once Marie's done here, we'll fly out to the cabin. It's a quick flight and it sounds like you might need us." Dylan sounded worried.

"Us too!" Maya chimed in. Her face shifted from joy to pain, and she placed her hand on her very pregnant stomach.

"You okay over there?" Emma waved her hand at the screen. "Ned, back up, I wanna see Maya."

"False alarm, the baby's just kicking like the dickens." Maya said. "We don't know if we've got a little tiger or a little dragon in here, but *man* is he strong." Maya fidgeted uncomfortably in her chair. "This little one is due any day now, assuming he doesn't just kick his way out." She smiled as she let out a small grunt. "This baby is going to have the weirdest family in the best way."

"We all know I'm going to be the favorite." Alec grinned. "This baby is going to be a computer *genius*. I just know it."

"Uncle Caesar will make sure he knows how to get the

ladies." Caesar slurped on a straw noisily. "Or fellas. Smooth moves are smooth moves, no matter what."

Emma laughed as everybody argued how they would be the best aunt or uncle. Tiger or Dragon, Maya's baby was going to be spoiled rotten.

"Okay guys, I'm going to see if Joe's calmed down." Emma hated to break away from the comfort of their happy chatter, but she knew she would procrastinate all night if she didn't leave soon. "Wish me luck."

She closed her laptop amongst shouts of "Luck!" and squared her shoulders. This was going to suck.

"Okay, Joe, I think we need to--" Emma stopped short as she entered the main room. Joe and Rachel's bags were neatly packed and placed by the front door, but nobody was around.

Something's wrong.

JOE LOOKED up at the night sky as wisps of grass tickled the back of his neck. The stars looked cold and alone in the unending blackness. The moon was just beginning to rise, a crisp sliver of white that stretched the bleak shadows of the trees.

Out on his own, away from Rachel's accusations and Emma's anger, he was finally able to regain some clarity. He didn't believe for a second that Rachel could be Sterling—Emma's evidence was *beyond* flimsy, and there was no way Rachel was a murderer—but he knew he shouldn't have blown up at Emma like that. Emma had never given him bad intel before, and he should have at least heard her through.

Joe sighed and stretched on the soft grass. *I can't believe*

I kicked her out of the Iron Claws. Once a Claw, always a Claw. That was their rule from day one. Even when Ned stopped riding with them to start his bakery business with Maya, he was still one of them. The fact Joe had so much as considered kicking Emma out, let alone actually gone through with it, was a sign of how badly he'd been worked up.

"I have to fix this." He got to his feet, determined to apologize to Emma, on his knees if necessary, to try and make up for his mistakes.

A dark shape passed across the stars and he looked up. Even with so little light, he recognized Rachel in her dragon shape. Her yellow scales were indistinguishable in the darkness, but he would know the pattern of her spines, the slope of her reptilian face anywhere.

Where's she going in the middle of the night?

He quickly pulled off his clothes and shifted to his dragon, launching himself into the air with a few powerful beats of his leathery wings. He dropped to just above the tree line, careful to follow Rachel at a safe enough distance he wouldn't be seen. It was dangerous flying so low in the dark, and Joe swooped and swerved to avoid the uneven treetops as he tried to keep up.

Miles fell away as they sped onward. Joe squinted as the lights of the city came into view and he could make out the outline of Rachel's dragon begin to descend. She dropped to the ground next to a small hut on the outskirts of town, and Joe quickly landed a short distance away before she could spot him. He shifted back to human, hiding his smaller form behind a nearby shed.

Rachel walked around to the front of the hut, already shifted to her human form. She reached for a pouch tied to her leg, and pulled a long, silk robe out of the bag. Joe noticed Rachel arranged the robe so it fell open past her breasts, the ties loose around her waist.

"I'm so glad you're okay," a man's voice said from Joe's left. Joe ducked behind the shed, but not before catching a glimpse of a tall man in a suit walking towards Rachel, his arms outstretched. Rachel made a happy, squeaking sound and Joe peeked around the shed to see her jumping into the strange man's arms. She wrapped her legs around his waist, holding him tight as her lips locked onto his.

What?

Joe sat still, shock running through him. Rachel was smiling and laughing, her tongue visibly probing the other man's mouth with glee. She was so different from the angry, screeching woman he'd seen in the kitchen earlier.

Several minutes passed before the two lovers unlocked, but they remained in constant contact, each gripping or caressing the other. The man ran a hand gently over her swollen right eye.

"I hate seeing this, my love," he said. "I can't stand knowing that I hurt you."

She covered his hand with hers and leaned into his touch. "You only did what I told you to, honey bear. My ex had to believe that Emma was violent if he would ever consider leaving her. You did what you had to do for the cause, and you know that makes me love you all the more." She reached up to give him a long, lingering kiss. "Don't worry, honey, all of this will be over soon and my revenge will be complete. Then we'll be free to be together forever."

The man nodded, running his hands down to cup her ass and draw her closer. "I know, baby, but this sneaking around is driving me crazy. How long do we have this time before you have to go back to your ex?"

She raised her eyebrow and caressed her finger along

the waist of his pants playfully before undoing the button of his fly. "Just enough time to have you inside me, baby. All this sneaking around gets me so *hot*."

"Oh yeah?" He raised an eyebrow in return, pulling open her robe and rubbing her clit. "So wet for me, my sweet Sterling."

"Oooo, call me that again," she moaned, freeing his cock and beginning to rock her body against his.

"Sterling, my sexy Sterling," the man said.

Joe turned away, he didn't need to see any more. He knew he should be angry, enraged even. His wife had been behind the brutal attacks on his family. She'd murdered innocent humans in cold blood, and why? Revenge?

But he wasn't angry. He felt more at peace than he had in *years*. He was free of Rachel forever.

He quietly jogged out of earshot and fished into the bag he always carried with him when he shifted, pulling out his phone. He pressed the top speed dial and held his breath as the phone rang once, twice.

"Where are you?" Emma blurted from other side of the line.

"Emma, I'm so sorry. I was wrong to say what I said to you--"

"Yeah, yeah," she interrupted. "I knew you'd come to your senses. But where are you? Are you safe? If Rachel's plan was to get you alone, it's likely a trap. Tell me you're nowhere near her."

He looked behind him. He was far enough, he could only see their outlines, but he could tell Rachel was riding her lover hard, oblivious to the world.

"I'm safe, but that doesn't matter. You were right. Rachel is Sterling. You need to contact the rest of the Claws, get them up to the cabin and--"

"Way ahead of you. I already called them and they're almost here."

A wide smile stretched across Joe's face. This was why he loved her and the Iron Claws. They knew him better than he knew himself.

"Thank you. I'm grateful you still had my back."

"Once we've defeated Sterling, we're going to have a strong talk, but I'm glad you're okay. Everybody's landing right now, so you better get here quick."

Joe could hear commotion in the background, the familiar voices of the other Claws calling out greetings as they arrived at the cabin. Emma called out to them and he heard a voice say, "Here, let me talk to him," and then the shuffle of a phone being passed along.

"Hey boss, did you finally come to your senses?" Ned asked, his voice quivering a little.

"Yeah, I'm sorry that I freaked everyone out. We're all okay," Joe said.

"You bet we are! You missed the news, Puff is legal now."

"What?" Joe cried, only remembering to keep his voice low at the last minute. He picked up the pace, sprinting to return to his family.

"Yeah, the High Council finally caved," Ned said. Joe heard an excited whoop that sounded like Caesar in the background. "Between Penelope and Marie's irrefutable medical evidence, and all the political shaming about dragons keeping such a valuable substance hidden, the High Council didn't have a lot of choice."

"That's amazing!" Joe said. "So, no more running or hiding?"

"Nope!" Ned cried. Joe could imagine Ned's happy grin even through the phone and felt struck with homesickness. After the last few days feeling alone and disconnected to the people who mattered to him the most, Joe couldn't wait to rejoin them.

"Tell the rest I'm on my way to the cabin now. We need to figure out how we're going to deal with Sterling."

"Right-o, boss. See you soon." Ned hung up the phone and Joe stored his away in his pack before swiftly changing to dragon form.

He was airborne in seconds, the ground falling away and the cool air roaring past as he sped toward the cabin at top speed. His marriage was over and he felt happier than ever. He needed to talk to Emma, but for the first time in years, he knew for sure that everything was really going to be alright.

EMMA PACED the boards of the cabin's living room, her heart racing as she waited. *This is it*. The front door opened and her breath caught. Rachel stepped into the room, her hands on her hips.

"You." Rachel's voice was laced with hate. "Joe! Honey, come help. She's going to hit me again!" she screamed.

"Cut the act, he's not here." Emma's fists clenched. *Just try something, bitch.*

"You've got a lot of nerve, sticking around here." Rachel spat. "You know my husband wants nothing more to do with you. He's done with you, skank." She leaned back against the wall, her arms crossed against her chest.

Emma felt a slow grin stretch across her face. "I think we both know he's done with *you*." She paused a beat, "...Sterling."

"Oh really? We both know that you haven't got a shred of evidence. You're not smart enough to unmask Sterling."

Rachel leaned in to whisper. "I'm far too smart for a nobody like you."

Emma stepped forward and felt a small flash of satisfaction when Rachel tensed. "I figured out your game fast enough. And I'll have the proof soon enough."

"Will you?" Rachel chuckled. "Honey, I've already gotten away with more than you could imagine."

"Like how you killed all those Puff users to make us think Puff was poison?" Emma asked. "Some masterful plan, making us think we were murderers for almost a whole day."

"And now I've succeeded at destroying the Claws," Rachel said. "My gods, it wasn't even that *hard*. A few raids here, a handful of murders there." She raised a meticulously-plucked eyebrow. "Not surprising really, you're just a mishmash of orphans and outcasts. Hardly a challenge."

Emma couldn't hold back a triumphant grin. "Outcasts with video cameras, you evil bitch."

Alec emerged from Emma's room, followed by the rest of the Iron Claws. Rachel backed away, trying to keep them all in view as the blood drained from her face. She finally fixated on Alec, who was holding a laptop with a live stream of the cabin showing on the screen.

Joe stepped out from behind Alec.

"This video is broadcasting right now to the Dragon High Council and the heads of all the shifter clans," Joe said. "They just heard your entire confession. Everyone now sees you for what you are: a murderer."

"A villain!" Penelope chimed in.

"The worst," Ned squeaked.

Emma bit back the retort of "pretentious sadist" sitting on the tip of her tongue.

Rachel looked around the room filled with smug faces

and she started to cry. Large tears rolled down her face and her shoulders started to shake. It would have been a better performance if Emma hadn't already seen the woman's smug satisfaction at destroying lives.

Rachel rushed to Joe, throwing herself at him. "Oh baby, everything I did, I did for you. For us!" She clung to his shirt, but he barely looked down, his arms firmly affixed at his sides. "Puff is going to be the downfall of us all, don't you see? The humans will abuse it, like they do everything else, and then come hunting us down when their supplies run low." She turned towards the rest of the Iron Claws. "Don't you all see?" She screamed.

"You're out of your mind." Joe's voice was surprisingly gentle as he stepped back from her to stand at Emma's side. Emma silently wrapped her palm around his and squeezed.

"You're so *stupid*." Rachel was so upset, her words came out in enraged pants. "You left our marriage to run around the country with these...*freaks*." Spit flew from her lips as she ranted. "We were great together, and you walked away just to help some filthy humans live? Why not save *rats* next?"

"That." Joe pointed toward Rachel. "That right there is why we would never have worked out. Not the Puff, not the Claws. *You*. You have no regard for human life. I-" He stopped short. "This marriage is *over*." The last word came out as a low growl so menacing Rachel jumped back from him.

An amused, formal voice came through Alec's laptop. "This is all well and good, but I don't believe you need to broadcast the whole divorce." They all turned to see the head of the Dragon High Council speaking to the camera. "I trust some of you are capable of bringing the former Mrs. Silver, alias Sterling, in unharmed?"

"Yes sir." Dylan saluted. He grabbed her by the arm, Caesar taking her other side as they hustled a glaring Rachel outside. The rest of the Iron Claws filed out behind, chatting happily, until Emma and Joe were alone in the cabin.

Emma turned to Joe, feeling so light she thought she might be able to fly without wings. His marriage was over. He was free.

"After all this time, we finally defeated Sterling." Emma sat down heavily on the sofa. "We're going to be safe, no more running. I can barely believe it."

Joe sat down next to her, reaching out to caress the side of Emma's face. "I can't believe I almost lost you." Joe's voice was almost a whisper. "Emma, I'm so sorry. I should have believed you right away." Joe stopped once Emma's fingertip touched his lips.

"Shh." Emma smiled. "As much as I love to hear how I'm right all the time, can we just clear up one thing?"

Joe nodded, still shushed.

"Rachel was the only reason we weren't together. Now she's gone. Does that mean--?"

Joe reached for her, pulling Emma close. Her lips finally found his and she tasted their soft skin for the first time. Her heart pounded in her chest like it was trying to escape. His lips were perfect; they molded around hers, claiming her and welcoming her. His lips felt like home.

She shifted closer, pressing herself flush against his body and then straddling him on the couch. His hands wrapped around her waist, supporting her as he sat up, her legs still wrapped around his hips. She couldn't stop kissing him, her hands caressing every inch of him she could reach. He carried her back to her bedroom, slamming the door behind them.

"I've wanted to do that since the moment we met." Joe gently laid Emma down on the bed, pulling off her clothes like he was opening a precious package.

"Oh yeah?" Emma teased. "What else did you want to do?" Emma didn't have the patience for precious. She ripped Joe's shirt off, grabbing for his belt.

"Everything." Joe kicked off his shoes. They bounced along the wooden floor with distant thumps.

"Everything?" Years of waiting left Emma desperate to touch him. She pressed against his warm body, pulling his pants and boxers to the ground, leaving them both naked and panting. "That's quite a few things," she teased.

"Yes. And I want to start with this." Joe's hands circled Emma's legs in winding patterns, getting closer to her core.

Emma was already soaking wet. She bucked her hips forward.

"Yes, Joe. Yes." She gasped as his fingers played closer to her wetness, massaging her inner thighs and stroking behind her knees.

Joe bent over to pepper her thighs with tiny kisses, his hands still roaming all along her legs. Emma whimpered and leaned back onto the covers, reveling at the feel of him.

This was what she had been waiting so long for. It felt unreal that she was finally here, with him. Emma kept waiting to wake up and realize that this was just another fevered sex dream.

Finally Joe's hot mouth found her clit and Emma cried out, gripping the bed's comforter. *Not a dream*. This felt too good to be a dream. She grabbed his head as sensation flooded over her in increasingly intense waves.

Joe's tongue danced along her slick folds, darting around her in unpredictable patterns. He sucked on Emma's swollen clit for a moment and was rewarded with her low moan. Slowly, he pressed a finger inside of her, moving in and out in a steady rhythm.

His tongue flicked at her clit as he moved inside of her, adding a second finger as her pulse intensified.

"Oh gods!" She cried.

"Let go, my love, I have you."

Emma could feel herself losing control, waves of delicious sensation finally growing so intense they all came crashing down at once in a thunderous cascade of pleasure. Her inner walls pulsed around Joe's hand. She screamed his name as she came, bucking against his fingers.

Joe pulled his fingers out and licked them clean, moaning as his tongue lapped at Emma's juices. His thick cock stood at attention, a tiny bead of precum glistening on the tip.

Emma reached up to slowly stroke the warm skin of his shaft. She'd seen him naked before, living in such close quarters with the Iron Claws she'd seen everybody undressed at some point, but this was different. He was magnificent.

She leaned forward and pressed her pink tongue to his tip, tasting his salty flavor. She ran her tongue all along his shaft, trailing ever closer to his swollen sacs. It felt so good to be close to him, to feel her power over him, that she felt the wetness grow between her legs again.

"Yes. Oh, Emma yes." Joe ran his hands through Emma's hair as she sucked him.

Emma took one of Joe's balls in her mouth and her tongue gently flicked all around it. She reached down to rub at her clit as she heard Joe's groans of pleasure.

"That's it, love, touch yourself while you're licking me." He groaned. "I want--"

She licked a trail back to his tip and loosened her throat,

taking him into her mouth as far as she could. Whatever he was going to say was cut off as he started to fuck her mouth in earnest. Emma loved it. She began to hum lightly as she sucked and teased him, moving up and down his length with increasing speed.

"Emma." Joe was panting. "Love, you gotta stop. I'm not going to be able to hold it in much longer. I want to cum inside you."

Emma kissed Joe's erection as she slid away, her hands trailing along his body. She shook with want. If she couldn't have his cock inside her soon, she was going to burst.

"Fuck me, Joe." Emma moaned. "Fuck me like you've always wanted to."

"Emma, I need you so badly." Joe pulled her back against his chest, kissing her neck as he gently positioned himself behind her. "I've always needed you." She shifted her hips backward, moaning when she felt the brush of his cock against her inner thighs. Leaning onto her hands, she thrust her hips toward him and Joe entered her from behind. His huge cock slipped into her slick entrance with little resistance.

"Fuck me hard, Joe."

Joe slammed into her, letting out a satisfied groan once he was fully inside her. He slid one hand around Emma's waist and rubbed her sensitive nub as he thrust within her.

Emma had never felt so connected, so complete. She pushed back in rhythm with him, her loud moans echoing across the cabin. Who cared if anyone heard them? They were finally together.

"Emma, I..." Joe gasped for breath. "Emma, I love you."

Emma's vision burst into bright lights and shooting stars as her second orgasm ripped through her body, even stronger than the first. She could feel Joe follow her over the edge, his body jerking as he came hard. It took a long moment to come back to herself, like she was waking up from the best dream she'd ever had. Joe pulled her backward until she nestled within his arms. She curled against his body, feeling his heartbeat against her back.

"I love you, too," she whispered. "Let's not wait another five years to do that again."

JOE FELT Emma turn over next to him in bed and blindly reached out to pull her naked body closer to his. They'd been together for a few months, but each moment still felt precious and new.

Sunlight streamed through the Iron Claws' new clubhouse window, the shaft of brightness cutting through the gap in the curtains to hit along the pillows. Emma curled closer to him, ducking so Joe's body blocked the light.

"Not waking up yet," she groaned.

"But you know what today is, right?"

"I don't care, I'm not moving yet." She wriggled her body until her ass was against his morning-hard cock. She turned around so she could throw a leg over his hips. "Well, maybe I'll move a *little* bit." She rolled her hips enough to rub the tip of his cock against her wet lips and Joe moaned.

"We did three rounds last night. You're going to kill me, woman." He laughed, already rolling over onto his back so she straddled his chest.

"But what a way to die, right?" She shifted so his cock was positioned under her core and he surged upward, filling her as she slid down so he was nestled inside her completely. "We waited so long for this, I'm not losing another second."

She bobbed up and down along his cock, her head thrown back in passion as she rode him. Her body felt perfect around his cock, warm and tight. He reached up to thumb her clit just the way she liked it. She cried out as she came around him.

He heard pounding on their bedroom door and Caesar's voice yelling, "Hey guys! You're late!"

"No, we're not!" Emma yelled back, picking up the pace as she rode Joe harder.

"Yes, you are! Your wedding starts in less than an hour!" Caesar called through the door. "This baby dragon flower girl will be dropping more than roses down that aisle if you keep her waiting much longer." The sound of Maya's newborn, Nancy, wailing on the other side of the door nearly broke the mood.

"It's our wedding, we can't be late. You all are just...early." Joe's voice came out in quick pants as he thrust upward. He could feel Emma was close, but he didn't want this to end soon. When Emma walked down the aisle, he wanted to see the post-coitus glow still in her cheeks.

"Never grow up, kid. Adults in this family have no consideration." Caesar's tone was light and bubbly as he addressed the baby. "And do I have to mention that it's unlucky to see the bride the day of the wedding?" Caesar said, sounding amused.

"Tell everyone to start on the open bar," Emma said. She reached behind her to caress Joe's balls and he groaned loudly. "We're going to be at least--" she paused, looking down at Joe with an eyebrow raised.

"Two hours," he finished. He rolled her over so she was on her back, her legs high enough to lock around his shoulders so he could push deeper at another angle.

"Oh yeah, that's it," she moaned.

"You two are impossible; you'll give the dragonling a complex," Caesar muttered, still loud enough for them to hear him. "You know I waited until at least before the reception to start my wedding sex."

They heard his footsteps recede down the stairway. Joe leaned forward to capture Emma's nipple in his mouth, massaging it with his tongue.

"I'm never waiting again," he said.

She bucked her hips against him, squeezing her inner muscles until they both screamed with pleasure. They fell apart just long enough to pull each other close for a long kiss.

"You know, we'll have to go down and get married sometime today," Emma said, running her fingers against his bare chest.

Joe shrugged. "Yes, we will. But that's for everyone else. What matters is you and me, together."

Emma nodded. "Forever."

Dear Reader,

We hoped you enjoyed **Her Biker Dragon**. We really love this world and creating more places and people to inhabit it. Many readers wrote asking; "What's up with Lola?" Well, stay tuned for more of Lola's mysterious meddling because the adventures at AUDREY'S (and the paranormal romantic interludes) aren't over.

When we first published this series, we got a lot of emails from fans thanking us for these books. Some liked certain series and sets of characters more than others. As authors, we love feedback. Your appreciation for this world is the reason why we keep writing books in this world.

Reviews are increasingly tough to come by these days. You, the reader, have the power now to make or break a book. So, tell us what you like, what you loved, even what you hated. We'd love to hear from you.

Thank you so much for reading **Her Biker Dragon** and for spending time with our wacky brains.

Have fun, everybody

Annie & Jess ("AJ") Tipton

MEET AJ TIPTON

AJ Tipton is the pseudonym of a writing team: Annie and Jess (Get it? "AJ." You get it). Corporate drones by day, we spend our evenings writing fantasies to astound, arouse, and amuse. Located in Brooklyn, we are total dorks and love it.

Want more stories of the bizarre and wondrous? Sign up for the new publications subscription list and you'll be the first to know when new books become available. There might also be other surprises along the way. Or just contact us directly at a.j.tipton.author@gmail.com

Our ideas for future books--everything from sex robots to ghost brothels--will keep us busy for many years to come, so follow along for the fun and let us know what series you like best. We love to hear from readers.

ajtiptonauthor.wordpress.com
ajtiptonauthor@gmail.com